Hidden
and Other Stories

Hidden
and Other Stories

Stuart M. Kaminsky

Five Star
Unity, Maine

Five Star Mystery
Published in conjunction with Tekno-Books & Ed Gorman.

September 1999

First Edition

Five Star Standard Print Mystery Series.

The text of this edition is unabridged.

Set in 11 pt. Plantin by Al Chase.

Printed in the United States on permanent paper.

Library of Congress Cataloging-in-Publication Data
Kaminsky, Stuart M.
    Hidden, and other stories / by Stuart M. Kaminsky.
       p.   cm.
    ISBN 0-7862-2034-1 (hc : alk. paper)
    1. Detective and mystery stories, American. I. Title.
PS3561.A43H49 1999
  813'.54—dc21
                                          99-27153

Table of Contents

Introduction

Two confessions: First confession, I love to write short stories. I love having an idea come to me and be able to sit down at this computer and bring it to life in one or two sittings and twenty-five or thirty pages. Second confession: I think writing a short story is easy, at least it is for me. It has always been easy for me. We'll talk about novels some other time.

No one will probably argue with my first confession. My second confession, when I have voiced it in the past, has brought on two responses.

Those who write for a living usually say something like, "You're right, but don't tell anyone. They think it's hard." Those who wish to write say, "No, writing a short story is difficult. Each word has to be honed and chosen carefully because you have so few pages in which to work. The diamond must be polished carefully before it is presented to the world."

Well, every story in this collection was written quickly and though I think some of them are far from perfection, I love them all. They were fun to write, even the most somber and serious of the lot.

From confession to six observations about the art and craft of writing short stories:

1. Serious stories are not more difficult to write than the lighter ones. I learned to write short stories by first reading

them, hundreds, thousands of them. Russian, French, English, Canadian, African. I devour them. If one wishes to write a short story, one should love them.

2. Short stories, when the moon is right and one isn't too full of chocolate mousse, come in a burst, a word, an idea. They spring into life and I let them appear on the page. They are evidence that something close to magic exists within us. They are not, in my case, calculated constructs. I marvel at their existence and when I am done with each of them I ask "Where did that come from?"

And I get no answer.

3. I seldom write a second draft. I will clean things up, change names, change something here and there. The child of my imagination is born.

4. The beginning and end are important to me. Sentence one relates to the last sentence of the story. The first paragraph relates to the last. I am about to write a story that begins with "The End" and ends "The Beginning." In the first paragraph there will be a man with a tattoo on his right bicep. The tattoo is old and fading. It is of Siamese twins joined at the hip. One twin is male, the other female. On the other arm is the faded tattoo of the sign for Libra, the scale. He will . . . ah but you and I will have to wait because . . .

5. I never tell anyone the story I am working on until it is written. I never even tell anyone what the story will be about. I want to give birth to it from the malachite egg, which grows in my imagination. I don't want to talk it to death, which leads to . . .

6. In *The Good, The Bad, and the Ugly*, Tuco, played by Eli Wallach, shoots a man who is in the process of telling Tuco how he tracked him down. Tuco looks at the dead man and says, "If you're going to shoot, shoot, don't talk."

Which leads to, "If you're going to write, write, don't talk." I write. Lesson over.

I've been writing short stories since I was twelve. At twelve I was pretentious. At eighteen I was precious and confessional. At twenty-eight I was commercial. At thirty-eight, I finally got it right. I began to have fun.

I am a storyteller first. I am a craftsman second. I will let posterity, if it has any interest, decide whether I am also an artist. I don't have all that much faith in posterity. It is too often wrong.

A number of paragraphs up I said that I learned by reading. It is true. There are so many great short story writers to learn from that I wonder why there are so many awful short stories written and published.

If you want to be a short story writer, first read Raymond Carver, Sherwood Anderson, Ernest Hemingway, William Faulkner, Richard Wright, Flannery O'Conner, Ray Bradbury, Isaac Bashevis Singer, Dorothy Parker, Bailey White, Harlan Ellison . . . and I am just sticking to Americans because of space, but Chekov, Gogol, Maugham. I must stop. There are hundreds.

Don't look for lessons in these works, just absorb them, lose yourself in them.

May you enjoy reading these stories as much as I enjoyed writing them and may you lose yourself in them as I did.

HIDDEN

Corrine did not scream. It was more like a vibrating moan followed by a little wail as she ran down the stairs. She didn't let out a real scream till she was out the front door. She had saved her scream till she was sure someone would hear her.

I had pressed the record button of the tape recorder the second I heard her open the front door. It took her four minutes to change into her working clothes and use the downstairs bathroom.

Once she called, "Mrs. Wainwright?"

My parents' room was always the first one she cleaned. This Tuesday was no different, at least so far, than the four years of Tuesdays that had gone before it. It took her ten minutes to finish cleaning my parents' room. She would have taken half an hour if she thought my mother was home.

My room was second.

It was when she opened the door and stepped in that she made the wailing sound and ran.

As it was, the first real scream from the lawn was just a loud extension of the moan. It was the second one that must have howled down the street and through the open front door back up to me.

It was a little after nine. A little before four, I had driven my dad's car to Gorbell's Woods, walked north on Highland for another half mile or so, and dropped my father's favorite hat at the side of the street. Then I walked the two miles back, making sure no one would see me, not that anyone but a peeping insomniac would have in Paltztown.

Corrine was screaming almost steadily now, but her screams weren't as loud. She was probably running down the street now, neighbors cautiously looking through their windows, afraid the Wainwright maid had downed more than a few too many.

They didn't know Corrine. She was born again. A boor. I know she had at least one married daughter, Alice. Alice had come to help her mother once about two years ago, when I was twelve. Alice must have looked like her father. Corrine was a bloated wobbler. Alice was a skinny snorter. I could only imagine what kind of bird Corrine's husband, the part-time reverend, looked like.

The first neighbor to come, five minutes later, was Mr. Jomberg, two doors down, retired, a heart condition. I didn't find out it was Mr. Jomberg until later, but I'm surprised he didn't have a heart attack when he opened the door.

I recorded Mr. Jomberg's "Holy shit" and his footsteps hurrying unsteadily down the stairs.

Can shit be holy? Why not? Would God bother to exclude it? Would God be sure to include it? I've had the feeling since I was no more than ten that God, if there was one, worked to create the universe and people and when it came time for the little things, the details, God just said, "The hell with it." And God had a lot to do. New worlds out there every minute. New stars born. Old stars dying. Busy somewhere in the firmament. I was a forgotten detail, a the-hell-with-it. I figured that out too when I was ten and I almost drowned in the pool. I shouldn't have been left alone. I hadn't had a seizure for almost a year and I was in the shallow end, but I shouldn't have been left alone. I felt it coming, felt what Dr. Ginsberg calls "the aura." I must have panicked, felt confused as my brain began to close down. Instead of heading for the side of the pool I took a step toward the deep end.

I woke up in the hospital. When I opened my eyes, my mother began "Thank God"-ing though she never went to church and committed many a sin of omission. My father was there, sighing deeply. He touched my cheek. My sister, Lynn, a year older than me, had been pulled away from her friend's house.

"You okay?" she said, looking bored.

I nodded yes.

"No more swimming alone," my father said.

My mother was supposed to have been watching me in the water. She had gone in the house to answer the phone. When she came out, I was almost dead.

That's when I decided I was a go-to-hell person.

You'd think that would depress a ten-year-old. If it did for a few seconds, I don't remember. I remember lying there and thinking, "If there is no God, only people can punish me for what I do. If there is a God, he doesn't care what happens to me."

That was my final seizure.

Before whoever listens to this says, "That was the big day. Trauma time. The day we can trace it all back to. If only he had been given therapy. But now we understand. We can put it in a box with a label and forget Paul Wainwright. Even his name is easy to forget."

The police came eight minutes and twenty seconds after Mr. Jomberg went ballistic. I imagined him and Corrine on the front lawn, screaming, dancing in a crazy circle. If they make a movie, I strongly suggest they include the dancing scene, at least as a fantasy.

There were two policemen, one a man, one a woman. In

case it's not clear on the tape, she said,

"Ahh, God."

He said,

"Jesus. Call in."

"God," the woman repeated.

"Billie, call in," the man said with a quaver in his voice. "I'll . . . I'll check the house."

They both left my room. I was hungry. I reached into the box next to me and took out two slices of bread. I put individual American cheese slices in the sandwich and placed the plastic that had covered them in the plastic container. I quietly snapped the container closed.

It's a little after one in the morning now. I can record all of this whispering into the microphone.

I had thought this out carefully. Lots and lots of premeditation.

In the ceiling inside my closet is a small trapdoor. It used to be the only way to get to the crawl space when my parents bought the house. They dormered the attic and made it a giant room for Lynn. I didn't mind. I like small spaces. Once I went with my mother and sister to Baltimore on the train. I think it was to console my Aunt Jean when her son died, but maybe it wasn't. I was just a kid, maybe three. My mother and sister complained about how small the sleeping space was in our little private room, especially when the two beds were open. I was in the upper. Even at three there was hardly enough room to turn over. I loved it. Wrapped in the dark.

The trapdoor in my closet. I hadn't forgotten. Walls were put up in the attic, on each side, to make it look and feel more like a room. The walls created unreachable spaces behind them. Narrow front-of-the-house to rear passageways. The trapdoor was forgotten by everyone but me. I locked my bedroom door and scrambled up, almost every night. I climbed quietly so Lynn wouldn't hear. I'd store things in the space and take naps in the darkness. One afternoon when I was home alone, I made a small hole in the wall, a very small hole so I could see most of the room. Then I went into Lynn's room and used the hand vac from the kitchen to pick up the few pieces of wood shavings I'd made making the hole.

I think of things. I plan ahead. I have a complete supply of nonperishable canned foods and drinks up here and a sealable plastic bucket where I can put my garbage. I chose foods that would have the least detectable smell. I have blankets, two pillows, and almost all my clothes piled neatly a few feet away. I have the small battery-powered television set that my parents kept in their room. And I have battery replacements. I checked with a flashlight for bugs for weeks before the morning I killed my parents and sister. The crawl space was clean.

The hardest part, the part I'm most proud of, is the fake ceiling, exactly the size of the closet ceiling. It fits perfectly. I made it in my room, tested it to see if it would work, how it would look. When I go through the trapdoor, I can reach the false ceiling where I prop it over my clothes rack. I reach down, pull the false ceiling up by the spring and handle I screwed into it and set the spring and bar in place in the trapdoor to hold the false ceiling in place. If someone looks in my closet, they'd see a ceiling. The only danger is if someone reaches up ten feet and pushes the ceiling. Not likely, but if they do climb up, the ceiling will wobble a little. They might think it's a little odd, but that's all.

There is plenty of air in my crawl space. Lynn's walls are wooden slats on plasterboard or something like that. There's a space between each of the slabs of plasterboard, a small space but enough.

But back to this morning.

Twenty more minutes and more police and a doctor.

"I've never seen it this bad."

"Walters case, seven, eight years ago. Five in the family. Father did it. Ax, hammer, teeth. Bodies, parts all over the apartment."

"Before my time, Barry."

"Father's still in the funny farm, I think. God, will you look at this?"

"I'm lookin', Judd."

I know what you're thinking. I'm not squeamish. I'll talk about it. You're wondering what I do for a toilet. Two things. I've got an emergency plastic bowl, a big one, with a pop-on top. If I can make it through the day, I'll go down at night, tonight, and use my own bathroom. I thought of everything. I made a checklist. I have a copy of it with me with a penlight and a supply of penlight batteries and even some replacement bulbs. I have books for during the day. All kinds of books, any kind of book, nothing that could form part of a puzzle to come up with a simple profile.

"He reads mysteries. That explains it."

"He reads romances. That explains it."

"He reads histories. That explains it."

"He reads about knights with lances. That explains it."

And then, from below, clear, the one with the rough voice,

"This is the son's room."

"No sign of him unless some of these parts. No head, nothing that looks like a kid."

"You got enough pictures there? I'd really like to get the hell out of here."

"You wanna wait in the hall? Wait in the hall. I don't want some lawyer coming back at me a year from now. This is a big one."

"We either find the kid's body in the next hour or he did it."

"Prediction?"

"Experience. For Chri—Doc, what'd he do to that one?"

"Bad things, James. Let me work here. Go look for the boy, clues. Stop bothering me so I can get this done, these bodies out of here and back to the hospital."

Two men left, out looking for signs of me. The doctor, left alone, talked to himself, probably into a tape recorder. I heard the click. It's on my tape. He said it was a pre-autopsy report, an "on-site." He talked slowly, forced himself to talk slowly or he had trouble breathing: "All three victims are nude. Preliminary cause of death on female, age approximately forty-five, massive evisceration. All hair, from head and pubic area, shaved roughly, probably after death. Decapitated. Body on the floor. Head on the bed. Preliminary cause of death, male, same age, massive, repeated blows to the cranium, extensive brain damage. Multiple stab wounds. Preliminary cause of death on female, age fifteen to twenty, repeated, traumatic penetration of . . . No sign of bullet wounds on any of the victims, but the condition of the bodies is such that clinical examination will be necessary."

He clicked off the machine and said,

"Animal. Animal."

A few minutes later, the one with the rough voice and one or two others.

"Jesus," said somebody.

"That's what they all say. Look around. Take it in. Do your job. No blood in the hallway or anywhere else. They were killed in here. I'd say they were shot first."

It was hard to hear the rest of the conversation. Someone was using a machine, sounded like a vacuum cleaner, in my room. I think they said,

17

"Neighbors don't report any noise, but . . ."

"You think after he killed the first one, the next one just came in here, saw the body and let herself—"

"Or himself . . ."

"Probably killed the man first. Easier to deal with the women."

"What kind of kid lives in a room like this?"

"Shit, what kind of kid does something like this?"

"Place looks like a cell. No pictures, things on the table. Black blanket and pillows. I'll bet his clothes are neatly piled in the drawers and lined up perfectly in his closet."

The sound of a drawer opening.

"What'd I tell you?"

The sound of someone opening the closet drawer right below me. I held my breath.

"I should have bet," the rough-voiced man said right below me. "It's the kid."

New voice, shaky.

"Sergeant, wagon's on the way for the bodies. Can they bag 'em?"

"Ask the doc," the rough-voiced one said, closing the closet door and making me strain now to hear what was going on in my room. The closed door had one advantage. It cut out most of the smell.

"Call in from Commer and Styles. They found one of the family cars. Identified by contents in glove compartment. Over in Gorbel's Woods, just off Highland. Driver side door open. Half a block farther, heading north, they found a hat on the side of the road. A kind of Greek fisherman's hat with the father's name on the sweatband."

"He's heading out of town. On foot."

"Why the hat? Why'd he take it? Why'd he toss it? Why'd he leave the car?" asked the sergeant with the rough voice.

They were all good questions.

"Can we go now, Sergeant? I mean downstairs."

"Go. I'm stayin' awhile."

Footsteps leaving the room. A faraway sound of an ambulance siren. What was the point of the siren? What was the hurry?

The sergeant was breathing hard enough for me to hear him through the floor and door. He said something, too soft for me to hear, but it was angry. I'll listen to the tape later, maybe weeks from now when I can turn up the volume. I'm curious. Can you blame me?

Downstairs people were talking, arguing, using our phone. Beyond the wall two feet away from me, a pair of footsteps tracked around Lynn's room. I put my eye against the narrow slit between the plasterboard and planks. I caught a glimpse of blue uniform on a woman's body.

"Pretty kid," said a young man's voice.

I was sure he was looking at Lynn's photographs of herself and her friends, resting on her dressing table.

I couldn't see him or the policewoman who answered,

"Not anymore."

They didn't stay in Lynn's room long. No more than a minute after they left I heard new voices below in my room.

"Oh, Lord . . ."

"They told you what it was like, Nate."

"Yeah, but . . ."

Footsteps coming up the stairs.

"We set the bags. We set the gurneys. We—"

"Room's been printed and vacuumed," the doctor said. "That torso and the head go in one bag. Girl and the hand go in another bag. The woman in the corner . . . I'll help you."

"Never done anything like this," said the one called Nate. "You know that, Russ? Old people who die in their sleep. Kid gets shot. Husband knifes . . . Nothing like this. Not in this town."

"Give me a hand," the doctor said.

The sound of a zipper. Good-bye, Dad?

I watched the eleven o-clock news, watched carefully. They won't really clean the room for a day or two. They'd close the door when the bodies were gone and seal off the room, probably seal the whole house. Teams of police, possibly even South Carolina state troopers, possibly the FBI, would tear off tape, open doors, take more pictures, look at the blood, start looking for clues about where I might have gone.

They will find, in my second-from-the-top dresser drawer, under my sweaters, on the right, my notes and maps of New York City. I have circled neighborhoods with different color markers and made notes about them as places to visit or find an apartment. I have never been to New York City, never want to go. It's dangerous. It's dirty. It is where I want them to look for me.

Short-term plan: Be careful. Use the bathroom only late at night when I'm sure the house is empty.

Long-term plan: When I run out of food and clean clothes in about three weeks or a month, in the middle of the night, I climb down, use the large-container Krazy Glue to fix the false closet ceiling in place, and then get my bike and helmet wrapped in plastic and hidden five blocks away under the Klines' back porch. I wait till morning and, dressed like a morning biker complete with helmet, goggles, and armed with only a water bottle, I pedal out of Platztown, eating fast food on the way to Jacksonville, where I buy clothes, a shirt here, jeans there. I have $2,356 in my wallet. Most of it money I earned working in the Kash and Karry. Some of it from my mother's purse and father's wallet. I even know how to get a new identity, a Social Security card, a driver's license. I've seen it on television, read two books about it.

It has gone pretty much the way I planned. Busy with the police for about three days. A crew of women, Polish or Russian or something, came in to clean the room. After the cleanup, there were fewer and fewer until one day no one came. Days and nights reading, watching game shows, talk shows, movies and the news using my earphones. The Channel Seven News, the team "on your side," called what I had done "gruesome" and "beyond belief" after the national news anchor in Washington soberly reported on the horrid dread. People in Platztown are locking their doors and sleeping with their guns on the night table for fear I am still lurking in the night. There are photographs—of me looking like a grinning nerd, of my parents and Lynn looking like the next-door neighbors of Rob and Laura Petrie.

The sergeant with the rough voice was part of a press conference on the second day. He looked fat and tired. His hair was curly and gray, and his sports jacket and unmatching trousers were badly in need of burning.

The mayor spoke at the conference, attended by reporters and television crews from as far away as Charleston and Raleigh. The mayor assured the world that the "person or persons who committed this monstrous crime would soon be caught." The chief of police was careful in answering a reporter's question. He said that I was certainly a prime suspect, but that I might also be the fourth victim, buried in the woods or, he hinted, kidnapped for the kidnappers' pleasure. A television reporter from Channel Seven asked, "What if he had help?"

"No report of anyone in town missing," said the chief with a knowing smile.

"Then whoever might have helped him might still be in

town," said the reporter. "One of our own kids."

"Not likely. We think Paul Wainwright is in New York City or soon will be," the chief said.

"How do you know?"

"Why New York?"

"Documents found in the suspect's room," the rough-voiced sergeant, identified as James Roark, said.

"What documents?"

"Did he leave a diary?"

"He left his family dead, naked, and in little pieces," Roark croaked.

At that point Channel Seven went back to Elizabeth Chanug in the studio. According to Elizabeth, there were "apparently reliable" reports that the police knew with certainty that I was already in New York and they had narrowed the search down to certain specific areas in the city.

My favorite part, I almost missed it, was on Channel Ten. They interviewed people who knew me.

Mr. Honeycutt, the school principal, to whom I have not spoken more than twice in passing: "A quiet boy. Outstanding student. Not a lot of friends."

Miss Terrimore, the guidance counselor, a sagging lump of a creature trying to hold herself together with tailored suits: "Without revealing confidences, about all I can say about him is that he was a bright, defensive, and clearly troubled boy."

She had talked to me twice, and both times she popped menthol cough drops and barely looked up from the report she was filling out. It was in-her-office, how-you-doin'?, that's-fine, next. I could have waved an Uzi in front of her, and she would have wiped her nose and said, "How you doin'?"

Jerry "Turk" Walters, Turk the Jerk, dresses like a rapper,

belongs in the crapper: "Paul was in two of my classes this semester, three last. I sat near him 'cause everything is alphabetical, you know. And our names are close. Paul didn't talk much. Good student. A weird smile that gave me chills. No close friends. No real friends I knew about. But he helped me out a few times."

Helped him out by letting him copy my homework regularly for two semesters.

Milly Rugello, pretty and mellow, dressed now in yellow, lips fine red and full for the camera, vacant eyes faking feminine concern: "I wouldn't say we were friends. Actually, I didn't talk to Paul much. He was kind of creepy. But he never made any trouble."

Creepy? Hindsight of the stupid. I was never, never creepy. I was clean-teethed and clean-clothed and normal, laughing when I should laugh, writing essays the teachers wanted, lamenting, although with regret and not anger, the plight of the hungry throughout the world, the spread of AIDS, the pervasiveness of bigotry. Man's inhumanity to Man.

I went to basketball games, football games, pep rallies, and even took my cousin Dorothea to the sophomore dance. Theme: A Touch of Springtime.

Milly Rugello
Lips like red Jell-O,
Dressed all in yellow.
Hardly ever said hello.
Rugello, Milly
Skin like a lily,
Brainless and silly,
Oh, what I'd like to do to you.

Mr. Jomberg, breathing heavy, trials of the heart and emphysema, dressed for the occasion in worn jeans and a flannel shirt with dominant reds and blacks, thumbs in his pocket, mountain man, folksy, neighborhood wise man: "Wainwrights were decent people, always a good morning. The girl was bright, always friendly and polite, not like a lot these days. The boy?" Mr. Jomberg shook his head sadly, "An enigma. Always polite, showed a little interest in my garden, seemed to get on well with my dog. It's all a shock."

Enigma? Had Mr. Jomberg run to his thesaurus? Did he have an untapped vein of the mother lode of mindless clichés? Interest in his garden? Did Mr. Jomberg live in Fantasyville? And the dog? I seriously considered eviscerating the snarling, foul, filthy-toothed rag.

Connie was kept from the cameras. A good thing too. She would have been useless, though she might have had a good word or two for me. I was always polite to Connie, I was always polite to everyone.

Day by day Channel Seven has even less and less about me and what I have done. The national news abandoned me after three days. Channel Seven dropped the story today. There was no new news about me. There was nothing to report.

I've come down cautiously around two in the morning every other day, listened to be sure no one was in the house, used the toilet, washed myself, dried the bowl with toilet paper I had brought down with me, flushed whatever had to be flushed down, and gone quickly back to the closet.

The first time down, on the third day, I had been, I admit it, just a little excited. Not frightened. Adventure. Challenge. Danger. I stopped in the middle of my room, the light of a three-quarter moon letting me know that the room had been cleaned, something I already knew from the sounds of the day. Bed against the wall, stripped to the springs. Dresser in the corner, everything cleared from the top. Desk empty now.

During the day, the policeman with the rough voice, James

Roark, had brought my Aunt Katherine through the house. I heard the door to my room open.

"You gonna be all right, Mrs. Taylor?"

She didn't answer. She must have shaken her head.

"I'll just stand here and give you a hand if you need it."

Shuffling. A cardboard box opening? My imagination. Drawers opening. Things being swept into the box, clunking hurriedly off its sides. Aunt Katherine breathing hard. Her husband, my father's brother, had left her and Dorothea when I was a little kid. I wondered if he would read about this or see it on television or if he were dead. "Were dead." Got that? Subjunctive. Feed that to Mr. Waldermere if you find it. You taught me well, Mr. W. I listened. Promising future, huh, Mr. W?

My room looked like a tomb, drenched in gloom, waiting for the boom of doom, growing smaller, driving me into the corner where I could curl up like a pre-abortion in the womb.

I climbed back up and sealed myself in.

It is two weeks later on a Tuesday at two-twenty in the morning. I just dropped a green garbage bag of dirty clothes and another green garbage bag of food and garbage onto the floor of the closet. I propped the fake ceiling against the rods from which all my remaining clothing had long since been removed, and climbed down sneaker quiet. It took me fifteen minutes to seal the ceiling. I'm drenched in sweat. It's a hot night and the air conditioning isn't on. Why should it be? I left the television, radio, and all but one of the books sealed in the crawl space. I took a paperback copy of Lord Byron's poetry, which I've stuffed into my back pocket. I also took this tape recorder. I plan to chronicle my journey through life. Tape after tape after tape. Hundreds of tapes, maybe thousands. I'll leave them right out in the open, neatly catalogued, telling visitors that I plan to publish them someday.

Three years, five years, ten years, half a century from now when the house is remodeled or torn down—if it was not demolished in the next two months because no one wants to buy it—some unintentional archaeologist would discover the traces of my deception in the crawl space.

Will they marvel at my cleverness or just call me mad? I have no illusions about people.

I am putting down the crinkling garbage bags to open the door. And then down the stairs, out the back door, through the alley, dropping the bags in the Dumpster outside of Rangel and Page's Supermarket. Pickup on Wednesday morning. After that, with the coming of dawn, the morning biker, head down, tools down the highway and what I really am remains . . .

hidden.

Paul Wainwright walked gently down the stairs, feeling his way in the near total darkness, garbage bags tapping against his back, tape recorder clutched in his hand. In the living room, the nearby street lamp let a slash of filtered light through the downstairs curtained windows.

Paul had taken four steps toward the kitchen when he heard his father's voice say,

"Put them down gently, Paul."

Paul dropped the bags and turned into the darkness of the living room.

"Go sit in the chair by the window," his father said.

Paul's knees turned to pudding. For as long as a minute, he didn't move, and then the voice again from his father's favorite chair,

"Sit, Paul. Now.'

Paul made his way to the chair near the window and looked toward the voice of his father in the darkness.

"I've got to know why," his father said wearily.

"You're not my father," Paul said.

"And for that I thank God," the voice said.

"You're Roark, James Roark. Sergeant James Roark."

Roark had almost dozed off when he heard the sound above him. A thud, followed by another thud. The thudding sounds were followed by shuffling and the slap of something—wood, plastic—against something hard. It could have been a burglar, but Roark didn't think so.

For the first week after the murders, he had slept two, three hours a night in patches. His wife had reminded him that they were going to visit their daughter at Mount Holyoke in two weeks and he had to apply for the vacation time. He had said yes and forgotten and then, when it came time to pack and leave, Roark had said no. He had to stay behind. He had to find Paul Wainwright.

His wife hadn't argued. She had seen Roark like this only once before, when they lost their first child before he reached his first birthday. Best to leave him alone. Best to let him heal. Best if it worked the way it had more than twenty-five years ago.

When his wife had left, Roark had taken his vacation and slept during the day with the sun coming into his room and the phone turned off. At night he had gone quietly to the Wainwright house, let himself in, and sat in the living room waiting, hoping for the boy to return, sure at times that he would, just as sure more often that he would not. He was certain that the boy had not gone to New York City. The hints were too obvious, the maps too hastily circled, the blood on the corner of one map that of the dead father, strongly suggesting that the maps had been put in the drawer after the father's murder. There had been no evidence of a young man of Paul's description going through any nearby town or getting on any bus, train, or plane. The family's second car was still in the garage. No, the chances were good that Paul Wainwright was still somewhere in or near Platztown. They had searched, asked and found nothing, and so Roark had clung to the hope that the boy would come back home when he thought it was safe, would come back home for clothes, hidden money, a last look. Nothing much, but Roark had a feeling. His feelings had been wrong in the past. Wrong more than they were right, but he had nothing to go on and a real need to justify the nights he was spending in the Wainwright living room. And now came the realization that Paul Wainwright had been hiding in the house, two floors above him for more than two weeks. In the slash of light from the window, the boy looked white and thin, his dark T-shirt pulsed with his beating heart.

"What's in your hand?" Roark said. "Hold it up."

The boy held up a small tape recorder.

"Put it next to you on the window ledge." Roark went on rubbing his stubbled cheeks.

Paul put the tape recorder on the ledge.

"Now," Roark said, "play it."

"I—" Paul began.

"Play it," Roark insisted, and Paul pushed the rewind button. The two sat listening to the hum till the machine clicked and Paul hit the Play button. Twenty minutes later, the machine clicked off.

"Doesn't explain much," Roark said.

"That's all there is," Paul said.

"There's no why to it," said the policeman. "I need a why."

"When I was ten," the boy said, "I discovered that I had no feeling for anyone, none. My friends, family. They meant nothing to me. I didn't like them. I didn't hate them. I was just better than they were, smarter because I wasn't tied down by the confusion of—"

"Bullshit," Roark interrupted.

"No. That's the truth."

"Why did you, for chrissake, rape your own sister before you—before you—?"

"Because I could do it. I could do anything. I was excited by the power, the blood," the boy said evenly.

"And your mother, Jesus, kid, what'd you tear out her heart with, your bare hands?"

"And a knife," the boy said.

"Last question. Why did you have to stab your father not once but six times?"

"Fifteen," the boy said. "I stabbed him fifteen times."

"The tape is bullshit, isn't it, son? You wanted to find a way to get caught and have someone listen to it. If I hadn't caught you tonight, you'd have found a way to get caught."

Paul Wainwright tried to laugh, but it came out as a dry, choking sound.

"No one raped your sister, Paul, and no one tore your mother's heart out, but you're right. Your father was stabbed fifteen times."

"I killed them," Paul said, his voice breaking. "And I almost got away with it."

"Nope," said Roark. "Nothing about your life fits the kid on that tape or what happened in that bedroom. You want to know the way I figure it?"

"No," said the boy.

"I'll tell you anyway. You came home a week ago Monday night from the Tolliver game. No one around but your father. He said something like, 'Let's go up to your room. I've got something to tell you.' You were feeling good, thought it was good news, bad news, who knows. You got up there and opened the door and saw what he had done to your mother and sister. You went wild with fear, anger. You hit him with the lamp, and when he went down you took the knife from his hand and you stabbed him, once for every year of your life."

"The fake ceiling in the closet," the boy tried. "It took me—"

"Hell, you're a kid. My daughter had a hiding place in a cupboard. You've probably been climbing up there for years, hiding out, spying on your sister."

Paul started to get up.

"Sit down, son," Roark said. "And don't get up till I get some more answers. I understand why you killed your father. He'd been seeing a shrink in Charlotte for a couple of years now. Plenty to show that he was a man in need of help. Between you and me and without the tape running, I'd say you could get yourself a good lawyer and sue the hell out of that shrink for not seeing where this was going."

"I killed them," the boy repeated.

"Why? I mean, why did you climb up there? Why did you make the tape? Why did you want us to think you'd killed them all?"

The boy was shaking now.

"I killed them," he repeated.

"Take it easy. You cold?"

Paul shook his head no.

"Let me give it a try," Roark said. "My father's still alive and I've got kids. You wanted to protect your father's name."

"I should have seen it coming," Paul said softly. "The little things he did, said. The anger, crying. I should have seen. My mother should have seen and my sister too, but they're not . . . they weren't . . ."

"As smart as you," said Roark. "It was your fault he killed

them because you're smarter than they were and you should have stopped him?"

Paul said nothing. He hugged himself and began to rock in the filtered light from the street lamp.

"What about it being his fault, your father's?"

"He was sick. Someone should have helped him. He was a good husband, a good dad."

"We're way out of my league here," Roark said. "I'll try once and leave it to the pros. You killed one person, your father, who murdered your mother and sister and was trying to murder you. You're not responsible for what he did. There's nothing you could have done to stop it 'cause there's no way you could have known he would lose it. Plenty of people see shrinks and behave wacky. I saw a shrink for years and I yelled at my family and behaved like an—you'll excuse my French—asshole."

The boy kept rocking, tuning out. Roark had seen it before. He got up from his chair and moved to the boy's side, looking down at him. Roark took off his jacket and put it around the shivering boy's shoulders, though the room was warm and muggy.

"Let's go," the policeman said, helping the boy up and pocketing the tape recorder.

Paul gave him no trouble. They stepped past the two green garbage bags.

"I just thought . . ." Paul started and looked around the room. "I just thought . . ." he repeated, looking up at the thick Irish face of the policeman and trying to speak through his tears, "that there are some things, some things that should stay . . ."

And the policeman finished as he put his arms around the boy,

". . . hidden."

IN THUNDER,
LIGHTNING OR IN RAIN

"We don't have a hell of a lot of time here, Doc," the old man said, removing the bicycle clips from his rain-soaked pants.

Carl Lenz sat back behind his desk and looked at the old man who tucked the clips into the pocket of his frayed denim jacket and said, "I was thinking the same thing."

The old man, who had identified himself as Max Horner, had appeared at Lenz's door less than five minutes earlier. Carl hadn't heard the bell or the knocking. His wife had nudged him and whispered,

"Carl, there's someone at the door."

He felt her nipples against his back, groaned comfortably and tried to ignore the insistent reality of the banging door.

He opened his eyes and found the red numbers on the bedside clock telling him it was just before two in the morning.

"Morrie," he whispered hoarsely, sitting up.

Connie reached over and touched his naked thigh, her fingers moving between his legs.

"Come back soon," she said softly. "I'm awake now."

He sat feeling her hand slink away, her moist mouth on his bare back. And then another knock, louder.

"I'll get rid of him," Carl promised.

"Good," his wife whispered.

Carl had fumbled for his robe, put it on and tied it, trying to come awake. If it weren't for the demanding knock, Carl could have more than accommodated his wife's suggestion. They had been married for six weeks and Carl had begun to worry about keeping Connie satisfied. He was only forty, but she was ten years younger and apparently always willing and usually eager for his body.

"Coming, coming, coming," Carl muttered as he made his way down the stairs.

The knocks were more frequent now, more frenetic, and behind them he thought he heard the sound of falling rain.

"Morrie?" he asked through the closed door.

"Morrie?" came a man's voice from beyond. "Hell, no. How 'bout opening the door, Doc? I'm dip-tar soakin' out here and time's running out."

Carl looked through the small window in the door and saw a tall, thin old man with curly white hair looking back at him. Rain was beating down. The path was wet and glistening in the glow of the porch light. The man on the other side of the door looked reasonably fit. Carl Lenz was in good shape and reasonably confident of his body, particularly when the potential threat was an apparently unarmed old man. Beyond the man, propped against the black metal railing to the left of the stone steps, was a bicycle.

Carl opened the door.

"Horner," said the old man holding out his hand. "Max Anthony Horner, pedaled down from Providence, took half the night. Truck almost hit me a few miles back."

Carl took the extended hand and felt even more confident. The handshake was firm, but there was a slight tremor and the enlarged knuckles that signaled arthritis.

"Come on in, Mr. Horner," Carl said, pushing the door closed and cutting off the sound of steady falling rain.

"Obliged," said Horner looking around.

Carl put on his best I'm-listening smile, hands in the pocket of his silk robe, and looked at the man.

"What can I do for you, Mr. Horner?" he asked.

"Wrong question," said Horner running his tongue over his uneven upper teeth. "Wrong question. What can Max Horner do for you is the question of the night. Nice house."

Horner looked around in the dim light of the reception area. The house was old, an eighteenth-century farm that Carl had rebuilt; well, he had supervised its rebuilding. Lenz's nearest neighbor was the man who had sold him the farmhouse, Morris Geckler, a former patient. Geckler had asked remarkably little in cash for the farm, but it had become clear soon after renovation began that Morris Geckler now assumed he had free psychotherapy available to him at any hour of the day whenever the Lenzes were in town.

"Can we talk somewhere?" said Horner, rubbing his hands together.

"Is this going to take long, Mr. Horner?"

"Probably. Up to you. I tell my story quick as I can. You listen and make up your mind. I got reason to hurry. Good reason."

The skies had raised the stakes beyond the door and the sound of heavily falling rain hit the windows. A clatter of metal against stone let Carl know that Max Horner's bike had fallen. Horner didn't seem to notice.

"This way," Carl said, moving through the open door at his right. Horner followed him.

Carl turned on the light and closed the door behind them.

"Cozy like," the old man said, and took two steps toward the black leather chair across from the desk.

"How about . . . ?" Carl said, moving behind the desk.

"About? Oh, the chair. Don't want it wet. Got you, Doc. Nice chair. Nice room."

"Used to be the living room," said Carl, sitting behind his desk. "Now . . ."

"Office," said Horner, moving to a straight-backed wooden chair and sitting. "Nice. Kind of work away from work. Do most of your writing up here?"

"Most," agreed Carl. "Would you like a drink?"

"No time," said Horner. "Mind if I close the drapes?"

There was one large bay window in the room. Beyond it lay the yard with its gentle slope leading to the woods fifty yards beyond. There was nothing to see now but the rain hitting the window.

"No," said Carl.

The old man rose, moved to the window, peered out into the darkness for a moment, and pulled the drapes closed. Then he turned and faced Carl.

"Read your book," the man said, putting his hands behind his back and facing the desk.

"Which book?" asked Carl.

"All of 'em, cover to cover and back again. Last one is the one though."

"A *Longing of Witches*," said Carl.

"That's the one," Horner said. He returned to the wooden chair and sat slowly.

"You bicycled from Providence in the rain to tell me how much you like my book?"

Horner laughed, a nervous old-man cackle of a laugh.

"Knee slapper," he said. "Don't get me laughing here, Doc. Not a laughin' matter, and laughin' gets me achin' on a night like this. Chill, you know. Old bones. Old bones."

"Sorry," said Carl. "I'll try to be more serious."

Thunder cracked far beyond the woods toward the ocean. There was a fireplace in the corner. When the old man left, Carl decided, he would get the fire going and bring Connie down to make love in the heat on the soft bearskin rug. If he started the fire now, the old man might take it as a signal that Carl was ready to talk till dawn.

And then Carl realized that if the storm kept building, he wouldn't be able to send the old man back into the night. He would probably have to put him up in the attic bedroom.

"Your book's okay far as it goes," Horner said and turned his chair slightly so he could take in both Carl and the draped window. "Owes a lot to Ernest Jones."

"I acknowledge that in the book," said Carl. He leaned forward, folded his hands, and placed them on the dark polished oak of his desk to examine this ancient scarecrow of a man who came in the middle of the night to discuss Ernest Jones.

"You got it right why people want to be witches, warlocks, such like that," Horner said, pointing a long arthritic finger at Carl. "Hell, who wouldn't be tempted to make other people do what they want, sex and all, power of life and death, live for hundreds of years taking over other people's bodies. What you got wrong is that not all people who think they're witches are nutcase loonies, Doc."

Carl could see where this was going now. He began to formulate a plan for tucking Horner away for the night and locking him in the attic room till he could drive him back to Providence in the morning.

"You mean there really are witches," Carl said while he surreptitiously checked the old schoolhouse wall clock over the fireplace with the expertise of the experienced therapist.

"Heard this one before I guess," said Horner, looking around the room and shaking his head.

"Frequently, Mr. Horner. Almost all the people I've dealt with who have this fixation think either they or someone else is a witch, vampire, werewolf, or whatever. It's the rare one who thinks there's something wrong with his or her belief."

Horner was shaking his head through Carl's brief speech. He jumped in as soon as he could and said, "We don't have time here for what-ifs and who is and isn't nuts. They're comin' for me. Can't be too far behind."

"Who's coming for you, Mr. Horner?" Carl asked.

"Who's coming? Why the goddamned witches, that's who. Coven up near Providence. Few from as far away as Maine. Been fighting them all my life. My father before me and his mother before him. Way before Salem. Back in Wales. They're strongest when it's raining. Big storm. Harness the energy. Do their stuff."

Carl did his best, which was professional and damned good even at two in the morning, to make it appear that he was giving the old man the benefit of the doubt. It was a tight line to walk, but he had walked it before. Don't buy the argument. Remain open-minded but skeptical.

Then, above the rain, he heard a knock at the office door, and Connie entered wearing her matching silk robe. It was partly open at the neck and when she saw Horner she pulled the front of the robe closed.

She looked pale and quite beautiful. Her short, straight dark hair fell sleepily down her forehead, partly covering one eye.

"Are you almost done?" she said.

"Almost," answered Horner cheerfully before Carl could answer.

"Mr. Horner and I will be done soon," Carl said.

Connie said, "Soon."

"Soon," Carl repeated. "Mr. Horner and I are fine."

Connie stepped back and closed the door behind her.

"Lovely lady, the missis," said Horner.

"Thank you, Mr. Horner," said Carl. "We're in agreement on that one."

Stuart Kaminsky

"But not on the witches?" asked Horner, stretching out his legs. A joint cracked. "Age does that. Sorry. Okay, I'll get to the point. They know I've come for you. Gettin' old. Need new blood to help fight 'em. And you're this close to believin' 'cause you got the background. I studied you."

Horner had moved his hands almost together to show how close Carl was to believing. Carl thought the distance should be much, much greater between the hands if they were truly to represent how close he was to believing in witches, but he nodded.

"And they're coming after you because they know you're going to recruit me to carry on the fight against them?"

"Somethin' like that," Horner agreed, running his hand through his hair and closing his eyes.

"Part of it's that they found me just a few days back," said Horner. He opened his eyes and looked toward the draped windows. "I was hiding pretty good, pretty good if I do say so myself, and between you and me, Doc, there's nobody else gonna say it."

"And . . . ?"

"They mean to kill us, Doc," he said. "Pure and simple."

"Kill us?"

"Dead. Come right through that window or the door maybe. Shoot us dead."

"Shoot?"

"Crossbows," said Horner calmly. "They use crossbows. Tradition. Ebony bolts."

"Because . . . ?"

"You mean, why are they gonna kill us, not why are crossbows traditional?" said Horner, biting his lower lip and looking down at his gnarled hands.

"Let's start there," said Carl, leaning back and leaving his hands open. He now had the feeling that the old man might,

38

just might, get a bit violent as he went on.

"It's sort of my fault gettin' you and your wife involved. No, not just sort of, it is my doin'. I'll own up to that right now. But done is done, right?"

"Done is done," agreed Carl. "If this coven is right behind you, why aren't you more worried?"

"I am worried. I'm so damned scared I'm near heavin' up what little I got in my stomach." Horner got up and moved to the window. "I'm scared, but I'm not panicking. Big difference."

Carl watched the old man reach for the drapes and then change his mind and turn around.

"I've been at this a long time," said Horner. "There're things to do to get us through the night, through this storm. Daylight comes, they'll back off and we'll have time. Now we better get goin'. I'll move the chairs and rug back so . . ."

"Hold it," said Carl, getting up.

Thunder rattled close by.

Horner, who had begun to move a chair, paused and looked at him.

"Right," said Horner. "What the hell am I thinkin' here? You're not convinced. No point tryin' to force you."

Horner took three long steps to the door and switched off the light.

The room went black.

"Put the light back on, Mr. Horner," Carl said calmly.

"Don't panic on me here," Horner said. "I'm just tryin' to make my case."

A crack of lightning hit nearby, bringing a burst of light that penetrated the closed drapes and illuminated the face of the old man across the room. The face was pale, eyes deep in their sockets, white hair in shock.

"The lights, Mr. Horner," Carl said, coming around the

desk, confident that he knew the room better than the old man.

"Go to the window, Doc," Horner said softly. "Just you humor me. I'll stay right here."

"I . . ."

"Ain't gonna hurt, Doc, for you to look out the window."

"I look out the window," said Carl, moving toward the window with his back to it, "and you turn the lights back on and leave the furniture alone."

"You give a good look and I turn the lights back on. You got it."

Carl wished he was wearing something more than the silk robe. His gray suit would have been better. His sweat suit would have been acceptable.

Thunder cracked again and Carl reached for the drapes.

"Just a little. 'Nough for you to see."

Carl pulled the drape back no more than two inches and looked out into the darkness and rain.

"There's nothing out there, Mr. Horner."

"Give it a chance, young man, give it a chance. They should be comin' any minute. Should be signs of 'em."

A slight rumble and a nearby crack of lightning shook the windows. Carl let the drape fall closed. He turned around and faced the darkness.

"You saw something," Horner said confidently.

"What's going on, Horner?"

"What'd you see?"

"I don't know."

"They're coming from the woods, right?"

"I think I saw some figures near the trees."

"Hooded figures," said Horner. "One of 'em carryin' somethin'."

"Look . . ."

"No, Doc. Best you take another look, satisfy yourself it

wasn't some mirage or somethin'."

Carl turned and opened the drapes again. He waited. Waited. The nearby thunder. The pause. The crack of lightning. And no doubt. There were figures. Four. Five. Maybe six of them. Hooded, one of them carrying something, moving slowly, carefully, their robes just touching the top of the grass.

He let the drapes close and turned. The lights came on. Horner was moving as quickly as his body would allow. He grabbed the chair.

"What you think, Doc? I'm givin' you a cock and bull or the gold eagle?"

"Hold it," said Carl, moving forward and grabbing the old man's wrist. "There are people out there. And they are heading toward the house. That doesn't prove . . ."

"Don't see you got much choice here," said Horner, looking down at the hand holding his wrist. "People dressed in robes carrying crossbows coming toward your house. I'd say they mean us no good."

"Shit," said Carl. "I don't . . ."

Carl let go of Horner's wrist and moved back to his desk to reach for the phone.

"Do you no good, Doc," said Horner, putting the wooden chair near the window. "They see the same movies you do. Phone lines'll be cut. Besides, by the time you got help, it'd all be over and you, me, and the missis would be dead and dragged away."

Carl picked up the phone. It was dead. He stood holding it and watched as Horner pushed the leather chair across the room and threw the bearskin rug over the desk.

"Give me a hand here. It'll go much faster," said the old man.

"I don't know who those people are, but we're getting my

wife and getting into my car and getting the hell away from here."

"They got to your car by now, Doc. First thing they'd do, even before the phones."

Horner was looking at the space he had cleared in front of the fireplace.

"Nice floors, good wood. Maple," said Horner. "Best get the lady now."

"Wait . . ." Carl began.

"No time. Unless you got a gun, but I know you don't believe in usin' 'em. Said so in your book, the one about violence and TV. Trust me and we'll make it through."

The two men looked at each other now. A beat.

"I'll get my wife."

Carl moved quickly past Horner and ran up the stairs.

"Connie," he whispered into the darkness of the bedroom.

"What?"

Carl made his way across the room to the window and looked out across the field, squinting into rain and night. He urged on the lightning, willed it, wished it, but it didn't come.

"Carl?" Connie said behind him.

Carl saw or thought he saw something move outside. Near the shed in the glint off of rusting metal.

"Con, put on your robe and come downstairs, fast."

"What are . . . ?" she began and he heard her moving out of the bed.

"No light. Don't turn on the light."

"No light?" she asked, sitting up and reaching for her robe.

"Trust me."

"It's the old man. What's he doing? Does he have a gun?"

Carl went back to the bed, found his wife and began to guide her to the door.

"No gun, Con. I'm not sure what's going on, but there are people out there."

"Out? On our lawn? Who?"

They were in the hall now, on the landing next to the bathroom. The night light downstairs illuminated Connie's face as she stopped and looked at her husband. She was beautiful in any light.

"There are people out there who think they're witches," Carl said as calmly as he could.

"Carl, are you sleepwalking?"

"Con, there are people out there."

"Oh God, crazies. Your book."

"My book and Horner, the old man downstairs."

He took her warm, small hand, and hurried her down the stairs and into the office, where they found Horner on his knees, a bottle of dark red liquid in his now red-stained hands. Horner had moved the chairs. The rug, Carl saw, was draped over his desk. The old man was putting the finishing touches on a yard-wide five-pointed star he had painted on the wooden floor. He put a cork in the bottle and pulled a leather bag, ancient and dark, from the pocket of his denim jacket.

"What the hell are you doing?" Carl shouted.

"Pentagram," said Horner. "I've done better. Done worse too. 'Pends on how much time I got."

Carl looked at his wife, who stood wide-eyed, mouth partly open, looking at the floor.

"Blood of the lamb," Max Horner said.

Above the sound of driving rain, Carl heard the handle of the front door turning.

"Stand over there," Horner said as he poured white sandy grains from the bag. "Inside the pentagram. Right there."

"Carl," Connie said, looking at her husband.

43

Something rattled the window behind the drapes.

"Best step over here," said Horner, pointing to the space on the floor. "Makin' a halo around you with holy powders from the Holy Land. They can't touch you inside it."

"Wait, now just wait," Carl said, holding up his hands as the old man completed the circle of sand around the five-pointed star of blood. "Did they have you in a hospital in Providence? Did you get out of a hospital . . . ?"

Horner shook his head no and said,

"You think maybe I'm some kind of escaped nut and those people out there are a squad of keepers with straitjackets and stun guns, somethin' like that?"

"Something like that," said Carl, holding Connie close to him.

"Pull back the drapes, Doc," Horner said with a sigh. "It's a risk, but can't see no way I can force you."

Carl eased Connie's hands from him and moved to the window. He took a deep breath and pulled back the drape. On the other side of the rain-streaked window stood a figure in a dark robe. The hood of the robe covered the figure's face. And in the hand of the robed figure was a crossbow. Carl Lenz let the drape close, stumbled backward, and took his wife in his arms.

"I don't understand," he said, looking at Connie and then at Horner.

"Nothin' more to understand," said the old man. "Just time to do."

A pane of glass in the bay window broke. A crash of metal against wood sounded from beyond the closed office door in the direction of the front hall.

"Carl," Connie whispered, her voice cracking, her body trembling. "Let's just do what he says. Please."

She took her husband's hand and stepped into the circle of

sand at the center of the pentagram. Carl followed her as Horner stood back and checked his handiwork.

"I think I got it all," Horner said as the sound of breaking glass and wood resounded behind him. "Take off the robes. Throw them outside the circle."

"What are you talking about?" Carl cried, holding Connie close to him. He could feel the rapid pounding of her heart.

"Bridge. They can use it like a bridge. Anything. Clothes, jewelry, any such like. Hurry."

Carl hesitated.

"I don't think . . ." Carl began, and then stopped.

Horner had pulled a small, shining gun from the pocket of his denim jacket. The gun was aimed at Carl's chest.

"No time to argue here," said Horner.

Connie took a step back, took off her robe, and flung it toward the bearskin on the desk. She was panting in fear, trying to catch her breath. Carl tore off his robe and threw it beyond the circle. He held Connie again now, skin-to-skin, breast-to-chest, feeling her heart beat, tasting her breath.

The sound of a thud and a crunch of wood came through the closed door.

Horner moved quickly, a pocket lighter in one blood-red fist, the gun in the other.

"Stay close together and close your eyes," he said.

Horner's down-home accent seemed to have disappeared, but Carl had no time to examine the observation.

"What about you?" asked Carl.

"You'll just have to carry on for me," said Horner with a cockeyed smile. He flicked the lighter, and knelt to set the sand afire. The flame moved serpentlike around the circle, sending a blazing wall around Connie and Carl Lenz.

"I love you," Carl whispered. He closed his eyes as he heard a body crash through the bay window and the office door crash open. The heat was searing.

Connie whispered something back, but he couldn't make out the words. She shivered in his arms. He held her close and kissed her, soft, warm, and deep. He felt a sudden jerk inside and tried to open his eyes, but they refused to respond. Voices surrounded him and the heat was gone. The heat was gone, but he felt suddenly stiff, aching.

Carl Lenz opened his eyes and saw three hooded figures in front of him, he heard the crackling of flame behind him. Cold wind billowed the drapes in front of the broken bay window.

Carl turned to the sound and heat of the flames, and reached out for Connie. Across the room in the circle of flames, in the center of the five-pointed star, he saw himself, naked, clinging to Connie, kissing her. He saw himself turn, and the face he had seen every morning and night in the mirror smiled at him.

"No," screamed Carl Lenz, looking down at his gnarled, bloodstained arthritic hand holding a gun. "No."

Carl moved as quickly as he could toward the flaming circle, and raised the gun toward the body that had been his. He felt a sharp pain in his back, a piercing pain that sent him sprawling into the desk. His fingers found Connie's robe on the bearskin as he dropped the gun. Carl Lenz in the body of Max Horner rolled toward the hooded figures. One of them held a crossbow. There was no bolt in the bow, Carl knew the bolt was embedded in his back.

Carl tried to speak. Blood blocked his throat. He coughed and raised a hand toward Connie. Carl felt the life in this body ebbing as one of the figures took off his heavy robe. Beneath the robe was a man—not a young man, but a bald man with a middle-age belly. The man threw his robe on the flames and stamped them out.

Carl watched the man help Connie and the creature who had taken his body step out of the circle and look at him. The creature in his body held Carl's wife close to him.

"Who are you? What is this?" asked Connie. A second figure, a thin woman in glasses with her hair tied in a bun, handed Connie her robe.

"This man," said the being in Carl's body, pointing at Carl. "He came here, pulled a gun, made us get in that circle. What's going on? And who the hell are you people?"

The third robed figure in the room slowly, somberly, reloaded the crossbow with a black bolt. In the doorway to the office stood another hooded figure with his hands folded like a monk in flowing sleeves.

"We're members of the Order of St. Robert," said the woman as she handed the man inside Carl's body Carl's robe. The man put on the robe. "Our order is dedicated to finding true witches and warlocks and destroying them. That man," she said, pointing at Carl in the body of Max Horner, "is a warlock. It is the night of confluence, the thirteenth of April. If the heavens and hell collide and thunder, lightning and rain prevail, a witch or warlock can take the body of another and discard his own."

"I don't believe this," said Connie, looking with disgust at the agonized dying body of Max Horner.

Carl tried again to speak. Tears came to his eyes as the man in his body put his arm around his wife and kissed her comfortingly above her ear.

"No," Carl managed to croak from the floor. "I'm Carl Lenz."

The bald man and the thin woman turned to him.

"He's gone crazy," said Connie. "You're all crazy. He's no witch. He's just a lunatic. You're all just lunatics."

Connie put her head against the false Carl and wept as he

held her tight. The bald man and the woman looked at each other and nodded.

"Inquisition," said the woman, turning to Connie.

"Inqui . . . what are you . . . ?" the man in Carl's body said incredulously.

"He may be telling the truth," said the woman. "The pentagram was drawn. The flame was lit. He may have had time."

"To do what?" asked Connie.

"To take one of your bodies," said the man.

"Take my body?" asked the false Carl, pointing at himself.

"Or that of your wife," said the woman.

"Inquisition," said the man.

Carl, dying in the body of Max Horner, gasped.

"Doctor Lenz, ask your wife questions only she could answer and tell us if she answers correctly."

"Hold it," said the man in Carl's body. The crossbow rose toward his chest.

The creature in Carl's body looked at the dying Carl, shrugged, and turned to Connie.

"What did you wear on our wedding night?"

Connie looked at the people facing her and then at the crossbow now pointed in her direction.

"Silk," she gasped dryly. "Pink, one piece."

"The last time we went out to dinner," asked the false Carl. "Where did we go and what did I eat?"

Connie gulped, paused, thought for an instant and said, "Martoni's, last Friday. You had the filet mignon and a Caesar salad."

"This is Connie," the false Carl said with a sigh of exasperation. "And this is ridiculous. This man is dying. I'm a doctor. If you'll just let me . . ."

"Now," said the woman, ignoring him and addressing Connie. "You ask them questions. Do not tell us who is right or wrong till they've answered all the questions. You understand?"

Connie looked at the false Carl, who nodded his agreement.

"I've got to think," said Connie, biting her lower lip. "I've . . . My mother gave us a wedding present. What is it?"

The woman turned to the false Carl, who said, "A crystal vase. It's in the hallway."

Carl, in Horner's body, shook his head and gasped, "No, a quilt, handmade quilt. On the bed upstairs."

"Next question," ordered the thin woman in glasses.

Connie looked at the two men, the one dying, the other her husband.

"My favorite movie," Connie asked.

The false Carl smiled sadly and said, "*The Way We Were*."

Carl, on his knees, blinked away tears and tried to swallow blood and bile; he mouthed, and then managed to painfully cough out, "*Lost Horizons*."

"One more," said the woman. "Time for only one more."

"What did I tell you I want for my next birthday?" Connie said, her eyes moist, darting from person to person around her.

"The French designer dress we saw in the window of Saks," said the false Carl.

"Pearls," Carl tried to say through the puffed lips of Max Horner. Nothing came out. He tried again. Still nothing. Rage filled him. He clenched his fists and managed to spit out, "Pearls."

"Enough," said the woman. "Identify your husband, quickly."

Connie looked at the dying, crumpled figure on the floor

and then at the man in Carl's body. Carl blinked once and watched in disbelief as Connie moved into the arms of the body snatcher who had answered every question incorrectly. She kissed the false Carl, kissed him with open mouth and tears flowing.

Carl felt himself being lifted from the ground. He tried to speak but was too weak. He blinked in agony as he was carried toward the door and heard the woman say,

"No one will believe you if you tell about this."

"We won't tell," the false Carl promised.

Carl wanted to howl in death as he saw his wife nod in agreement. And then Carl closed his eyes, sensing only movement and nausea and then the spray of rain and the chill of night as he was carried out. His foot kicked the bicycle Horner had come on only an hour earlier.

"Do not die," a man's voice said in his ear.

"Be very quiet," a woman's voice whispered in his other ear.

Carl opened the eyes of Max Horner and felt rain on his dry lips. Before him, he saw something familiar and yet unfamiliar, and then he realized that he was standing outside his office window, his broken office window looking at the billowing drapes.

"Do not speak," came a voice so soft that Carl was not sure he heard it.

And then he heard other voices, his own voice, the voice of his wife from within the office.

"Too long," said Connie. "Too long."

"As quickly as I could," he heard the man in his body say. "The body was not spent. The signs weren't right till tonight."

"Shhh, I know," Connie said, and there was silence.

The wind billowed the drapes and through the opening he

saw himself and Connie naked on the floor on the bearskin rug, mouths together, bodies together. He knew he was about to cry out, but a hand covered his mouth to stop him.

"I took this body in April," said Connie, rising over the body of Carl Lenz, "and you come back to me in April. The circle is complete."

The drapes closed again and low, chanting voices surrounded Carl. The hand came away from his mouth and the chanting voices rose.

Again the wind and the drapes parted. The man in Carl's body looked toward the window and Carl found himself once more gazing into his own eyes. Connie noticed nothing, caught up in her passion.

Carl shuddered. The body of Max Horner shook as death entered his open mouth. Carl closed his eyes as the chanters shouted something harsh that sounded like a long ZZZZZZZ. The pain in his back departed, replaced by a softness and a feeling of life between his legs.

Carl opened his eyes and found himself looking up at Connie, who was arched backward in ecstasy, a satisfied smile on her face.

She looked down at him as he felt himself releasing in horror an uncontrollable animal heat. And in her eyes at that moment, there was recognition. Though she too couldn't stop, he knew that she knew.

"Connie," he groaned, and she roared in pain as the bolt entered her long, white, beautiful neck.

And the rain stopped falling.

THE FINAL TOAST

Holmes was not himself that night.

Some time before dawn on a weekday morning in the winter of 189—, he burst through the door of our lodgings at 221B Baker Street, London West. Without removing his coat, he sat opposite me in a straight-backed wooden chair and looked about as if he were seeing the room for the first time. I must confess that I had been dozing in my armchair over an article in *The Lancet* on treatment of infection from saber wounds. It was not that the article had failed to hold my interest but that I had pondered over it beyond the moment when I could muster sufficient energy to rouse myself and prepare for bed. I remember telling myself that I would simply close my eyes for a few minutes and then, refreshed, awaken to prepare myself for a comfortable night's sleep.

When Holmes came through the door, my eyes shot open and I experienced a moment of confusion.

"Holmes," I said, reaching down to retrieve *The Lancet* from the floor where it had fallen, "I thought you were on your way to Glasgow, thought you'd almost be there by now."

Holmes sat back in the shadows of the final embers of the fire, which I'd stoked halfway through the article that had been my undoing. With his fingers forming a temple before his face, he stared at me in a way that I found quite unnerving.

In the half-light, his features looked a trifle too sharp, his voice sounded a bit too precise, as if he had been tightened by some Godlike puppet master. My face or manner must have betrayed me, for Holmes said,

"What is it, John? You look as if you've seen . . ."

"Nothing, Holmes. Nightmare. Surprise at seeing you, that's all."

Holmes rose suddenly, removed his coat and dropped it on the chair.

"A good cigar, John. Shall we smoke in the darkness while I tell you of the singular adventure that began this morning?"

"Well . . . yes," I agreed, as Holmes moved to the humidor. It was on the mantle next to his unanswered correspondence, which was secured to the dark wood by a jackknife. He opened the humidor and rattled the empty can.

"It seems," he said wearily, "that we will have to forgo the pleasure of tobacco."

"Pity," I said with a yawn, "but you have never been particularly dependent upon the weed in any case. I'd offer you some cigarettes, but since you never . . ."

"Quite true," he agreed, returning to the chair as I rose rather languidly. "I'd like to get to the heart of my misadventure. As you know, I received a letter imploring me to come to Glasgow immediately, and in the letter . . ."

". . . was a ticket for the morning train and a sum of cash," I said, rummaging around the room for something I urgently wanted to show him.

"Seventy pounds," he said. "A somewhat odd sum. But the letter was urgent."

"And," I added, finding what I was looking for in a drawer near the window, "the puzzle posed rather intriguing."

"Rather," he agreed, watching my movements. "John, you appear a bit nervous. Would you like me to make some tea before I go on? This might make one of your more interesting tales about my exploits."

"Sorry, Holmes," I said, returning to my chair with my hands snugly in the pockets of my purple Randipur smoking jacket." I'm sorry, there is nothing remaining from dinner for you to eat. I had no idea you were coming back. There are half a dozen eggs left on the sideboard, but I know how you dislike . . ."

A look of distinct distaste came over his sharp features, as if he had smelled something foul.

"I can do without the residue of barnyard fowl," he said. "Shall I tell you of the case or not? I must say, John, you seem oddly preoccupied whereas I anticipated that you would be agog over this conundrum."

"You have no idea of how intrigued I am by your whereabouts this day," I said, sitting up. "But may I first ask you what I believe to be an important question?"

"Ask away, my dear fellow," he said, brushing his hair back with his palm.

With that, I rose, removed the Webley handgun from my pocket, and aimed it squarely at his chest.

"Who are you?" I asked.

His face was lighted from below by the final embers of the fire. The last remnant of coal cracked and crackled, but I did not look away or flinch. I hoped I looked as unworldly to him as he did to me.

"Who am . . . Good Lord, John, how much have you had to drink? I'm Sherlock."

"Sherlock Holmes does not refer to himself as Sherlock," I said evenly. "Sherlock Holmes never calls me John. Sherlock Holmes knows full well that the cigars are kept, not in the humidor, but in the coal-scuttle. Sherlock Holmes has a passion for eggs. Sherlock Holmes would not refuse cigarettes when he was involved in a case. In fact, he would accept any form of tobacco."

"Pray, continue," the man said, eyeing my weapon carefully and returning to the chair on which he had draped his coat.

"The light is poor, but your nose is a bit too sharp, your hair a bit too dark, your cheeks a jot too full and there's something . . ."

"About the way I walk and talk," he said.

"That also," I agreed, backing away. "You are a devilish approximation, I'll admit, but I know Holmes too well and I've seen through your sham. Now tell me what has become of the real Holmes or I shall fire upon you with no hesitation."

I expected many things, a lie, a confession, a warning, but I did not expect him to do what he did next. He laughed. The laugh was deep, quite natural. His hands clasped in front of him.

"You missed several things, Watson," he said. "For example, most people walk listing to one side or the other depending on which hand they favor. It is a slight thing in all save the elderly. We are often aware of it in others without consciously knowing that we are aware. I have made it my business to be consciously aware of such things. What others carelessly call instinct, I know to be unconscious observation. Thus, though you have not been consciously aware of it, you know that I normally walk without listing in either direction. That list, by the way, is what causes men lost in the desert to wander in circles. Actually, the diameter of the circle of a wandering man, judged by his footprints in the desert or on a moor, should be enough to tell you his approximate age and height. It can certainly tell you if he is right-handed or left-handed. General Kitchener . . ."

"Rubbish," I said, holding up my weapon. "You'll not get by on such rubbish. Where is Holmes?"

"I also put lifts in both my shoes to give me an extra quarter-inch over my normal height," he went on, walking to the Persian slipper on the table and filling the pipe he had removed from his pocket with tobacco stored in the slipper's toe. "The weapon you are holding is a two-and-a-half-inch barrel, .442 model 1872. It has no ejector rod. Spent cases are removed by removing the cylinder entirely, a rather cumbersome method which makes the weapon a chore to fire and clean. You don't wish the boredom of cleaning such a weapon and, as I know, you've never fired it and possibly are not even sure if a spent round now resides in each chamber. Are you satisfied, Watson?"

"Not in the least," I said. "But I am impatient and concerned about Holmes."

"Then let me put your final fears to rest, my friend," he said, and with that he removed something from the bridge of his nose, removed two small balls from his mouth, wiped his face with a handkerchief from his coat pocket and sat down to light his pipe.

"Holmes," I cried, "what is going on? What is the point of this bizarre charade?"

"Put away your gun, throw a few more coals on the fire, and pour some tea," he said comfortably. "And then I will explain."

Holmes, for I now knew him to be Holmes, began by removing a neatly folded sheet of paper from his vest pocket as I carefully placed the coals on the fire. When I had turned from the fire, which crackled suddenly to life again, I wiped my hands on the rag we kept near the mantle and took the sheet from his outstretched hand.

"It's a newspaper clipping," I said, folding it open with my back to the fire so I could read by the resurgent flame. I had moved to turn on the gas lamp but Holmes had stopped me.

Holmes puffed at his pipe and nodded before speaking.

"An advertisement from *The Thespian Chronicle*," he explained, looking not at me but into the fire. "Are you familiar with the publication, Watson?"

"Can't say that I am," I said, trying to read the fine print.

"It is a monthly publication, four sheets devoted primarily to advertisements for theatrical professionals, musical acts, touring players, stage hands, the like," he said. "I might have missed this piece, though I occasionally scan the publication, were it not for one of the Baker Street Irregulars, a rather clever lad named Chaplin whose parents are in the theater. Little Charlie has a sharp eye. Read what he directed to me."

The ad was simple:

"Wanted. For one morning's work. Excellent pay. Discreet actor who can impersonate a well known London consultant. Applicants should be slightly over six feet, quite lean, with sharp, piercing eyes and a thin, hawklike nose. Chin should be prominent and with a squareness which marks the man of determination. Appear at 13 Bellowdnes Road at 7 A.M. sharp, Monday."

When I looked up, Holmes was puffing away and staring at the fire.

"Well?" I said, handing him back the clipping which he took and replaced in his pocket without looking up.

"What do you make of the advert, Watson?"

"Make of it? Someone wants an actor for a sham of some kind and I suppose you want me to observe that the actor being sought bears a resemblance to you."

"Watson, that description is taken directly from your very first published tale chronicling my endeavors. Whoever wrote that hoped that those who answered it would know they were to engage in portraying Sherlock Holmes. The fact that my name is not mentioned, that the pay is to be high and that it is a singular job suggests . . ."

". . . a possible nefarious purpose," I supplied, "but it could also be some kind of a prank or even a promotion for some public house. It could be many things."

"It could be many things," Holmes agreed, "but when we combine the ad with the letter urging me to an intrigue in Glasgow—an intrigue which would have me on a train away from London at the moment my double was to be chosen, and the following morning, when, I assume, he was to be used—and we have a very promising situation."

"Promising indeed," I agreed, sitting back in my chair to face him, "but promising of what?"

"That was what I determined to discover," Holmes said, his face covered by a soft puff of gray smoke. "I told you and Mrs. Hudson that I was on my way to Glasgow. I even went to the station, boarded the train and traveled one stop, on the chance that I was being watched. I then hurried back by coach to audition for the role of Sherlock Holmes. I might add that it was the most difficult deception of my career. I've been many things, a drunken groom, an aged Italian, a simple-minded clergyman, but to be myself was the ultimate challenge."

"I can't see why," I said. "You simply . . ."

"Nothing simple about it at all," he cut in. "I had to assume that whoever placed that ad knew what Sherlock Holmes looked like, had probably even seen me, watched me closely. So I had to resemble myself but not be myself. Imagine for a moment, Watson, that you had to masquerade as John Watson, M.D. What would you alter? Are you aware of how you walk? How you cock your head to the right when you are puzzled, as you are doing now?"

I straightened my head and nodded, seeing the problem he laid before me.

"Can you alter your speech slightly but not too much? And how do you alter it without losing the resemblance to yourself?"

"I find this all very confusing, Holmes," I admitted. "Why not simply go to the address and confront whoever was there? I would gladly have joined you."

"And we would have discovered nothing," he sighed. "When we walked through the door, whoever was there would almost certainly have a covering story, a lame one perhaps, but no law has been broken. No, if I was to discover what this was about I would have to play the role. Besides, the suggestion of illegality in the ad, the fact that my name was not mentioned, and the fact that such steps had been taken to get me out of London convinced me that a crime was in the offing."

"And so you donned the disguise," I said.

"And so I did," Holmes agreed.

"I arrived at Bellowdnes Road just before seven," Holmes went on, looking into the fire as if he were seeing again the events of that morning. "There were two others seeking the role. The first was obviously ill-suited for the part, much too tall and not only thin but tubercular. Of the three of us, judging by his cough and threadbare coat, he was most in need of employment. The other aspirant was closer to the mark, somewhat better dressed and about my height, but his nose would never do . . . too flat, obviously the result of several years of professional pugilism. We stomped in the cold early morning till the door opened and we were led in by a woman who kept her face covered with a shawl as if she were suffering from a cold."

"And she was not," I said.

"Decidedly not," Holmes agreed. "We were led into a stark parlor where a man sat behind a table. The man and woman, who never identified themselves, questioned us, had us walk around, dismissed the emaciated actor after giving him a sovereign for his trouble and interrogated the former pugilist and I rather closely. For a few moments it seemed well within the realm of possibility that I would not be awarded the role of Sherlock Holmes. The other fellow was quite good, and I had to be careful not to betray myself."

"What finally got you the role?" I asked, assuming that Holmes did, indeed, receive the part.

"My thinly veiled zeal to do whatever had to be done, whether it be legal or not. When asked about our backgrounds, the pugilist erred in the direction of good citizenship. I, on the other hand, hinted at brushes with the law of which I preferred not to converse."

"And so," I said, urging him on. "You got the part."

"Let us say that I proved to be the most appropriate actor for the role," he said, and then paused to look at the bowl of his pipe. Outside, the clop-clop of a horse and coach some distance away punctuated our silence.

"All right, Holmes, for God's sake, what did they want of you, or of the impersonator of Sherlock Holmes?" I finally asked. My irritation had several causes, the tension of the situation, the late hour, a winter's twinge around the war wound in my leg. I threw the remnant of my cigar into the fire where the orange flames wrapped around it.

"Let me make you some tea, Watson. You seem particularly on edge this evening." Holmes began to rise but I waved him back.

"Just tell me what happened," I urged, and then I'll go to bed."

"To bed," he said, looking first at me and then toward the window beyond which the sound of the horse and cab were drawing closer. "I'm afraid not. I believe before the hour of seven I shall be in need of your able assistance. To answer your question, when the other thespian had departed, I was questioned further about my willingness to engage in less than legal acts and then informed that I was simply to dress like Holmes in clothes which would be provided—the very clothes I am now wearing."

"They do look like those you normally wear," I admitted.

"I was to go to Dartmoor Prison in the morning, just before seven, and deliver to prisoner Malcom Bell a small vial hidden in the cuff of my coat. The man and woman said that as Holmes I would certainly be admitted to see Bell and that Bell would be expecting me."

"But you are responsible for Bell's being in Dartmoor and his awaiting execution," I said.

"Precisely," Holmes went on. "The scheme is brilliant. Who better to make a delivery to a condemned man than the person who put him behind bars."

"Bell vowed to kill you," I reminded him.

"Yes," agreed Holmes. "I've grown devilishly hungry. I believe you do have something left from. . . ."

I got up and hurried to the sideboard where some scones and a small brick of cheese sat covered by a white cloth. I carried the small platter to Holmes, who put aside his pipe and began to eat. Between bites he went on.

"I was told by the couple that my visit to Bell would be an act of mercy. Bell would be hanged on Tuesday morning, publicly hanged, and a man of his ego . . ."

"Who had been responsible for the deaths of six people," I put in.

". . . would prefer to thwart the hangman," Holmes continued. "The vial, they said, contained a strong, tasteless poison, which Bell would welcome. My pay was to be twenty-five pounds immediately and an additional twenty-five upon completion of the job. The final payment would be made at the same address where the audition took place."

"I see," I said.

"Do you, Watson? Capital. It took me a while to see."

With this Holmes popped a piece of cheese into his mouth and magically produced a small vial which he held between thumb and forefinger. By the light of the dancing flames, the vial seemed particularly menacing, as if the amber liquid within it were alive with virulence. Holmes eyed me momentarily and then flipped off the cork top of the small glass container. Before I could move, he put the vial to his lips and downed the contents.

I gasped and started out of the chair.

"Holmes, what kind of insanity is this?"

Holmes smiled up at me, replaced the cork and handed the vial to me.

"Watson, kindly refill this vial with claret. We may have some use for it."

"I must say, Holmes," I said, taking the vial. "That was a poor jest. You've obviously already removed the original contents and replaced them with some harmless concoction to stage this musical hall turn."

I looked at the vial and at my friend with what I hoped was the stern rebuke of an injured relative.

"No, Watson, I assure you. The liquid I just downed was the same as that given to me by the man and the woman this morning. I did, I confess, open the vial earlier to smell and taste the contents. It was claret with more than a touch of quinine."

It was then that I realized the room was growing brighter.

The sun was coming up. I walked, vial in hand, to the table near the window, where a decanter of claret stood alongside an identical decanter of sherry.

"You have been hired for fifty pounds to deliver a harmless drink to a condemned man?" I asked as I carefully poured the claret.

"No, the total cost, including the train ticket to Glasgow and the retainer for the mystery I was supposed to solve there, is closer to one hundred pounds."

"To deliver . . ."

". . . Sherlock Holmes into the hands of the man who has vowed to kill him," he said. "Malcom Bell has studied me well. He used his two accomplices to lure me into the challenge of playing myself. He knew I could not resist. I'd have arrived here much earlier, but I first tracked down the boy, Chaplin, who readily admitted that, while he recognized me in the description in the advertisement, the ad had been brought to his attention by an actor, a tall, thin man with a flat nose, who had simply commented in Chaplin's presence that he was going to try for the role."

"The man who almost won the role, the pugilist," I cried. "What an extraordinary coincidence."

"Coincidence? Hardly. Charles Chaplin was chosen to bring the bait to me. I have no doubt that the pugilist followed him to our apartments to be sure he delivered the paper. Had he failed to do so, I am sure they would have found another, perhaps less subtle, means of bringing the ad to my attention. Remember, Watson, Bell has had nothing to do for the past three weeks while awaiting execution, other than to plan his revenge. Now, may I suggest that you load your Webley and come me with me."

"To Dartmoor?" I said, moving to retrieve the pistol.

"To Bellowdnes Road," he corrected. "After we take care

of the tall gentleman who is certainly lurking somewhere on the street to be sure that I appear at Dartmoor and that the show go on."

Less than fifteen minutes later, Holmes went out to the street and moved to the corner. I watched from the window in the growing light. Holmes was dressed warmly for the chill morning. As he turned the corner, a figure stepped from a passageway below and moved in his direction. I hurried to the door and down to the street to follow the man. We wandered the streets, a strange trio playing follow the leader, with Holmes in front. We met few on the streets, except for those slouching to early jobs and a handful of deliverymen. One drayman's cart, carrying coal, scuttled down the cobbled street as Holmes suddenly turned in a direction that was clearly not going to take him toward transportation to Dartmoor. The tall man following Holmes quickened his pace and I did the same. Somewhere near Old Surrey Lane, Holmes turned into an alleyway. The man following him hastened to catch up. I managed to reach the mouth of the shadowy dead-end alley just in time to see Holmes turn to face the man who appeared to have him trapped.

"What game are we playing here?" the man said in a voice that sounded scorched and dry. He advanced on Holmes menacingly, right hand thrust deeply into his right coat pocket.

"Trap the criminal," Holmes answered, his legs apart, his hands clenched at his sides.

The taller man laughed and kept advancing on my friend. From his right pocket he drew something that looked like two bars of metal.

"Bell's going to be disappointed," the man said. "He wanted to do you in himself."

I stepped into the alley and raised my Webley, aiming

squarely at the back of the man who now stood no more than four paces from Holmes. He was bigger than Holmes by several inches, heavier too, and not only did he have the experience of being a boxer, he also had what might be lethal weapons in both hands. In spite of Holmes's admonition, delivered before we left, that I should move temperately, I was prepared to fire before the man took another step. However, before he could take that step, or I could pull the trigger, Holmes bounded forward, ducked right, threw two punches to the man's middle section and then alternate punches with right and left hands to the man's face. The metal bars in the gnarled hands of the bigger man clanged to the alley stones as he fell back in a sitting position and turned his head in my direction with a look of complete astonishment.

Holmes lifted the startled man to his feet and produced a pair of cuffs, which he clasped around the man's wrists.

"Rather a dangerous move," I said, putting the gun away as I stepped toward them. "I've witnessed your boxing skill before, but it was lucky you . . ."

"Luck, Watson?" he said, turning the confused pugilist toward the opening to the street and pushing him forward. "Since when have you known me to rely on luck? This man's right hand is badly used and his left hand virtually normal, which made it evident that as a boxer he favored the right and would certainly punch with it first. I, therefore, moved to his left. His nose, as you can see, has been broken several times, indicating that he would not be particularly vulnerable to a single blow to the nose. Therefore, when I moved to his left, I threw a blow to his kidney and another to his solar plexus, directly at the point where his lungs would give up much of their supply of air. He was quite helpless when I delivered the next two blows to the nerves in his cheek and neck."

"Forgive me, Holmes," I said with some sarcasm as we returned to the street and began to search for a constable. "I should never have assumed that you might need my help."

"On the contrary, Watson, I had to determine what weapon he had with him, if any. Were we dealing with fire-arms I would have welcomed your shooting him squarely between the shoulders. I'm an observer of human nature, an amateur in the realm of human anatomy and a consulting detective, but I am certainly not a fool."

Finding a constable and explaining the situation proved to be a bit more difficult than Holmes would have liked, but find one we did, an older fellow nearing pension who recognized Holmes and was glad to be of service. Less than an hour from the time we had left 221B we were standing before the doorway on Bellowdnes Road. Holmes, in spite of the fact that he had not slept for at least twenty-four hours, looked quite exuberant and awake.

"Won't they have cleared out?" I asked as he reached for the door.

"Why should they?" he said. "I'm not to make my appearance at Dartmoor for another hour. They believe they have fooled me and will be waiting for confirmation of my death at the hands of Malcom Bell from the gentleman we just turned over to the police. Ready your weapon, Watson. The end of this singular case is at hand."

He tried the handle of the door, which did not open, and then knocked loudly. The door was flung open almost immediately and Holmes reached forward, pushing it even further to reveal a heavy, dark woman in a black dress.

"What are you doing here?" she asked indignantly.

"Returning this," he said, revealing the vial.

"This is not . . ." she began, but was interrupted by a man's voice from the shadows of the interior.

"Enough, Rose," the man said. "He knows."

"Kindly step forward," I said evenly, aiming my Webley into the darkness and trying to appear as if I could see him clearly. Fortunately, he limped forward into the dusty half-light of the small entranceway.

"I assume you are both relatives of Malcom Bell," Holmes said.

"I'm his sister Rose, and this is my husband, Nicholas." the woman said. Then, suddenly, she began to sag and the man behind her moved forward to support her.

"I'm afraid," said Holmes, "Malcom Bell will have to take this final disappointment."

A cold slash of air chilled my neck and I followed Holmes into the house, closing the door with my shoulder while I kept the pistol at the ready.

"Not quite," the man said, leading his now-sobbing wife to a coarse wooden chair. "Rose isn't weeping because you caught us. Malcom thought you might be too clever. He has a vial of real poison hidden in his cell. Whether he had the chance to do you in or not, if you showed up at his cell he planned to switch the vials."

"So that I would be accused of having smuggled in poison," said Holmes. "If I survived or died, Malcom Bell would be credited with having bested me. And if I didn't show up?"

"If you don't show up before seven, Malcom, precisely at the hour, will take out that hidden vial and drink a toast to you and the hangman. He may not get his revenge, but he will avoid the noose and your justice."

"Quick, Watson," Holmes said. "The time."

I pulled my watch from my pocket and replied, "Seconds to seven, Holmes. I don't see what we can . . ."

Holmes pulled the vial of claret from his pocket, opened it and said, "Tell me when it is precisely seven."

The slumping woman, the man and I exchanged puzzled

looks, but approximately ten seconds later I said, "Now. It's seven."

Holmes held up the vial and said, "To a formidable opponent whom I will be both pleased and saddened to lose."

And with this he downed the amber liquid to the very last drop.

BITTER LEMONS

Warren Hlushka had the kind of face that made people say, "He'll never win a beauty contest." In fact, that's just what the bartender at the Cascadia Lounge on Broadway said to me when Warren burst nervously into the perpetual darkness of the bar, bringing an unwelcome blast of sun behind him and reminding me there were hours to go before I called it a day.

"Close the door," the bartender called, and Warren shifted the weight of the oversized book under his arm, pulled himself together, and closed the door. Then he squinted, blinked, and tried to adjust his eyes to the amber darkness.

Warren's nose was pushed to one side as if his face were permanently pressed against a store window. His large popping eyes made him look amazed at even the most inconsequential contact with other human beings. Warren was short, bald, and so thin you wondered how well he could stand up against an evening breeze off the Pacific.

Coils Conroy, the barkeep, was wrong. Warren had heard his beauty contest comment. Warren had won a beauty contest in Baker, Kansas, when he was a kid. He proved it to us by dropping what proved to be his family album on the bar and opening it to a brittle, crumbling, yellow newspaper clipping. The clipping showed that a boy named Warren Hlushka, son of Peggy and Marcus Hlushka, had won the

1912 Baker County Fair Best Looking Child ribbon. A photograph of a smiling blond boy with yellow curls looked up at me. I turned the album around so Coils Conroy could see the clipping. He looked at it sourly, grunted, and turned away.

"That's me all right," Warren insisted. "That's me right there, Mr. Marlowe."

I turned the album back around to look at the pretty young woman in the photograph holding the hand of the little boy. She wore a little hat and held her free hand up to her face to shield her eyes from the sun.

I looked at the kid in the picture and then at Warren. The long eyelashes were still there and the features, they were there too, but exaggerated, grotesque.

"And that, holding my hand, is my mother," he said. "And there, in the next picture, that's my father, he's holding my baby sister, Louise. I want you to find her for me. That's why I came here looking for you. I thought it through, came looking for you. You're not in your office so . . ."

"Your sister?"

"Sister, right," said Warren, looking in amazement at the photograph as if he had never seen it before.

"The one you want me to find?"

"The one," he agreed. "I want to see her. I got something important to tell her."

"What?" I asked, unwilling to reach for my beer and not offer Warren one.

"Can't tell you, Mr. Marlowe," he said, lowering his voice and glancing at Conroy to be sure he wasn't listening. "Family stuff."

"How long has it been since you saw your sister?" I asked.

"Louise?" he asked and then considered the question as he bit his lower lip. "Twenty, twenty-five years maybe. I got a letter."

70

He turned album pages quickly, passing photographs, postcards, matchboxes, and even candy wrappers.

"Here," he said, triumphantly slapping the page with his palm.

I had come down to the bar to nurse a beer after a long morning of listening to the radio and reading the newspaper from cover to cover, including the car ads. The phone hadn't rung. The mailman hadn't brought a desperate cry for help, and no one had knocked at my door pleading for my services. I was tired from doing nothing. I wanted to look at Conroy's homely face and feel the cold moisture of an amber beer bottle. I didn't want to think about going back to my office or my apartment.

I had nothing better to do, so I listened to Warren Hlushka.

Warren fidgeted around, behind, and nearly on top of me, pleading, giving information as I tried to read the letter.

"Letter's from Louise," he said, pointing at the neatly scripted name in the corner of the envelope neatly pasted next to the letter.

"I know," I said.

"She's not in Baker, Kansas, anymore," he said. "I called, asked. Long time ago. I looked for her a couple times, I asked."

"This letter's almost twenty-five years old," I said.

"I know. I know. I told you," he said, shifting from one foot to the other and looking around the bar. There was no one there but me, him, and Conroy. "I just want you to find her for me. Tell me where she is, is all."

"She's gone, Warren," I said gently.

Conroy walked over, examined my almost empty, and looked at me.

"Another?" he asked.

71

"On me, Mr. Marlowe, on me," said Warren eagerly.

"No, thanks," I told both of them.

"You want privacy?" Conroy asked me, looking at Warren and making it clear that he would lead the man and his album to the door if I gave the word. Coils had lost his patience and most of his left leg in Guadalcanal. Warren was shaking his head no. I couldn't tell if the no was for Conroy, in response to my saying his sister was gone, or in answer to the prodding of some private demon.

"No, thanks," I told Conroy. "Warren and I are old friends."

I had known Warren for a couple of years, but we weren't friends. He did odd jobs in the neighborhood, washed windows, ran errands, swept up in exchange for free food from the restaurants, an odd pair of shoes or pants from a shoe store or clothing store, and a place to bed down in the basement of the building where I had my office.

I was now engaged in the longest conversation I had ever had with the man.

"I got drunk, Mr. Marlowe," Warren said as Conroy shrugged and turned his back on us to clean some glasses. "I got drunk to get up the nerve, you know. Then I was ashamed of being drunk so I sobered. So my head is hurtin' fierce."

I gulped down the last of my beer, patted Warren on his shoulder, and got off the bar stool.

"She's gone, Warren," I repeated. "Get drunk again and get some sleep."

"I've got money," he said, stepping back to dig into both pockets of his faded blue pants. Crumpled singles, fives, and tens appeared in his gnarled fists. He piled them on the bar next to his album and went back for more.

"See," he said. "I can pay."

More dollars. Lincoln and Washington looked up at me

from the top of the heap of bills. They were on Warren Hlushka's side and I found them convincing.

"What's the discrepancy here?" Conroy said, turning back to us, towel in one hand, glass in the other.

Warren was hyperventilating now, his large eyes fixed on my face, waiting for the answer to all his prayers.

"Life's savings," he said earnestly, his face pressing against the window of his expected failure. "All I've got. I'm not asking for favors here. Oh no. I'm hiring just like any Joe. You too busy? Okay, but I'm a . . . a . . . ."

Warren wasn't sure what he was and I didn't want to tell him.

"Give me a bag, Coils," I said, and Conroy shook his head and reached under the counter in search of a bag, his eyes never leaving the pile of bills, mine watching him. He came up with a brown paper bag and handed it to me. I shoved Warren's money into it and handed him the bag. He offered it to me again.

The last time I had met a client in a bar I wound up finding a woman for him. The situation wasn't quite the same. Warren wasn't about to break heads the way Moose Malloy had done. And I didn't figure to nearly get myself killed the way I had done looking for Moose's woman. Besides, I needed the money now, but more important I needed to have something to do.

"Twenty a day and expenses," I said. "If I don't find her in five days, I give it up and you promise to give it up. Deal?"

Warren went stone still.

"Give me fifty in advance," I went on. "I'll bill you for the rest if there is a rest. I'll need your album."

Warren shook himself out of his funk, smiled, and reached past me for the album. He handed it to me.

"That's business," he said, brushing his bald head in

memory of long-departed hair and digging in to pull out my advance. "Alls you got to do is find her, tell me where she is. I'll do the rest."

"I'm closing for lunch," Coils Conroy said behind the bar as he removed his apron. "Place's a morgue."

I drove home with Warren's album on the seat next to me and his fifty bucks in my pocket. My car needed work. It was pitted with acne, but fifty dollars wouldn't cover the body work. When I got through my door, I took off my jacket and tie, turned on the table fan next to my chessboard, and sat down to look at the Hlushka family album. I wondered once or twice if I were doing a good deed or conning a sap who would never make it off the bottom rung of life. I wondered, but I didn't think about returning his fifty.

Warren's album contained six more photographs of Louise. She was about fifteen in the most recent one, a pretty girl in a white Sunday dress with a big white bow in her short auburn hair.

Judging by Warren I guessed his little sister would be in her mid-forties now. The one letter Warren had shown me didn't help much. It was post-marked Baker, Kansas, and said that Louise was thinking about getting married and that she and her fiancé were considering a move to California. She asked if he could come home for the wedding. The address on the envelope indicated that Warren had lived in Dayton, Ohio.

I played through a Capablanca game from the 1921 international, had a cheese sandwich, took a shower, and went to bed early, turning the fan toward me. I had no trouble sleeping.

In the morning I shaved, stopped for a carry-out coffee and donut from a hole-in-the-wall called Casey's on La Cienega. Casey's coffee was awful, but his wife made great donuts. I took donut and coffee to my office, gathered in the three letters waiting for me in the morning mail, went to my desk, pulled over the phone, and got to work.

Two phone calls later I was talking to a woman named Ethel Murray at the *Baker Weekly Dispatch*. Ethel didn't sound young, but she did sound impressed by a long-distance phone call from California.

"Ethel," I said, "your editor, Mr. Stanfield, said you might be able to help me. Sometime back in May or June nineteen twenty-one a woman named Louise Hlushka probably got married in Baker. I'd like to know who she married and where . . ."

"Alton Cash," she broke in. "Married by Reverend Sawyer at the First Methodist."

"I'm impressed," I said.

"Needn't be," said Ethel. "I'd like to string you along, tell you I have one of those photographic memories like the boy in *American Weekly*, but it's not in me. I was Louise's bridesmaid. Not a big wedding, but I stood up and so did Alton's brother Jess."

"Where are Louise and Alton?"

"California," she said

"Big state," I said, tucking the phone under my chin and reaching for the morning mail.

"I'll narrow it some," she said. "Alton said he had relatives in some place called Bay City. You heard of it?"

"I've heard of it," I said, opening a phone bill and shoving it in the lower right-hand drawer of my desk. "You have a picture of the happy couple or Louise alone? That's my final request and I'll send you five dollars for your time and effort."

"I'll take a look," she said, "Mr. . . . ?"

"Marlowe," I supplied.

"Why are you looking for Louise after all these years? If it's about the Taylor girl, believe me it was an accident. I knew Louise. She had a temper, yes, but under it. . . . It was the rumors, the talk, that drove them off, not any fancy job. Alton was doing just fine in Baker."

"What did Alton do?"

"He was chief of police," Ethel said.

"Ethel, put together whatever you have on the accident and on Chief Cash. I'm sending you a check for ten dollars. You can cash it before you send whatever you find. Louise's brother is looking for her, just wants to make contact, and I'm helping him out."

There was a long pause, a sigh, and Ethel said, "I thought Warren was dead by now. I'll see what I can find for you and get it in the noon mail tomorrow. No charge. Just if you see Louise, tell her Ethel Murray said God bless."

I told her that if I had the chance I'd give Louise Cash her message. I thanked her, gave her my address, and hung up. It could have been easy from this point on. Bay City was less than thirty miles from where I was sitting. I'd had some runins with the police there, but that was a few years back. It could have been easy, but it didn't work out that way.

The second of my three morning letters was an ad for the latest in sidearms. I junked it. The last letter I didn't open. I recognized Terry's handwriting from the address. I junked it and pulled a Bay City telephone book from the same drawer I'd put the phone bill in.

There were five Cashes. No Alton. No Louise. I tried all five. Two were Negroes. Two were surly and said they didn't have any relatives named Alton or Louise. The fifth was a lonely old man who didn't want to lose this lucky contact with a fellow human. He said he thought he had a cousin Louise from the East but she had never come to Bay City. He suggested I come see him. He would make lunch and we could talk it over. I thanked him and said I'd get to him if I needed more help.

Warren Hlushka came by just before noon as I was leaving the office for lunch. He played with his sleeve, looked at me in wonder, and asked if I had found anything yet. I gave him what I had from Ethel and the phone book.

"There was some trouble back in Baker," I told him. "Something to do with a girl named Taylor. You know anything about it?"

"Me?" asked Warren.

"Unless Eisenhower just walked in behind you, yes," I said.

"I don't know anything about anything," he said.

"Your sister and her husband probably left because of the Taylor business," I explained. "Probably changed their name, that is if they even moved to Bay City. I'm waiting for some information from Baker. It'll take a few days to get here. No charge till it does."

"You favoring me, Mr. Marlowe?" he asked. "Or is that the way of it? You're not trying to give me no free ride?"

"It's the way of it, Warren," I assured him and went out for lunch.

I didn't quite forget about Warren and the Cashes for the next two days but I did manage to push them into some dark space while I helped out on an insurance stakeout for the World Detective Agency. It was an around-the-clock surveillance on a trio of ex-cons who'd probably taken down a Brink's truck in Encino the month before. World called in free-lancers like me to fill in while the regulars were out beating the bushes. After two days, somebody at World decided we had the wrong men or it was costing too much. I was given a check for fifty bucks and the offer to join the staff. I took the check and turned down the job.

The package from Ethel Murray of Baker, Kansas, was under my door the next morning. It helped. There were newspaper clippings of the Cash-Hlushka wedding. Alton had gotten married in his chief's uniform. He looked lean, trim, and proud, and his smile showed a small gap between his top front teeth. Louise had been married in a white dress. Her hair was short, her face pretty and clean, and her body full but not quite plump. There were no other pictures of Louise but there were several of Alton over the next year and a half after the wedding. He'd aged quickly. The Taylor case, on which there were four clippings, probably helped age him. Sharon Rose Taylor, twenty-four, had fallen or been pushed out of a window of the Equity Building, the tallest building in Baker, which meant that she had fallen about six floors at most. Alton and Louise had been with her at the time. Their tale was full of holes, but Cash was the chief of police and he'd said Sharon Rose had gone inexplicably mad and leapt out the window. Sharon Rose's father, according to the clippings, was incredulous in spite of the fact that his daughter had spent a few weeks in the state mental hospital earlier that year. The county coroner's inquiry accepted Alton and Louise Cash's story. The town of Baker might have had more trouble with the tale than the county coroner. Three months after Sharon Rose Taylor's death, according to a small clipping, Alton resigned as chief and announced that he had been offered a big job in California.

That was it. Not much, but something. I drove to Bay City with the windows open, half dreaming in the heat, not thinking about the drive. The smells of Los Angeles guided me. Each neighborhood has its own smell and look: the dry summer dust of the string of flatland towns; the suburban grass and steep hills as you head west; the smell of salt and the craggy coast as you hit the ocean and the coast highway. I drove south down the western end of the continent. This was as far as you could go, as far as your dreams would carry you in the United States.

Bay City was full of people who had run as far as they could go. It had been taken over more than thirty years earlier by men with dollars and guns who made a profit from the dreamers and high rollers. Bay City was known as the place where you could buy anything if you looked right and kept your mouth shut. I'd had a run-in with a Bay City cop named Degarmo some years back. Degarmo had been one of the dreamers. He was dead now, but Bay City was still alive, though the high rollers weren't rolling quite as high as they once had.

I drove straight to the police station, a freshly cleaned stone three-story at the end of a park. The lobby was empty and the polished stone floors recently scrubbed. The rubber soles of my shoes squeaked as I went through the door marked Inquiries/Detective.

The place had been through some remodeling since I had been there last. A counter ran from wall to wall protecting the police from the public. The desks beyond the counter were steel and small, with a few cops and robbers strewn around the place. Behind the counter facing me was an old cop whose face I remembered but whose name I couldn't place. He was overweight and uncomfortable in his stretched and starched uniform complete with tie.

He looked me over, didn't show any sign of recognition, which was fine with me, and decided I wasn't high priority.

"You got a problem?" he asked.

"Looking for a guy," I said, leaning on the counter to face him. He was my height, about six feet, but I had the feeling he had once been taller. I pulled out a clipping of Alton Cash and shoved it toward him. The old cop looked down at the clipping and then looked up at me.

"Old picture," he said.

"Very old," I agreed. "But he has the kind of weathered face that probably doesn't change much and that space between his teeth wouldn't go away."

The old cop scratched his head and looked at Alton's picture again.

"What's your angle?" he asked.

"I'm a friend of the brother-in-law," I said. "Brother-in-law is sick, very sick, probably dying back in an L.A. hospital. Hasn't been in touch with his sister for more than twenty years and suddenly got a line on her in Bay City. This friend wants to see his sister before he dies."

"Simple as that?" he asked, pushing the clipping back at me. I took it and returned it to my pocket.

"Simple as that," I said.

He looked around to see if anyone was watching and then whispered, "New chief here. Cleaning up. New image. I'd retire now if I had the years in. Collar's killing me. Can't afford to retire without the pension."

"Can I contribute to the pension fund?" I asked.

"Don't see why not," he said. "Private donation. Say, fifteen dollars."

"Say ten," I said, pulling out a ten and letting him see me palm it in my right hand.

"Ten," he said. "Name's not Cash like it says under that picture. Calls himself Dyson. He was on the force here. Quit some time back. You're lucky you ran into me. Most of the young vets around here wouldn't know him."

"How do I find him?" I asked.

He looked around again, held up a finger to show I should wait, and then slouched around the corner. I watched the neatly dressed cops at their desks talking quietly on their phones for about three minutes till the old cop came back. He leaned toward me.

"Four-four-six Oleander Drive. Go back to Central and then right almost to the docks. You'll see Oleander on the right about the same time you see the Pacific. That's his last address. Your guess is as good as mine if he's still there."

I reached over, shook his hand, and felt him take in the ten dollar bill with the skill of an expert. There was nothing more to say. I went back outside and headed down Central.

Oleander wasn't hard to find. It was one of those run-down side streets on which some developer had thrown up one-story white-frame houses back in the 1920s for the first wave of newcomers working in the Bay City shipyard. Ten years after they were built the flimsy one-stories were ready for the wrecker. Twenty years later they were occupied by Negro families where the breadwinners were women who cleaned house for the grifters in the estates higher up in the hills. Thirty years later the houses of Oleander Street were sagging and dying. A few of them had been shorn up and coaxed like punch-drunk pugs into standing up for one more round. Four-four-six Oleander didn't look as if it could take another punch. The porch sagged and the paint flaked. The screen door had been patched so many times that it looked like modern art, and the dirt lawn with only a barren lemon tree on it had long ago given up the hope of grass.

I parked on the curb of the cracked concrete street and looked over at the two Negro kids about six who had been tossing a tin can back and forth till I got out of the car. The boy crinkled his nose at me and the girl squinted. As I hit the steps of four-four-six, I heard the girl say, "He gonna see the witch."

I knocked at the peeling frame of the screen door. The door shook and threatened to come loose. Nothing. I knocked again.

"Keep knockin', mister," called the girl from across the street. "They home. They always home."

I kept knocking and eventually I heard a shuffle from inside. It stopped. I knocked again and the shuffle moved toward the door and then the door opened, but just a crack.

"What?" came the man's voice.

I couldn't see the face in the shadows through the thick mesh.

"Mr. Dyson?" I asked.

"So?" he asked.

"My name's Marlowe. I'd like to talk to you for a minute. I just came from police headquarters in Bay City.

"It's about your wife," I threw in.

The door stopped closing.

"My wife isn't well," he said.

"I've got a message for her," I said.

"No," the man said, slamming the door.

"Mr. Dyson," I called through the closed door. "I think you're going to have to deal with me, either now or tomorrow or the next day. I can keep coming back and draw a lot of attention to you, or you can let me in and get it over with."

If he hadn't opened the door, I would have left and gone back to Warren with my report. But he didn't call my bluff.

"That's tellin' him, mister," the girl across the street called.

The door opened and I went through the screen door into a darkened hall. I could see the thin outline of a man in front of me. He backed away and I followed. When we stepped into a small living room, there was enough light coming through the drawn shades to see that the man was dressed in a badly faded blue shirt and equally faded blue pants. His mouth was partly open and his teeth were bad but they were all there and there was a gap. In his right hand he held a Smith and Wesson

.38 with a six-inch barrel, a favorite with cops.

The most striking thing about Alton Cash was that I knew he couldn't be more than fifty, but he looked at least twenty years older. His hair was white, his shoulders bent, his eyes a vacant, faded blue.

"Who are you?" he asked.

"Name is Marlowe, just the way I told you."

There were chairs to sit in, even a sofa, but they were old with a washed out, ghostly pattern and I was sure the dust would rise from them if I sat. He didn't ask me to sit and I didn't want to.

"He sent you, didn't he?" Cash asked, pistol leveled at my stomach. "He sent you to find us."

"He?"

"Her brother," he said.

"I want to talk to your wife," I said.

"No," he said.

Something stirred in the doorway and I turned to the sound of sagging wooden floors. My eyes met the deepest, darkest and most melancholy brown eyes I had ever seen. The eyes were set in a soft balloon of a face resting on a huge, neckless, round body. Louise Hlushka Cash walked with a cane to support her mass. Her breathing was pained and labored.

"He's from Warren," Alton said.

Her eyes opened wide with fear.

"He wants to talk to you," I said.

"We know what he wants with her," Alton said.

"Warren," Louise croaked.

"We've spent our lives hiding from him, Louise," Alton said with almost a sob in his voice. "I'm beginning to think our lives aren't worth that damned much anymore."

With that he gave me his full attention.

"How much he paying you to kill us?" he asked.

"Kill you?" I asked. "He doesn't want to kill you. He wants to see his sister."

"His sister is dead," Louise Cash said, sagging into a nearby chair that groaned under her weight.

"Dead?"

"Her name was Sharon Rose Taylor," Louise said. "My parents adopted Warren. The Taylors adopted Sharon Rose when their mother abandoned them."

"Whole family was a little mad," said Alton. "Sharon Rose thought I was in love with her. She said I'd promised to marry her. Louise and I went to see her where she worked in the Equity Building in Baker. We told her we were getting married, that she had to stop bothering me. And then . . ."

"She acted crazy, threatened," said Louise, her eyes looking beyond me into the past. "I lost my temper . . . I said things . . . and she . . ."

"Went out the window," I finished. "That's . . ."

"Crazy?" Alton said. "Damned right. She'd written to Warren telling him lies about me, about Louise, and when Sharon Rose died he blamed us for it."

"And he was right," said Louise softly.

"He wasn't," wailed Alton. "We didn't know she was that crazy."

"We should have been more gentle with her," said Louise to no one.

"We've been over it and over it," cried Alton. "You want to die now? You want this man to shoot you?"

"I don't care anymore, Alton," she said. "We ran from him when he came for us in nineteen twenty-nine or thirty, and we ran from the other man he sent when the war started, and . . ."

"I'm not here to shoot anybody," I said, but the Cashes

weren't listening to me. They were off in a conversation they must have had a thousand times on a thousand nights and afternoons.

"No more, Alton," she said. "No more."

Alton's hand dropped slowly as he spoke and the gun pointed toward the floor. I wanted to tell them to forget the whole thing, and then I would just go back to Los Angeles, return what I had of Warren's money, and tell him it was over. And that's what I would have done if Alton had given me a chance to explain. What he did instead was lift his .38 and take aim at me. I recognized the look in his eyes. I'd seen it before. It was a look that said, "I've got nothing to do with what's going to happen next. I'm somewhere else. When it's over, I'll come back and I won't even know what I've done."

The look gave me a fraction of a second to throw myself to the floor before he fired. I rolled further into the room when the second shot came and I heard a wheezing groan, a groan that sounded like a punctured tire. I was on the dusty floor against the wall waiting for Alton to take a third shot at me when I heard his pistol clatter to the floor.

I looked up to see Alton shuffling over to Louise, who was slumped forward, a rivulet of blood snaking down her once-white dress. I got to one knee and lunged for the gun but Alton didn't notice. He was trying to stop the massive body of his wife from sliding onto the floor. He didn't have a chance. I picked up the gun by the barrel.

"She's dying," he wailed.

"She's dead," I corrected, walking over to him as Louise Cash rolled onto the floor.

"I killed her?" he asked, looking up at me.

"You killed her, Alton," I confirmed.

"She'd be alive if you hadn't come."

"That's one way of looking at it. Where's the phone?"

"No phone," he said.

He sat cross-legged on the floor cradling his dead wife's head in his lap. The dust in the house and the taste of death got to me. I went for the door and into the sun still holding the .38 by the barrel. The bright hot day hadn't gone away. Nothing had changed in the few minutes I'd been in the tomb the Cashes had lived in. The two kids across the street were looking at me, probably wondering about the gunshots but not too surprised to hear them in this neighborhood.

"You got a phone?" I asked.

"Nope," said the girl, "but there's one in Robinson's store up the road. Anybody dead?"

"Most of the people who ever lived," I said.

The Bay City police came about twenty minutes after I called them. An address on Oleander gave them plenty of reason to move slowly. I turned the pistol over to the cops, who showed little interest in a routine domestic incident, and said I was just passing through the neighborhood when I heard the shot and went in. I told them I didn't know the Cashes, that I was just a good citizen, a former employee of the Los Angeles district attorney. I gave them Alton Cash's .38 and left a false name and address in L.A. in case they wanted to get in touch with me. Alton was too far out of it to contradict me or pay any attention. He had been waiting and planning to go mad for more than half a lifetime. His moment had come.

I drove back to Los Angeles slowly and made my way to the Cascadia Lounge where Coils Conroy was behind the bar. It was late afternoon and the place was alive with a crew of construction workers who were tearing down an office building nearby. I ordered a Scotch straight and nursed it. Warren Hlushka came through the door about an hour after I did.

"Figured I'd find you here," said Warren behind me over
the sound of two of the construction workers arguing about
whether a major league baseball team belonged in Los Angeles.

"You figured right," I said without turning around.

"Any luck, Mr. Marlowe?" he asked, squirming onto the
red leather bar stool next to me.

"Not for Louise Cash," I said. "She's dead."

Behind us a construction worker had dropped a couple of
dimes in the jukebox. A band blared out and I wanted to
leave.

"What?"

"You're too late, Warren," I said. "You can't kill her.
She's dead."

"Kill her?" he asked, those eyes wide with confusion. "I
didn't want to kill her. I wanted to tell her I forgave her. I was
bad to Louise, Mr. Marlowe. I said bad things to her when
someone died. I tried once to have someone find her, tell her I
was sorry, but she ran away. I tried to find her myself but it
was no go. I wanted to forgive her."

"For what she did to Sharon Rose?" I asked over the noise
of the jukebox and the arguing construction workers.

"Yeah," he said. "I said bad things and I been real sorry
for a long time. I wanted to tell Louise I was sorry."

I looked at Warren and I could see from his battered face
that he was telling the truth. Alton and Louise Cash had
spent most of a lifetime running from nothing but their own
guilt.

"I guess I got no sister now," Warren said. "Had two sisters most of my life. Now I got none."

"You've got change coming, Warren," I said, pulling out
my wallet.

He put his hand on top of mine to stop me.

"No favoring," he reminded me.

I shrugged and put the wallet back.

"Let me buy you a drink," I said.

"Just a beer will do," said Warren, looking around the bar in amazement. "You got any brothers or sisters, Mr. Marlowe?"

"No," I said, trying to get Coils Conroy's attention.

"Too bad," said Warren softly. "Too bad."

I hardly heard him. The air was full of music.

PUNISHMENT

Peasants and poverty-stricken students, peddlers and beggars moved around the tall man who stood in the Hay Market of St. Petersburg on that hot August afternoon in the year 1867. The tall man did not seem to notice the crowds, the dank choking smell of human sweat, the voices of housewives haggling with peddlers, whose carts carried everything from wilting vegetables to thimbles and thread.

There was something forbidding, something foreign about the man. He was, perhaps, forty-five years of age, thin, well dressed in a dark suit complete with the stylish tie of the period. He was certainly the best-dressed person among the several hundred who scurried and cried, sold and bought, coughed and fled. Beggars would normally have besieged him with pleas and sad stories, showed the place where arms and legs had once been attached, given the names of their consumptive wives and tubercular children. But the American's face was too forbidding to approach, hollow-cheeked, hair yellow—white and gray eyes focused beyond the cart in front of him owned by Yuri Kolodonov.

Business had not been particularly good for Kolodonov that day. He had brought his fifteen-year-old daughter, Natalya, with him in the hope that her clear skin and blue eyes would draw lustful husbands to his cart, where they would guiltily buy a set of four blue bowls and a quintet of brown cups made by the Kolodonovs in their own kiln and with their own hands right here in the city.

At first, the presence of the tall, well-dressed man had given Kolodonov some hope. He did not remember when the man had appeared, but he did remember the moment when he had looked up and saw him there. Kolodonov had smiled. He had nodded to Natalya to smile, but the tall man did not smile back and he did not approach.

After an hour as the sun dropped ever so little, Kolodonov decided that the man would not approach and buy but would only look from a distance. His presence became annoying. An hour later it became oppressive, and he feared that the tall man was driving customers away.

"Ask him what he wants," Kolodonov finally told his daughter as he pretended to rearrange his wares in the wooden cart.

Natalya did not look at the tall man. Instead she looked at the cart of Sofia Ivanova, who was doing a brisk sale in dirt-covered radishes that promised to send her home well before darkness came.

"I'm afraid," said Natalya stealing a glance at the man. "He may be mad or ill."

"Nonsense, nonsense," puffed her father. "He is a gentleman. He simply wants to . . . to be coaxed. I think he is shy, a foreigner."

"I'm afraid," Natalya repeated.

"And I am your father," said Kolodonov, touching his beard to remind himself that his age and station gave him the right to send his offspring off to face pale strangers. And Natalya obeyed. She wiped her hands on her smock, adjusted her blue blouse, assumed a smile she did not feel, and made her way past a pair of fat but dwarfishly small women with baskets under their arms who were arguing about whose turn it was to make dinner the next day.

"Sir," Natalya said, standing before him.

He looked down at her, a touch of irony in the corner of his mouth or, perhaps, only the illusion of a wasted smile. An argument exploded at a nearby cart. Two voices, both men, rose loud and animal-like. The tall man did not seem to hear though Natalya could not help glancing toward the squabble.

"Sir," she repeated, "could I help you?"

This time he did smile, a smile that indicated even to this most unworldly girl that he believed he was beyond help of any sort.

And then the man answered in a language which might have been gibberish but was, in fact, English:

By a route obscure and lonely,
Haunted by ill angels only,
Where an Eldolon, named Night,
On a black throne reigns upright,
I have reached these lands but newly
From an ultimate dim Thule—
From a wild weird clime that lieth, sublime,
Out of Space—out of Time.

"I don't understand," Natalya said as the man's right hand came up and touched her arm. She stepped back and into a woman with a child who mumbled a curse. The man's long fingers gripped her arm. Natalya turned to her father for help, but he was engaged with a customer. Natalya was considering a scream when a man's voice, a bit high-pitched, said,

"Edgar Allan Poe."

And then a hand came out, a white pudgy hand. It touched

the hand of the tall man that gripped Natalya, and the tall man released her.

"That was in English, something by the American Poe," the man with the pudgy hand said. "Somber man. My English is poor, but I recognize the pattern, remember the words but can't place them."

The tall man's face did not change. Natalya looked at her rescuer, and though she was grateful as she fought to keep from touching the place where the tall man's fingers had bruised her arm, she was not impressed.

The man was well dressed, about forty, short, fat and clean-shaven. His hair was short, and he had a large round head that was unusually bulbous in the back. His soft, round, snub-nosed face was yellowish in color as if he had seldom ventured out into the daylight. He was definitely smiling, the smile of a man who has a secret and longs to share it with you. There was something decidedly feminine about the man except for his eyes below almost white lashes, moist eyes that were quite serious. Something in those eyes told Natalya to turn away now and return to her father.

When she made her way through the crowd to the cart and looked back, the two men were gone. Her father paused in his sweating effort to persuade an uncertain woman to buy the bowls. He looked up, saw the tall man was gone, and nodded approvingly to his daughter. She did not respond.

For the first time in her life, the possibility of death had looked down at her and touched her. Though it was hot enough to cause the old to seek shelter from the sun, Natalya shuddered and crossed herself.

"My name is Porfiry Petrovich," the small man said, guiding the tall man out of the Hay Market and toward the river. "You speak Russian, I hope. My English is poor."

"My Russian is also poor," the tall man said in Russian with a voice so dry that it seemed to have gone unused for years.

"But it is better than my English," said Porfiry Petrovich. "I go to the market often to see the faces, feel the life."

The tall man grunted as they walked.

"Actually," said Porfiry Petrovich, "that is not true. I seldom go to the market. I don't like the smell. Look there. See. They're putting in gas lights on the main streets. Civilization. St. Petersburg is becoming like Paris. You want to see the city? I can . . . Are you all right?"

The tall man had stopped and was breathing heavily.

"Wound," he said. "During the war."

"The war?" mulled the fat little man. "You are an American. You mean your Civil War. You were a soldier? Which side?"

"Confederacy," said the man in English.

"Confederacy," Porfiry Petrovich repeated as crowds moved past them. "That was the South?"

"Yes," said the man.

"You were an officer?"

"A colonel," said the man, finding his breath. "Bullet in the lung. Still there."

"Your war fascinates me," said Porfiry Petrovich. "I'm fond of reading all military histories. I've missed my proper calling. I should have been a soldier, not a general, a Napolean or your Grant—I'm sorry. Your Lee, but I might have been a major. Yes, a major."

The tall American was ready to move again.

"What is your career, if I may ask?" the American said.

"I'm a lawyer," said Porfiry Petrovich with a deep sigh, as if the confession would lose him his new and closest friend. "And you?"

"Ulysses," said the man, walking again at the little man's side.

"I wander. I made a living as a soldier and a cotton farmer. That was when I was alive. I died in the war. My wife, my daughter, died in the war."

"I'm sorry," said Porfiry Petrovich. "I myself am and have always been a bachelor. Look, look there. The cathedral. The czar himself goes to the cathedral."

The tall man grunted and Porfiry Petrovich suddenly stopped and pulled him down so he could whisper into his ear.

"The truth is that the czar seldom goes to the cathedral. Tonight he will probably go. A member of his own guards was found dead not far from here yesterday. Murdered. Service will be today. Perhaps the czar will attend. Perhaps he won't. His wife, the czarina . . . but that's another story, Colonel Franklin, another story for a quiet . . . here, here, a cafe I know."

Though he was half the size of the tall American, Porfiry Petrovich dragged him through the wooden door and into a noisy, smoke-filled room in which a haggard woman with stringy hair was playing French-sounding songs on a concertina.

"Smells in here, but the food is good," said Porfiry Petrovich, leading him to a wooden table that was almost clean though it would never be rid of the smell of fish. They sat and Porfiry Petrovich waved furiously at a bearded waiter and called for drinks and food.

"You've never been in here before," the American said, fixing his eyes on the smiling little man who was surveying the room.

Porfiry Petrovich raised his hands, palms open to show that he had been caught in a lie.

"And you knew my name," said the man. "I didn't tell you my name."

Porfiry Petrovich grinned sheepishly and said, "Valve is badly off in that concertina, a distraction. I think the woman is too drunk to notice."

"You're a policeman," said Franklin without emotion.

"An examining lawyer in the department of investigation of criminal causes," said Porfiry Petrovich, shaking his head. "A person of no consequence. Ah, the food."

The waiter with the beard plopped two plates on the table, the smell of onions and chopped fish rose before them. Cucumbers lay sliced around the fish. A large square of dark, rough bread rested heavily on the edge of each plate.

"Vodka, Colonel?" Porfiry Petrovich asked. "I seldom drink, but today, a new acquaintance. Wine?"

Franklin sat unsmiling and silent.

"Make it wine," Porfiry Petrovich told the waiter. "Good wine. Take no liberties with my palate."

The waiter did not bother to respond but walked away to the call of other patrons. Porfiry Petrovich began to eat, carefully pronging pieces of fish, onion, and cucumber, ushering it to his mouth with a piece of bread.

"What do you want?" asked Franklin in Russian.

"Want? From you? To practice my English. To learn about your war. To show a cultivated visitor around our historic city. I like to talk. It is my passion, my need. I live alone, have few acquaintances outside of my profession."

"How did you find me in the market?" Franklin went on, this time in English.

Porfiry Petrovich paused in mid-bite to understand and translate the words.

"Eat, you have nothing on your bones. I have too much, I confess.

"I was looking for you. I went to your hotel. Your name, obviously American or English, was in the registry. The names and home addresses of all visitors to St. Petersburg are brought by each hotel to central registry.

"And I happened to be looking through the registry on a case and saw your name. I was intrigued."

"A case?" said the American ignoring his food as the little policeman finished his own.

The waiter brought a bottle of red wine and plunked it with two glasses on the table. Porfiry Petrovich inserted a finger into his mouth and poured the red liquid into the two glasses.

"Fish bone," said the inspector. "There, I've got it. Yes, a case. The same case I mentioned a little while ago. Might interest you. Count Nicolai Bognerov, one of the czar's guards. Murdered. Strangled. Obviously by someone very strong, very determined. The count, though confidentially he did drink, some say to excess, was not a small man. He fought in your war. On the side of the South. Small group of Cossack volunteers led by the count, an adventure, a lark, who knows, maybe deep conviction. You never ran into him in your country?"

"No," said Franklin.

"No," repeated Porfiry Petrovich. "If you are not going to eat . . . ?"

Franklin pushed the plate toward the inspector, reached for the wine, and downed it in one gulp.

"No, no, no, my friend," sighed Porfiry Petrovich, "not on an empty stomach. You'll lose control. Say things you might regret. Believe me. I know the cheap wine of such places. Trust me."

And then the inspector laughed. He laughed so hard that bits of bread sprayed from his mouth. He reached for the wine and drank it to stifle his laughter. The room was so crowded and noisy that no one but Franklin heard or saw the display.

"Forgive me," he said, tapping his chest. "The drink, the food, the company. I'm already a bit giddy."

"How did you find me in the market?" asked Franklin.

"I told you," said the inspector, wiping a tear of laughter from the corner of his right eye. "I went to your hotel and . . ."

". . . and they knew I was in the Hay Market," Franklin said in slow, precise English. "How would they know where I had gone?"

Porfiry Petrovich pushed his plate away, poured more wine for both of them, and folded his pale fat hands on the table in front of him. Beads of sweat evident on his forehead.

"I followed you," said the inspector.

Franklin nodded almost imperceptibly and took a drink.

"May I ask you a question? Tell me if I'm prying and we'll go. Would you like to see where we work, where criminal investigations are pursued? But that is not the question. Actually, I have two questions."

"Ask," said Franklin, after finishing his second glass of wine.

The bottle was already almost empty.

"First, when and why did you learn to speak Russian?"

"I began to learn in the hospital where I was treated after I was wounded at the end of the war," said Franklin. "I had business in Russia."

"And you have taken care of your business?"

"I have," said the tall American.

"I'll not ask you what that business is," said Porfiry Petrovich. "It is not my concern."

"I'm not sure I see how you determine what is and is not your business," said Franklin.

"Second question," said Porfiry Petrovich, "Why were you standing in the market and looking at the peddler and his daughter?"

"She looks like Melinda," said Franklin, pouring himself another drink.

"Melinda? Your daughter? Wife?"

"Perhaps both. Both were named Melinda."

Porfiry Petrovich nodded.

"And they died in the war?" Porfiry Petrovich said, almost too softly to be heard over the noise.

Franklin answered with a nod.

"Come, you are a military man. I want to show you something."

Porfiry Petrovich whispered, a finger to his full, pale lips.

"Is this an order?" asked Franklin softly.

"An order? You mean in connection with my? . . . no, no. A request. A plca for help."

He stood and Franklin leaned over to drink one final glass of wine. Porfiry Petrovich pulled out a rouble note and dropped it on the table.

"My treat," he said. "My pleasure. Worth it for the company and to get away from that desk. This way."

The fat little man made his way around the tables and to the door with the tall man following him, still steady on his feet, still military of bearing in spite of consuming most of the bottle of wine without food.

Back in the street Porfiry Petrovich stamped first one foot and then another.

"Circulation," he said. "Returns the circulation. The sun is still well in the sky. Does it stay light in the summer till late at night in your country?"

"No," said Franklin following the little man.

"Blessing and a curse," said Porfiry Petrovich with an exaggerated sigh. "More hours to fill. Darkness is an excuse to be alone."

"I believe you said you are a lonely man," said Franklin as they crossed the street behind a large rambling cart and avoided the recent droppings of a horse.

"Yes, lonely," admitted Porfiry Petrovich, "but sometimes a lonely man enjoys his solitude. Though of course solitude, only oneself for company, can result in strange thoughts, delusions. Only last year, not far from this very spot, a young student murdered two old women with an ax. Solitude had created delusion. A sad sight. Are you a solitary man, Colonel Franklin?"

Colonel Franklin did not answer as they turned a corner side by side.

"There, right there, that entrance," said the inspector pointing at a large double wooden doorway with large hasps. The stone building looked ancient.

"You recognize it?" asked Porfiry Petrovich with a smile.

Franklin did not answer.

"I only ask because the style of the building is very English and I understand many of the city buildings in your Charlotte and Natchez are . . . Here."

Porfiry Petrovich opened the door with a key and ushered Franklin into the near darkness.

"Is your wound bothering you? Watch your step. See the light to the left? Walk carefully. It's a courtyard near the steps. I'm right ahead of you."

Their footsteps echoed across the stone hallway as Franklin followed the outline of the inspector and his eyes began to adjust to the near total darkness. As they approached the stairs, the light from the courtyard gave him a reasonably clear picture of the wooden stairway that arched upward.

"Can you move ahead of me?" said Porfiry Petrovich, panting as they reached the second landing. "I'm not a military man and my legs . . . I'll catch up. Fourth landing. Door on the right. What I have to show you is in there."

They moved upward, silently except for the sound of their footsteps on the creaking stairs, the tortured breathing of Colonel Franklin, and the panting of Porfiry Petrovich.

Ahead of the inspector, the American had stopped on a landing and turned to his left. The inspector caught up with him as Colonel Franklin stood in front of a door waiting. Porfiry Petrovich caught his breath and looked at both the man before him and the door.

"Strange," said the inspector.

"What is?" asked Franklin.

"I told you we were going to an apartment on the fourth floor. You stopped on the third."

"Sorry," said Franklin, moving back toward the stairs.

"No," said Porfiry Petrovich. "The error was mine. This is the right door. Perhaps you miscounted?"

"Perhaps," said the American softly.

The inspector moved to the door, inserted his key, and opened it.

The two men entered. The room was large and surprisingly light with a window facing east. The furniture was fashionable, solid tables, chairs, and desk, a wood-trimmed sofa and two comfortable chairs covered in satiny red material with little red buttons. The walls were lined with military paintings except for one small bookcase toward which Porfiry Petrovich moved. "Right here," he said. "It's right here. The murderer wasn't interested or simply overlooked it."

"Murderer?" said Franklin, remaining erect near the door,

the only sign of his drinking a small band of moisture on his upper lip.

Porfiry Petrovich stopped suddenly, turned to Franklin, and hit himself in the forehead with the open palm of his right hand.

"The heat. The wine. Forgive me once again," he said, resuming his move toward the bookcase. "This is the apartment of Count Nicholai Bognerov. His family has an estate not far from the city. It was in this very room he was murdered yesterday, right there by the desk. The desk drawer was open. Something had been taken from it. You might look in the drawer while I find the book . . . here it is."

Franklin did not move. He stood on the corner of a once-elegant but now faded Oriental rug and watched without passion.

"You don't want to look in the drawer? Very well. I'll tell you. It is filled with photographs, some of them on those etched metals the French invented. Most if not all of them appear to be from your country. Soldiers in uniform, women, even children."

Porfiry Petrovich looked up and thought he saw the gaunt man shudder.

"You might know someone . . ."

"Thank you, no," said Franklin.

"Very well," said the Inspector with a wave of his hand to dismiss the offer. He moved to the sofa and gestured to Franklin to join him and still the American did not move. Porfiry Petrovich held the book up so the light from the now orange sun would hit the pages as he flipped through them in search of the passage he sought.

"Do you like the ballet, Colonel?" the inspector said, slowing down the pages just a bit.

Still no answer.

"I am fascinated by it, but, alas, I'm usually too busy. The passage. Right here. This is the count's diary. Listen. I'll read slowly. It's in Russian." He read: " 'This morning we followed General Smith into Charleston. We were attached to the 17th Cavalry. The goal was to drive the Union troops under Dunsteader back and provide time to join the . . .'

"I'll skip a bit of this," said Porfiry Petrovich, "and pick it up, let's see, here: 'The house had been part of a cotton plantation but did not look as if it had been tilled since the early days of the war. My cossacks and I were detached, alone. There were only women in the house and one wounded man who spoke with the accent of the North. I took him for a deserter and determined that the women had harbored him and were, therefore, traitors. I shot the deserter, and, as we had done before, I left the women to the cossacks. We dined in the house and the next morning set fire to it before moving north to join General Smith.' "

Porfiry Petrovich looked up. Franklin was rigid, at attention.

"Is that passage familiar to you?" he asked.

Franklin did not speak.

"The last entry in the diary is January 6, 1864," said Porfiry Petrovich. "Two weeks before the count returned to Europe. I understand that he left rather hurriedly and had to leave many of his belongings behind. I have spoken to the woman who has cleaned this room every day for six years. She tells me that this diary was not here yesterday morning before the count died."

"And?" asked Colonel Franklin.

"Who knows? Perhaps she simply never noticed it or the count moved it from someplace else yesterday just before he was murdered. Or, and this is the theory I wanted to ask you about, perhaps the murderer put the book on the shelf."

The sun was definitely dropping now and shadows had

fallen over Franklin's face, masking it.

"Why?"

Porfiry Petrovich stood now and placed the book in his pocket.

He began to pace the room with one hand behind his back as if he were about to dictate a letter.

"Perhaps the diary was left in your country," he said. "Perhaps it got into the hands of someone who, by the count's own words, had wronged that person. When he had finished murdering the count, the killer no longer needed the diary. He returned it to the shelf, a final gesture. The act of completion. You see where I am taking this?"

And Franklin said nothing.

"Do you have just a little more time? One more stop?"

"I have nowhere I have to be now," Franklin said.

"Good," said Porfiry Petrovich and led him out the door.

The sun was almost gone when they entered Porfiry Petrovich's office in the department of investigation twenty minutes later. A few clerks were in the outer offices, but the inspector's room was empty. Porfiry Petrovich moved ahead to light the two lamps on the desk. The lamps were helped by the uncovered windows, which caught the last of the sun.

Franklin stood just inside the door. The room was neither large nor small. Porfiry Petrovich moved behind his writing table, which stood before a sofa upholstered in checkered material, a bureau, a bookcase in the corner, and several chairs, all government issued, of polished yellow wood. In one corner was a closed door. Next to it was a heavy wooden clock with a gold pendulum that ticked loudly.

"My den," said Porfiry Petrovich. "Please sit. Tea? Coffee? It will take a few minutes only."

Franklin moved slowly into the room and sat on the sofa,

his eyes never leaving the inspector, who took the count's diary from his pocket and placed it on the writing table. He smiled and then opened the drawer of the writing table to pull out a small wooden box. He placed the box on the table, folded his hands, and looked at his guest dreamily. The clock ticked.

"My favorite time of the day," said Porfiry Petrovich softly. "Neither night nor day. The lost time. The time for contemplation and silence between the smile and the tear. I wish I could say it like your Poe. I'm pleased that we both admire your Poe."

They sat for perhaps ten minutes till the sun was completely gone and there was nothing but the clock and their own breathing.

Finally, Porfiry Petrovich opened the small box. He removed four flat and heavy rectangular objects and laid them before him on the writing table.

The silence was broken by Franklin, who stood suddenly, stepped forward, and pounded his fist on the writing desk.

"Sir," he said evenly. "These photographs are mine."

"They are," Porfiry Petrovich conceded without moving. "I took them from your room."

Franklin scooped the photographs up and shoved them in his pocket.

"Your wife and daughter?" the inspector asked, looking up at Franklin. "They do look like the girl in the Hay Market. And one of you with them. And the older woman?"

"My wife's mother," said Franklin. "Sir, I plan to leave this room now."

"Well," said Porfiry Petrovich with an enormous sigh and a wave of both hands, "I was hoping you could be of help."

"You plan to arres—" Franklin began, but Porfiry Petrovich sprang to his feet and interrupted him with, "Indulge me, Colonel, for just a moment, please."

Franklin hesitated.

"It is my theory," said the inspector, "that the count, who has a reputation for gambling, womanizing, and bad debts, a rarity in the aristocracy, had a confrontation with someone, perhaps one of his former cossacks, after a night of revelry. A neighbor reports seeing a tall man of military bearing enter the count's apartment slightly before the murder.

"That same neighbor reported that he heard the count speak to someone in a foreign language the neighbor did not understand. The death of a member of the aristocracy is not to be taken lightly. The life of a count is, as my superior said yesterday, worth that of a hundred peasants. My responsibility in this investigation, because of my humble ability to speak English, was to join others in questioning the handful of Americans and Englishmen in the city. You were the fourth I found. I have determined that you are quite innocent of any involvement in or knowledge of this horrible deed. It is possible that the savage murderer will never be brought to justice by man. He will have to stand before God. With that I am content."

And with that, Colonel Franklin, late of the Army of the Confederacy, sat back on the sofa and wept. For the first time since he had begun to watch him that morning, Porfiry Petrovich thought he detected a flicker of life in the gaunt man.

"There is a train to Moscow at seven in the morning," said the inspector, turning his chair to the window so that he could see the flickering lights of the city.

"I shall be on it, sir," Franklin said, dignity returning to his voice.

"Can you find your way back to your hotel?" Porfiry

Petrovich asked, still watching the lights of the city he loved.

"Of course."

"Have a good journey home," said the inspector.

Behind him, the office door opened and Colonel Franklin went into the hall, closing the door behind him. Porfiry Petrovich was alone with his ticking clock.

And before he could stop them and from where they came he knew not, lines of Poe came to him:

Thy soul shall find itself alone
'Mid dark thoughts of the gray tomb-stone—
Not one, of all the crowd, to pry
Into thine hour of secrecy.

THE BUCK STOPS HERE

"Can you guess what this is?"

We were standing in the storage room of the Truman Library in Independence, Missouri, early in July of 1957, and the question had come from Mr. Truman himself, who was pointing at a broken wooden beam about a dozen feet long leaning against the wall.

I couldn't guess what the beam was. I was tired when I had to be alert. Hungry when I should have been undistracted and attentive. I hadn't slept since my unit officer had pulled me out of a basketball game at a YMCA in Washington, D.C., the day before.

I stood, blearily looking at the beam and then over at the ex-president, who smiled at me, waiting for my answer. Truman was seventy-three years old, and although everyone from Franklin Roosevelt and President Eisenhower had referred to him as "little," the ex-president stood eye-to-eye with me, and I was slightly over five-nine. Truman wore a light suit and tie and looked dapper and alert with a white handkerchief in his breast pocket.

"Lieutenant?" Truman asked again.

"I don't know, sir," I said as he rested a hand on the beam.

"This," said Truman in his clipped Missouri twang, "is the beam from the White House that gave way under my daughter Margaret's piano. If it weren't for that piano and this beam, the major reconstruction of the White House might never have taken place. It took the fear of a piano falling on my head to get a few dollars to shore up the most important symbolic building in the United States."

"And that's why you want it in the Library," I said, looking around the room on what I hoped was the last part of the tour. I had a potential assassin to look for and some sleep to catch up on. My interest in history was not at its peak.

How had it happened? When my CO had called me out of the basketball game, I hurried down to the locker, took a fast shower, and got dressed in my sports coat, slacks, and solid blue knit tie. I was standing in front of Colonel Saint's desk within fifteen minutes of the moment he had summoned me.

Saint was drinking a cup of coffee. A matching cup stood steaming on the corner of his desk. He nodded at the second steaming cup, and I smiled and took it, even though I don't drink coffee. Saint never remembered this, but that didn't bother me. What bothered me was that he had made the friendly gesture. I was being prepared for something I might not want to hear.

"Have a seat, Pevsner," Saint said, reaching a stubby finger into his cup to fish out something tiny and even darker than the amber liquid.

Saint was fully uniformed, complete with medals on his chunky chest, his graying hair Wildrooted back and shiny.

"Thank you, sir," I said, and sat in the chrome-and-black leather chair across from him. Saint struck a pose, two hands clasped around his coffee cup. Behind him and over his head on the wall, a picture of President Eisenhower, in his five-star uniform, looked down at both of us benevolently.

"Carl Gades," Saint said, returning his finger to his coffee cup and fishing out a bit more of whatever it was that troubled him.

I didn't shake, shimmer, or show a sign when Saint looked up suddenly for my reaction. I just sipped at the bitter, hot liquid. I could see my face in the coffee. It was a bland, innocent twenty-eight-year-old face showing just what it had been trained to show: nothing.

"You know Carl Gades," Colonel Saint said, putting down the cup. "Damn coffee stinks. How can you drink it?"

I shrugged and kept drinking.

"I know Carl Gades," I said.

"You're the only member of this staff who has met him face-to-face who could identify him," the colonel said, folding his hands on his desk and looking down sourly at the coffee cup. "Kravitz wouldn't remember his mother if she wasn't wearing a name tag. Secret Service has no one who has ever seen him. They pulled your name out of the files. They can get things out of the files, off that damned microfilm, in a few hours now."

I had met Carl Gades only once and I didn't want to meet him again, but I was getting the idea that I might not have a choice. I hadn't made too many choices in my career for more than three years or, at least, that was the way it felt. I'd been drafted right out of UCLA and missed Korea by being pulled out after basic training and sent to Texas for Officers' Candidate School. After OCS I was sent to Washington for intelligence training, and a week after completing my training I was on a mission to Rome with a dyspeptic captain named Resnick. Resnick barely talked to me and barely briefed me. "Keep your eyes open," he had said, and then closed his and slept on the plane all the way to Rome.

My rapid rise in the military had been the result not of my great promise and intellect, but good breeding. My father was a retired Los Angeles Police Department captain, and my uncle was an aging, but still active, private investigator who had handled some delicate private jobs for people in high places. Oh, yes, there was one other thing that led to my success. I was a *hawk*. I hadn't known I was a hawk. There weren't many of us, and the intelligence services probably bragged to each other about the number of hawks they had.

A hawk is an individual who takes in everything in a scene, isn't distracted by the things that draw the attention of normal people. If I'm walking down the street and hear someone scream behind me, I turn around and see not only a woman shouting at a man running down the street, but I see each crack in the street, the color of the man's socks, the woman's straggling hairs, every window on every building, and the fern sprouting yellow fronds in a fourth-floor window across the street. I see and I retain.

It's a literal photographic memory. I don't remember words or conversations, just images, images fixed that can be recalled. Unfortunately, the images sometimes come back unbidden and they don't always bear any great significance. So, for whatever it was worth, I had this gift or curse, and I was of particular value in sensitive situations where photography would be valuable but for various reasons, usually location and security, photography wouldn't be feasible.

Gades had met with Resnick and me in the Piazza Popolo. Gades had worn a wide-brimmed white hat and a white suit. He had a dark mustache and beard and was careful to keep the top of his face and eyes in the shadow of his Marcello Mastroianni hat. Gades had insisted that we meet at the statue in the center of the Piazza so that no one would be near us but the people driving madly around the Piazza.

Gades was there to trade information. We gave him a name. He gave us a name. I don't know what either name meant. I was there to record and remember Gades, who, in broad daylight, insisted on patting us both down to be sure we weren't armed with cameras or weapons. He also informed us that he had people checking out the nearby buildings to be sure no one was lurking with a high-power telescopic-lensed camera.

Gades spoke no more than a minute in a raspy, disguised voice, and he gave his information first, confident that we wouldn't dare cross him, suggesting, in fact, that he rather enjoyed having people try to cross him so he could make examples of them and increase his value and public image.

Now, many murders—from Bombay to Kiev—later, Gades who had become even more cautious, was back in my lap.

"No photographs of Gades," Saint said. "Son of a bitch's too careful. You're the only one who might be able to identify him. Could you?"

I pulled out the fixed picture of that day three years earlier and went over it, the split second Gades had tilted his head up and shown his deep blue eyes, the other second when he had shown a profile, the freckles on his wrist, the turn of his left ear.

"I could," I said.

"Hot damn." Saint grinned. He turned and looked up at Ike for approval, and Ike seemed to give it. "We've got them by the short ones, Lieutenant."

"Glad to hear it, sir," I said, finishing the coffee. "Who have we got by . . . ?"

Saint leaned forward, straightened his tie, and grinned as he said, "Secret Service, FBI, all of them."

"I see," I said, "but I . . ."

"FBI got a phone conversation on a wired line," Saint said, pulling a manila folder out of his desk drawer and opening it. "Word is that Gades plans to assassinate Harry Truman. How do you like that?"

I didn't like it very much, but I was sure he didn't need me to tell him that.

"Why?" I asked.

"Revenge," whispered Colonel Saint, dramatically leaning toward me over the desk. "Gades's brother, Arthur, died in prison last month. Son of a bitch should have been executed. Tried to blow up a plane for who the hell knows why. Spent ten years in jail. Truman wouldn't let him out, turned down two appeals. At least, that's the way Gades feels about it, according to the FBI. It was his only brother. Things like that make would-be assassins careless. You know what I mean?"

"Yes, sir," I said, thinking of my own brother Nate, who was in college back in California.

"People are watching Truman, but they don't know Gades," Saint went on. "Fear now is that Gades probably knows we know. FBI screwed up the whole wiretap operation. Who knows? FBI, CIA, MI, everyone and his aunt thinks Gades'll move fast. You've got a military flight to Kansas City in one hour and a half. Sergeant Ganz'll drive you. I'd like you in uniform, highly visible. Stop off at home, change, and get your ass in gear. You meet Mr. Truman in his office in Kansas City first thing in the morning. 0800 hours. Questions?"

"And I'm . . . ?" I began.

"Hawk," he said, "spot Gades. Turn him over to the Secret Service. There'll be a couple of agents with Truman. You know Gades's reputation, and he's not likely to deviate this time. He does it himself. He does it in person. No bombs. Doesn't even like guns, though he carries one. Kills up close. Wants to scare the community. Does it, too. Kicks up his price. Let's get the bastard. Ganz has cash for you. Keep decent records this time, Pevsner."

That was it. His mouth moved from a broad smile to a thin enigma. I rose, saluted, took his return salute, and watched as Colonel Saint turned in his swivel chair, looked up at Ike and then, hands behind his head, looked out the window at the U.S. Post Office building across the street. Less than two hours later I was on an Air Force plane headed for Kansas City and drinking a Dr Pepper handed to me by a freckle-faced airman.

We landed at the Kansas City airport on a side strip reserved for military landings. I had picked up my uniform, but I didn't have time to change into it until I got on the plane. Before we landed I brushed my teeth and shaved.

Colonel Saint had given me enough money to last about a week if I was careful. If it took more, I'd have to ask. It might be a lot more. It might be forever if the FBI information was wrong or if Gades had changed his mind. I had the distinct fear that Colonel Saint wanted Gades so badly he might leave me to turn to fungus in Kansas City.

A khaki-colored Buick was waiting at the airport, and the driver, a Spec Four named Kithcart, took me to the Federal Reserve Building in downtown Kansas City, where he parked the car illegally and led me into the building where a pair of Secret Service men who identified themselves as Koster and Franklin took me to the elevator and up the stairs to Truman's office. Koster and Franklin were clean-shaven, gray-suited, about six feet tall, brown-eyed, closemouthed, and nearly bookends. I guessed they were both in their forties, but they could have been younger or older.

Truman came to the door to greet me. He shook my hand, a strong grip for an old man, and looked me straight in the eye.

"You're younger than I thought, Lieutenant," Truman said. "But so is everyone but Dean Acheson."

"Yes sir," I said.

"You know I was a captain in World War One?" he asked, walking to the corner of the room, putting a white hat on his head, and picking out a black walking stick from an upright black leather container near the window.

"Yes sir," I said.

"Let's go," he said. "I'm not changing my schedule for any two-bit gangster. I'm going to the Truman Museum back home in Independence. There's a construction strike all through this area, and some of the important work has stopped on the Library. Damn shame. Everything is ready for final plastering and floorings. Stacks, shelves, and exhibit cases may not be put in for the dedication. Some carpenters and painters are on job, but we are not on schedule. You ever been in the White House?"

Truman walked briskly past me and looked back at my face over his shoulder.

"Once, sir. I briefed President Eisenhower on a . . . a delicate mission with General Clark."

"I don't give a damn about the subject," said Truman, amiably gesturing for me to follow him through the door. "I just want to know if you're as good as they say you are. I assume you were in the President's office?"

"Yes sir," I said, following him out the door. He walked quickly to the elevator, flanked by the two Secret Service men.

We went down the elevator and out the building, heading over to a parking lot, where we got into a big, black Lincoln. I took in the street, the passing people, and saw nothing and no one I recognized. One of the Secret Service men sat with the driver. The other sat silently with Truman and me in the back seat.

"Microfilm," Truman said as I tried to shake off airplane

weariness. "At some point, thanks to microfilm, the Truman Library will have the best collection of presidential papers anywhere. You know that, until Hoover, people simply threw away presidential papers?"

"No sir," I said, which was true.

"One exception," Truman corrected, looking over his shoulder at me. "Rutherford B. Hayes, and who the hell cares about Hayes's papers?"

"I think you do," I said.

"You are right, Lieutenant," he said. "I care about Hayes and Millard Fillmore and Tyler. It's the office, Lieutenant. You put a man in the office, and it is his responsibility to fill that space with dignity. No man in his right mind would want to be president if he knew what it entails. Aside from the impossible administrative burden, he has to take all sorts of abuse from liars and demagogues. All the president is, is a glorified public relations man who spends his time flattering, kissing, and kicking people to get them to do what they are supposed to do anyway."

"I'll have to take your word on that, sir," I said, looking at the Secret Service man who scanned the road on the way to Independence and appeared to hear none of the conversation.

The trip seemed long, though Independence is only nine miles from Kansas City. When we hit Independence, we drove down Pleasant Street to the Truman Library, which clung to a knoll in the middle of thirteen landscaped acres.

"How do you like it?" Truman said as we got out of the car and the Secret Service men scanned the parking lot.

"Impressive," I said.

"Gift of the people of Independence," he said.

The Library stood on the highest point of the property, an arc-shaped building of contemporary design with an imposing portico in the middle. There weren't many windows.

We started toward the building. Truman's cane tapped on the stone path as we moved briskly, flanked by Secret Service men.

"Impressive," I repeated, hurrying to keep up with the ex-president.

"Too damned modern," he sighed. "It's got too much of that fellow in it to suit me."

"That . . ." I started.

"Frank Lloyd Wright," Truman said, picking up the pace.

I couldn't see much Frank Lloyd Wright in the building, and I was sure Wright hadn't designed the Library, but I said nothing, just scanned the building, landscape, and the workmen who unloaded a truck in the parking lot.

"Should have been Georgian," Truman said. "Neld got modern on me, and it was too far along to stop him when I realized it. I wanted it to look like Independence Hall in Philadelphia."

We strode through the doors under the portico and Truman led us past painters and repairmen who looked up at us. None of them was Gades. The ex-president opened a door and pointed through it with his cane.

"Step in," he said, "and tell me what you see."

I stepped in and found myself in the Oval Office, the same office in which I had briefed President Eisenhower two years earlier, or, at least, a near-perfect replica.

"The Oval Office," I said.

"Right," he said, motioning the Secret Service men to stay back as he joined me and closed the door. "But you're a falcon . . ."

"Hawk," I corrected, scanning the room.

"What's wrong with the room?" he said.

"It's not what's wrong that surprises me, Mr. President," I

said. "It's what's right. The mantel isn't a replica. It's the same one I saw in the White House."

Truman's laugh was a silent, pleased cackle.

"Perfect," he said, moving across the room, removing his hat, and placing his cane on the corner of his desk. On that desk near the window was a sign I knew about. It read: The Buck Stops Here. "It is original. When the White House was renovated and we moved into Blair House, I asked them to keep pieces they would normally throw out. That mantel was one of the pieces. I'll show you another."

He led me through the office and past more workmen, whom he greeted by name, and led me to the storeroom where he showed me the famous beam that I failed to identify.

"Stage props of history," Truman sighed. "So, young man, what do we do now?"

I held back a yawn and stopped myself from shrugging.

"Whatever you normally do," I said. "But with me nearby and a little more caution than usual."

"I've been threatened before in my life," he said, stepping over the beam and placing his hand on a table, a nicely polished table. "That is the table on which the United Nations Charter was signed in San Francisco."

I looked at the table, but it conjured up no images. I needed sleep or rest. He showed me other items: a wax figure of himself, a rug from the Shah of Iran, a bronze figure of Andrew Jackson.

"You think he has a chance of getting me?" Truman asked soberly but without apparent fear.

"Well . . ." I began.

"Forget it," he said. "I'm not going to get a straight answer out of you on that one. I'd rather not shock Bess when I go, and I'd like to see this place finished. Never did consider myself martyr material, either. We'll just have to see what

God decides to do with this one. I like to quote an epitaph on a tombstone in a cemetery in Tombstone, Arizona. 'Here lies Jack Williams. He done his damnedest.' "

"I'll do my damnedest, sir," I said.

"Almost nine," he said, looking at his watch. "Let's get back to the Oval Office."

He led the way through the storage room and back to the exhibit space, where the workmen stopped talking as we moved through, and into the Oval Office.

Truman went to the desk, opened it, and pulled out a bottle.

"Situation calls for a late-morning finger or two of good bourbon, wouldn't you say, Lieutenant Pevsner?"

"Yes sir," I said with a smile, though I disliked bourbon even more than I disliked coffee, but you don't let a former president drink alone if you're invited to join him.

I took the small crystal glass he pushed toward me.

"To your powers of observation," he toasted.

I raised my glass and took a healthy sip. Truman downed his in a single shot and pursed his lips.

"That will be my only drink of the day till nightfall," he sighed.

I finished my drink and tried not to make a face.

"And now," he said. "If you want to sit, walk the grounds, browse around, I've got work to do. You are welcome to join me for lunch at noon at the house."

I thanked him and went out the door, closing it behind me as he sat behind the desk.

The Secret Service man named Koster was standing outside the office, arms folded.

I nodded to him. He nodded back, deep brown eyes scanning my uniform. For the next twenty minutes I walked around the grounds. I ran into the other Secret Service man—Franklin—who was doing the same. We didn't speak. I was trying to walk off twenty-four hours without sleep and a stiff bourbon. It wasn't working.

Just before eleven a young man came running out of the Library toward where I was standing against an oak tree trying to look alert.

"Lieutenant Pevsner?" he said.

"That's right."

"Phone call for you. Follow me."

I followed him back into the building and into a small office not far from the Oval Office. A woman sat typing in the office and a phone rested on a desk off of the receiver. I picked it up.

"Lieutenant Pevsner," I said.

"Colonel Saint," he answered.

"Nothing here that I can see yet, sir," I said.

"Look again, Lieutenant," he said. "We have definite information that Gades flew to Kansas City one week and one day ago. He's been eating steaks and waiting for a chance to get Truman."

"He's not around here," I said, looking around the office at the woman typist, who reminded me of Bulldog Turner of the Chicago Bears, and at the secretary, who looked a little like Clifton Webb.

"Some FBI crackpot has an idea. Thinks Gades will make his move today, one month to the day Gades's brother died," Saint said. "Something about the date circled in an appointment book in a hotel room Gades might have been in."

"He might be right," I said.

"The time was noted," said Saint. "Three P.M. What do you think?"

"I don't," I said.

"Find him," said Saint.

"Will do, sir," I said.

Saint hung up, and I went outside to hang around. I didn't know how to find Gades. I watched people come and go—delivery vans, a mailman. None was Gades. I was sure of that.

Noon turned the corner and Truman came sauntering out of the building with Koster and Franklin close behind, looking everywhere. Truman tilted his head back so he could see me from under his hat and motioned at me with his cane. I followed him.

"Called Bess," he said. "Told her we'd be having company. You like fried chicken?"

"Like it fine," I said, walking at his side.

We didn't take the car, which made it more difficult for the Secret Service men and me, but it was a clear, not-too-hot day and the walk helped wake me up. The walk to the gabled Victorian house on Delaware Street was probably longer than most seventy-year-olds would like to make, but Truman did it talking all the way, mostly about Andrew Jackson.

"No sign of him?" Truman asked as we went up the wooden steps. He wasn't talking about Andrew Jackson this time.

"Not yet," I said.

"Wouldn't want him to try anything around the house," he said.

"I'm watching, sir," I said with what I hoped was a reassuring smile.

"There's watching and there's watching," Truman said, pausing at the porch and looking at the two Secret Service men, who had stopped at the bottom of the steps and were casually scanning the quiet street. "Sometimes you miss what's important because it's so damned obvious that you never consider it."

"I'll keep that in mind, sir," I said.

Lunch was hot and not too spicy. Mrs. Truman served the

lunch herself, but the cleaning up was done by a young woman wearing an apron and not meeting my eyes when I looked at her. The Secret Service men ate in the kitchen, though I found that Truman had invited them to join us.

"Last Secret Service fellows insisted on working shifts and getting their own food," Truman said. "These boys are less formal. Better that way. How's the chicken?"

It was fine, and I said so.

"Bess likes cooking, or so she says. Hated the White House sometimes. Plenty for her to do, but not the things she liked doing. It all happened too fast for her. One minute I was a failed Kansas farmer who couldn't keep a hat business open and in ten years I was a judge, a senator, vice-president, and president of the United States. Hard to believe. More peas?"

I said no thanks and checked my watch. It was almost one. If Gades was going to make his move at three, he'd have to show up soon. I was considering suggesting to Truman that we stay around the house till after three, but he rose, pushed away from the table, and announced that we'd better be getting back to the Library.

Mrs. Truman, who had joined us silently for the lunch, accepted my thanks and asked her husband to come home early.

"Margaret promised to call," she said.

"Then by all means I'll be back early," he said with a smile.

The meal hadn't made me more alert. I'd eaten lightly, but it was getting late in the afternoon and the walk wasn't having the effect I'd like. The Secret Service men, as always, were silent, and Truman talked animatedly about Hubert Humphrey and the Pope's promise to send the Vatican documents on microfilm as soon as they were ready.

"Don't know what I'll do with them," Truman said, the late-afternoon sun glinting off his glasses, "but you don't turn down an offer like that."

Nothing had changed at the Library. The same workmen were there. The secretary who looked like Clifton Webb was standing at the door to the replica of the Oval Office with a sheaf of papers in his hand. Truman took his left hand out of his pocket and took the papers and hurried into his office.

Koster ran a hand through his brown hair to make sure no loose strands marred the image. He took his place in front of the door and looked stonily at me to let me know that he wasn't up for idle conversation. Franklin scanned the narrow corridor and checked the doors. He turned to us, blinked his cold blue eyes, and nodded to indicate the place was clear. Then he wandered off to watch the rear of the building. My Timex told me 1400 hours was approaching. Saint's information seemed flimsy with Bess Truman's chicken, peas, and lemonade resting heavily in my stomach and a warm Missouri sun sparkling on the grass as I stepped in front of the building.

The whole Gades business seemed dreamlike, Colonel Saint's dream. I found an oak tree in front of the Library, loosened my tie, and sat in the shade where I could get a good look at anyone approaching the building on foot or in a vehicle. Birds above me chirped away, and once in the next hour I saw a cardinal and the second mailman of the day. I checked the mailman carefully. I'd once read a story by Chesterton about a criminal who disguised himself as a mailman because mailmen seem so much a part of the landscape. But this mailman was short and pudgy and definitely not Carl Gades.

I closed my eyes and began to go over the images of the day since I had arrived. I selected, checked faces and hands, and pulled myself up and awake when the image of Truman's dining room began to fade. My eyes scanned the Library, and I listened. Only the echo of a carpenter hammering away inside.

I had a sudden feeling of nausea. I wasn't sure what caused it, but I had to stand up. My legs were trembling. Maybe it was the lack of sleep, an allergy, or too much food for lunch; but something wasn't right.

"Sometimes you miss what's important because it's so damned obvious you don't see it," Truman had said.

Chesterton's invisible mailman. He'd been standing next to me, walking at Truman's right hand, looking at the former president's back through the window of the Library in front of me. The Secret Service man, Franklin. In the morning his eyes had been brown. Less than an hour ago they had turned blue. I was sure of it. I checked the images in my memory. Confirmed. I moved down the hill, straightening my tie, and went over other images. Franklin's nose, profile. Altered. Not quite Gades, but not unlike him. Little things could take care of that. And then I checked the hands. I stopped, closed my eyes, and compared Gades's left hand with Franklin's. A tiny white scar, a blemish the size of a tack head, the pattern of the veins. I started to run and checked my Timex. It was a few minutes before three.

I could have called for Koster, but I wasn't sure if Koster was Secret Service or Gades's helpmate of the month. So I ran behind the Library where Franklin was supposed to be stationed. He wasn't there. I considered running to the window of Truman's office and telling him to get the hell out of there, but I fought down the panic and the memory of lunch. I had no weapon. I hadn't expected to need one. The damned Secret Service was supposed to supply the firepower. I ran to the wall and crept along until I got to the window. When I looked inside, my head went light and I considered diving into a migraine.

Franklin was standing in front of Truman's desk and the

ex-president was looking up at him. Franklin was doing all the talking, but I couldn't hear a word. Franklin, hell, it was Gades! And he was looking at his watch. I leaned back against the wall and checked mine. If mine was accurate and his was, too, it was about three minutes to three. I hoped Gades's sense of poetic justice was operating.

I considered a leap at the window, but there were too many things that could go wrong. The window might not break or, if it did, I might be so cut up that I couldn't do anything except get myself killed along with Harry Truman. Even if I did get through the window and on my feet, I didn't think I was a hand-to-hand match for Gades. Gades liked to kill with a knife, but he was known to carry a gun. He might be impetuous, but he was no fool.

So, I hurried for the front of the Library, managing to trip once and rip the knees of my dress greens. There was no time for checking credentials. I went right for the Oval Office where Koster was standing. He looked at me, saw a panting madman with a torn uniform, knew something was up, and took a defensive position in front of the door. It was a good sign. A Gades man, knowing his boss was inside and about to commit murder, would have had his weapon out and would have put two holes in me by now.

"Hold it, Lieutenant," Koster said calmly.

I stopped, looked at the door to Truman's office, and hoped that it was reasonably soundproof. What was I doing? As I stood at an impasse in front of Koster, I pulled up the image of the original White House Oval Office I'd once visited. I found the door and fixed on it as I had left the room. The door was thick and solid. I did the same for the replica Oval Office behind Koster, recalling it from the second I'd looked at the door when I'd entered the room with Truman. It was equally thick. Knowing Truman's desire for detailed authenticity, I was confident that Gades and Truman wouldn't hear us in the hall unless we shouted.

"Koster," I said, trying to control my panting. "How well do you know Franklin?"

Koster tilted his head like a curious bird.

"Come again, Lieutenant?"

"When did you meet Franklin?"

I looked at the door and considered trying to rush past him, but I didn't see how I could make it even if I were lucky enough to catch him with a knee to the groin or an elbow to the stomach.

"Three days ago," he said. "He was assigned to bolster protection for the president when word came through that there might be an attempt on his life. What's your point?"

"Did you get a call? Did he have papers?" I asked, glancing at my watch. We had less than two minutes.

"Papers, a call came through," Koster said. "We talked. He . . ."

"His eyes changed color," I said.

"His eyes?"

"They were brown this morning. They're blue now. You think of any reason?"

Koster tried to remember his partner's eyes.

"Why?" he asked.

"Maybe the brown contacts bothered him. He had to take them out so he could see clearly when he killed Mr. Truman."

"Killed . . . Are you saying that Franklin is . . ."

". . . Carl Gades," I finished. "And I just saw him in there," I nodded toward the door, "with Truman."

"Let's find out," Koster said, reaching for the doorknob but keeping an eye on me. I didn't move forward. The door was locked. Koster considered knocking, thought better of it, and looked at me.

"The door's solid," I said, "but the frame is new. If we both go at it, we might be able to get it down."

"Might," he said. "Let's do it."

There wasn't much room to move. We got against the far wall and together went for the Oval Office door. Our shoulders hit together and mine went numb, but the frame splintered and we tumbled in. I went down on the floor. Koster kept his feet and look in the room.

Gades was standing next to the desk, a good fifteen feet or more from Koster. In his hands Gades held a small revolver. Truman sat behind the desk, his mouth a thin pink line.

"About thirty seconds," Gades said, aiming the weapon at us. "Then our little Mr. Truman will feel steel entering his bowels and he'll know a little of what it is like to die as my brother died."

I got to my feet shakily and stood next to Koster.

"Your brother died," Truman said, "because he was a murderer and he paid the penalty for that crime by living out what remained of his life behind bars where he belonged."

"You could have saved him," Gades spat, not taking his eyes from me and Koster.

"I made some tough decisions when I was in office," Truman said evenly. "That was not one of them."

"Shut up, old man," Gades said. "Shut up and watch the clock."

I wondered how much of a chance I'd have at surviving if I made a run at Gades. Not much. I might divert him enough for Koster to get his hands on him, but Gades had killed before. He could probably take both of us out in less than a second.

"Have you ever played stud poker?" Truman asked.

"Stud poker?" Gades asked, and then laughed.

"One card in the hole, four up," Truman explained. "Everything in sight but the hole card."

"You can talk till I put the steel in your belly, old man," Gades said. "What did you have for lunch? Ah, yes. Chicken. Let's see what it looks like when it comes running out on the floor."

Gades kept his eyes on us.

"The trick," Truman said, "is to get the other fellow looking at the wrong cards. It worked with Churchill. It worked with Dewey. It worked with Stalin, and by God, it'll work with you."

The next few seconds were a series of perfect images. I held them and savored them. I still have them in detail. Truman's hand had inched to the handle of the cane on his desk. He had been sitting absolutely immobile as he had talked. He had looked the old man, but in those few seconds, Harry Truman's cane swished upward under Gades's hand and Gades tried to turn the weapon in it away from us and toward Truman, who was on the rise. The gun hand went up in the air and the bullet cracked through the ceiling. Truman, now on his feet, brought the cane down with two hands on Gades's wrist. A bone broke with a sharp crack and the gun fell to the floor. Koster moved forward as Gades reacted by reaching into his jacket. The knife came out in the unbroken hand. Gades's teeth were clenched in hatred as he lunged forward over the desk. Koster was within a foot of the would-be assassin when Truman's cane cracked down on Gades's head.

Gades staggered backward, dropping the knife, and Koster hit him with a right that would have pleased Rocky Marciano.

"Little," grunted Truman, looking over the top of his glasses at the unconscious Gades on the floor. "Man doesn't know the game, he shouldn't take a drink in the dealer's parlor."

The hall was alive with people who had heard the door breaking and the gunshot. The secretary and typist and a few white-clad painters stood at the broken door trying to see what had happened.

"Show's over," said Truman. "Permanter, get that door fixed and call an ambulance. Everybody back to work."

They left reluctantly, missing Koster and me picking up the limp Gades.

"You did a fine job, Mr. President," Koster said, straightening his hair after he had secured Gades in a chair.

"Just be sure he's not playing possum," Truman said, looking up at the hole in the ceiling.

"He's not, sir," Koster said.

"Faced worse than that," Truman said, looking at the unconscious Gades, "Back in World War One. Hell, faced worse than that across the conference table."

"Still," I said, wearily wondering if Colonel Saint would be happy enough to pay for the new dress uniform I needed. "You took a big chance."

Truman grinned a broad campaign grin, leaned forward, and pointed to the famous sign on his desk that read:

THE BUCK STOPS HERE.

AMNESIA

She was doing a crossword when the newspaper fell on the table before her eyes. She pushed the newspaper to the side and asked, "Do you know a seven-letter word for loss of memory?"

"Amnesia," he replied and she looked up with a small grateful smile at the man who she recognized as one of the musicians in the Harry Codd Hydro Dance Band. She had assumed it would be him, the one who played the trumpet, the one with the dark hair parted in the middle whose collar always appeared just a bit too tight. He was about 50, perhaps a little younger, and even when he played upbeat songs like "Yes, We Have No Bananas" and "Don't Bring Lulu" there was a melancholy in his blue eyes that suggested memories beyond music.

"Thank you," she said, writing something on the crossword with the finely sharpened pencil.

"May I sit for a moment? We're on a break."

The woman did not look up. She gestured with her hand at the chair across from her and he sat. She took a small sip from the cup before her.

"You're not writing 'amnesia,' " he said.

At another table nearby a mother and daughter nibbled at melba toast and drank grapefruit juice. The daughter was at least sixty. The mother of a time long forgotten.

"It is not in this puzzle," the woman said, putting down the pencil and looking up, eyes unblinking, into the sad blue eyes of the man across from her.

"My name's Clark, Burt Clark," he said. "Work in the post office days. Trumpet at night."

"Leaves you little time for your family," she said.

"Wife's dead. Daughter's married. Lives in Surrey. Two kids. One's a little girl."

"I have a little girl," the woman said softly.

"I know," said Burt Clark. "Elizabeth, she's the day maid, says she saw a little girl's photograph on your dresser. Elizabeth's my brother Herb's daughter. You're . . ."

"Mrs. Neele, Teresa," the woman said, looking down at the newspaper that Burt had dropped on the table.

"Been watching you since you checked in a few days back, Mrs. Neele," he said. "Watching you sit here doing the crosswords, listening to us."

"You think I look sad and need cheering? I danced last night as you may recall since you have been observing me."

"You danced like I play," he said, glancing up as a couple, the husband just a bit tipsy, entered the room. "No heart in it. That's why I'm a postman, not a musician with some band maybe in London."

"I suppose there was something you wanted me to see in this newspaper?" she asked.

Burt Clark reached for the newspaper, pulled a pair of reading glasses from his pocket, tried to adjust his tight collar with his thumb and read:

"Missing from her home, The Styles, Sunningdale, Berkshire, Mrs. Agatha Mary Clarissa Christie, age 35; height 5 feet 7 inches; hair red, shingled part gray; complexion fair, built slight; dressed in gray . . ."

He paused, looked over the top of his glasses and continued, "Picture here. Looks like you."

"Others have made that observation in the past several days, Mr. Clark," she said pleasantly, the smile still on her lips.

"Some think as how she's dead, this writer who looks like you. Some say she met with foul play. Some say she's wandering with a seven-letter word that means loss of memory."

He leaned forward, removed his glasses, placed them in his pocket and said softly, "That daughter of hers and her husband must be worried. I know how I'd have felt and my daughter too if my wife, Constance was her name, had turned up missing."

"Were you a faithful husband, Mr. Clark? I'm sorry. That's a foolish question, a prying question and I can see the answer. You were."

"I was," he acknowledged. "And since I've been prying and you've been kind enough to hear me, you can pry."

"There's a hundred pound reward from that very newspaper for the person who finds Mrs. Christie," the woman said.

"I figure if she wants to be lost, she's got the right," he said. "I wouldn't touch such money. I would worry though about the husband and daughter."

The band members were slowly making their way to the small stand behind the potted palms. Burt glanced over his shoulder at them.

"Mr. Clark, I have a theory about Mrs. Christie. Would you like to hear it?"

"Very much," he said.

"I have heard that her husband has a . . . young woman, a woman named Nancy Neele."

"Relative of yours, Mrs. Neele?"

"Coincidence, Mr. Clark. Mrs. Christie does not wish to lose her husband, does not want her daughter to lose her father. It is my theory that Mrs. Christie has disappeared to bring attention to the situation, to the existence and threat of Miss Neele in the hope that when she is found the press will have unearthed this liaison and that facing public scandal, Miss Neele will retreat from the scene and Mr. Christie, seeing the anguish of his wife, will return to her and resume their marriage."

"Burt," a voice whispered from the band stand. "Five minutes."

"Got you," Burt whispered back. "Good theory," Burt said, turning back to the woman. "But I don't think it will do here. I've seen Colonel Christie's picture, heard a bit about him. Ask me, he's not the man to spend the rest of his life being the famous Miss Agatha's husband. If your theory's right, I think it won't work in the long run."

Burt rose.

"At the same time," the woman said, "I would think that Mrs. Christie may also have amnesia."

"Got to be careful about such things," he said, picking up his newspaper. "Had a friend. Tony Williams worked at the post office. Used to pretend he was a bit crazy, do anything. Got him laughs, attention. I warned Tony, but he said it was just a game, a fancy, and he smiled. Well, Tony's fancy kept up and took over. You see, he lost track of where the game ended and being real came back."

"What happened to Tony?" the woman asked.

"One night he went out on the street and started directing traffic with all his clothes off. Police came for him. You see, the fancy had taken over. I've got to go back for the last set. Waltz time."

"Thank you, Mr. Clark."

"My pleasure, Mrs. Neele."

"Mr. Clark," she added as he took a step away. "There comes a time when even the fancies are real. I very much believe that Mrs. Christie will be found very soon, that she wants to be found, wants to be rescued from her. . . ."

". . . amnesia," he supplied with a sad smile.

"Amnesia," she agreed.

While the Harry Codd Hydro Dance Band played "The Blue Danube" and the old mother and daughter whispered out of the room, the woman known as Mrs. Teresa Neele tried to finish her crossword. She found for the first time in her life that she was unable to do so, put it aside, and looked up into the blue eyes of Burt Clark, the postman trumpeter.

DRUP NUMBER ONE

The lock click-licked when Sklodovich inserted the broken bit of hanger into the keyhole and gave a sharp, confident twist. The door burped open.

Sklodovich, throwing his head back to clear the view through his overlong black hair, peeped out, scanned the empty corridor and darted into the slightly open door to his left with Arnold Trewitz, pink robe wrapped tightly, slippers flopping, right behind. The door closed with a snap behind them and Arnold found himself facing a lean bird of a man with saucer eyes bulging in soporific surprise, a look which Arnold was beginning to associate with patients at Japeth Psychiatric Research Hospital. Toucan eyes fixed on Arnold's flushed face before the man's white-gowned arm-wing swooped up to pull Sklodovich's shaggy head down to accept a whisper.

"A guy come in wit you," chirped the little man.

"I know. He's with me," said Sklodovich.

"You sure?"

"Yes. Are you?"

"Me? Me? Me?" The huge eyes seemed to be ready to pop—spreading, Arnold thought, a spray of aqueous humor which would fill the room. "What do you ask me?"

"He's with me."

"Good," said the little man, looking at Arnold and

scratching a few wisps of white hair on his bald head into Dirksenian dance. "Just want to be sure. Tell me," he whispered, clawing Sklodovich's sleeve into a crinkly mess, "are dey still out there?"

"No. Look for yourself." Sklodovich gently removed the hand from his blue polka-dot pajama sleeve.

"Me? Me? Me? Look out dere? No tank you, buster. Not me. What you tink I am?"

"Arnold and I have to see Dante," Sklodovich whispered.

"Ahnold?"

"This is Arnold. He came in with me."

"I see. Come wit me."

He hopped across the room which looked to Arnold much like the one he had shared with the big man who thought he was a Russian welder. One bed was neatly made. In the other, a large bulge under a crazy quilt shivered with fear, illness, or shock. The bird opened the closed door.

"They maybe ain't there now," he mumbled to himself as he pulled boxes out of the closet, "but open that door too wide and dey'll be dere so fast it'll make you pee-pee in your pants, I tell ya."

Sklodovich nodded, stepped into the closet and removed a loose-fitting plasterboard panel. Beyond the panel Arnold could see a white-gray tile floor with random cracks fissuring them without pattern. Arnold followed Sklodovich through the closet wall unsure of how he'd been covertly convinced to seek the aid of a vague, mad demi-deity named Dante. But Arnold had tried everything else to convince the seemingly deaf doctors that he had been brought to the hospital by a combination of bad luck and confused rhetoric. Why not Dante?

The bird whispered once more as he replaced the panel behind them.

"You tink I don't know dey out dere, you got another tink!"

"Who does he think is outside the door?"

"I don't know," said Sklodovich, looking around the washroom. "He'd rather not say."

Accompanied by the fugue of swirling water in a constantly flushing line of cleanser-odor urinals, Sklodovich moved to a toilet stall. Arnold paused, army memoried, but followed to see Sklodovich open a small, battleship-gray metal door above the seat.

"Up the pipe," he whispered, pointing his finger up the dark shaft beyond the door.

At first Arnold thought he had muttered a dark, empurpled curse against pipes and tubular constructions in his world of welded steel and international plots. Head-first, Sklodovich disappeared into the hole.

"Close the door behind you," his voice echoed as Arnold watched slippered feet vanish upward into blackness. Reaching into the void, Arnold felt a moist water pipe with which he pulled himself reluctantly after the fast fading sound above him. He closed the metal door and began to move, but the metal door had exhausted him before he began. Balanced, clinging to wet pipe with one hand and both legs, he had closed the metal door which had no handle on the inside, nothing but a protruding bolt which he struggled against with unprotected fingers. Fear. Total darkness. How many floors above, my god, how many floors below? Visions of zipping down into limbo like used razor blades down the shafts of hotel bathrooms. Could those blades ever be retrieved, thought Arnold. "And what of me?" Up. The ever-retreating sound of Sklodovich's powerful breathing.

Using the wall, a jagged mass of rough brick, and the protuberant interstices of ancient piping, Arnold inched upward.

Skinned right arm on an unidentified outcropping. Wet hands slipping, he rested holding the pipe and easing his ample rear against a somewhat smooth section of cold brick.

"Dr. Led."

The voice was sharp behind, in front, around him with the name of the unseen doctor who was responsible for Arnold's plight. Arnold turned his head in the darkness expecting to see a raven's green glowing eyes. A thin, dusty blade of light cut a line a few inches above his head. Brick dust itched his eye pressed tight to the slit. A broad white back filled the screen, shifted slightly and exposed the moist, uncomfortable figure of Dr. Lvov, the staff psychiatrist who had interviewed him.

"Funds for the staff party will just have to be collected this year from the staff," said the object of Dr. Lvov's gaze, and Arnold recognized the voice of Dr. Nobius-Led. He strained for a view of the head psychiatrist who had remained hidden from him behind a screen during a brief examination, but the slit was too small. "You all know I don't mind putting up the cash out of my own pocket, but I don't think the nonprofessional staff really appreciates it," Led continued. "In fact, I'm quite convinced that they resent it as a move of overt and condescending benevolence. They may equally resent our asking them for funds, but it will be a more controllable resentment."

Lvov opened his collar, pulled his tie down and made an unpleasant face.

"I assume you all agree," said Led. "If anyone feels that it is worth discussing, please see me privately. Dr. Lvov, I understand you want to comment on the Trewitz case before we subject him to the second phase of Drastic Recovery Undercover Project Number One."

"Simply," sighed Lvov, "he is not worth the effort of

DRUP. A borderline case, huh, at best with some minor manifestations which, I admit, are disturbing, but far from worth such attention considering our patient load."

"Dr. Lvov," said Led with a trace of petulance, "we have gone over this several times. It is precisely the patient's lack of extreme manifestation which makes him an ideal subject for this treatment. Our few experiments, as you are well aware, involved cases of extreme difficulty and yielded inconclusive results. Here we have a patient who is clearly borderline, clearly, if I may quote myself, 'balanced humanly on the razor blade which cuts a fine line between neurosis and more serious psycho-medical disturbance.' He may be able to exist indefinitely balanced, but he may also be sliced into schizophrenia."

"I think it highly unlikely," mumbled Lvov.

"The rest of us disagree," said Led sharply.

"I do not claim he is a median norm, but there are other cases . . ." Lvov trailed off, picking his nose while pretending to scratch it.

"Forgive me please, but there is a point which is likely to make a clarification of the issue." Arnold recognized the voice of the Indian resident, Dr. Randipur. Lvov, the only one Arnold could see, turned to look over his shoulder with irritation at the speaker who was known by patients and staff to be under the wing of Dr. Nobius-Led.

"The mother of this patient is quite willing that he be given transfer to the Garryowen Sanitarium as suggested, Dr. Led. This, I believe, is most sound. Therefore, it is this I suggest. We proceed with Dr. Led's most excellent plan of Drastic Recovery Undercover Project Number One, on a rapid basis, say twenty-four hours. If, after this time, we see no results which we find to be reportable in a technical report for the purpose of publication and further examination, I suggest that we then approve his transfer to Garryowen."

Lvov shrugged in defeat as Arnold willed him to make another defense, but if one came it was cut off from Arnold by a broad back which leaned against his viewing slit, cutting off sight and sound.

In total darkness, Arnold trembled, a victim of DRUP. But what was DRUP? If he didn't respond to it as expected (whatever response that might be), he would be shipped off to Garryowen. If he responded correctly, what was then in store? Perhaps endless rounds of DRUP and counter-DRUP. Perhaps eventually he would grow large eyes and fear unknown creatures lurking in the halls. Fingers and hopes slipping, Arnold moved upward with no thought but escape or possible confrontation with Dr. Led, a confrontation in which, somehow, he could convince him of the sanity of Arnold Trewitz.

Back aching, pajama bottoms slipping, he grappled upward. Palms blistered, he made an exhausted effort and found himself face to face with a long, thin man whose mouth hung stupidly and perplexedly open. A gray stubble beard surrounded the open mouth and circled a creviced tongue. Arnold almost lost his grip.

"Where have you been?" said Sklodovich, pushing the stunned creature from the opening and extending a hand to Arnold. Through the hole, Arnold found himself in another washroom and leaned against the toilet to catch his breath.

The man with the ugly tongue stood, still open-mouthed, with his pajamas at his feet and his arms wrapped tightly around his celery-stalk body. He had obviously been interrupted while seated.

"Let's go," said Sklodovich, walking to the door.

"Does he know what we're doing here?"

"He?"

"That man," said Arnold.

"I suppose not. Why?"

"Why? I think we scared the hell out of him."

"You think so?" Sklodovich said seriously. "Did we scare the hell out of you, fella?"

The man shook his head wildly.

"See, we didn't scare him. Now, let's go. If you see anybody in the hall, walk as if you belong here."

Without knowing how one walks in such a situation, Arnold followed him into the hall, leaving the bewildered man behind to make his peace with reality. Patients in the hall paid no attention, but a nurse paused and grabbed Arnold's sleeve. Sklodovich kept walking as if the situation didn't concern him.

"Don't you think you should take that robe off and get a clean one?" she said. "You look as if you've been crawling down a greased pole. I don't see how some of you do it."

"I don't know how it got so dirty. Must have fallen. I'll change right away."

"See that you do." She turned a corner and was gone.

Head aching, Arnold wobbled down the hall after Sklodovich who was waiting for him in a slight alcove. They ducked behind a pillar which hid a window covered by bars. Sklodovich opened the window and lifted two of the bars which easily slid out of the way. Easing himself out of the window, he beckoned for Arnold to follow onto a narrow ledge about ten stories above an enclosed courtyard. A thin rain was falling as Sklodovich helped him onto the ledge which tilted downward at a slight angle.

Sklodovich inched a few feet along the moist ledge, reached up to an old rainspout and pulled himself with one hand over the roof and out of sight. Arnold sighed and followed, remembering the voice of Dr. Led. As he reached the rainspout, his foot slipped and his already blistered hands released the spout.

"Not in my pajamas!" Arnold screamed as he felt Sklodovich's powerful grasp on his left wrist. Detached, Arnold glanced down to watch his slippers plunge, dance, and bounce into the rain and out of sight. Sklodovich lifted him—robe flapping, pajamas slipping—easily over the top, jarring him only slightly. Lying on the bepebbled asphalt surface, water streaming into his mouth, Arnold felt an acrid tear mingle with the rain.

"I'll carry you the rest of the way."

"No thanks." Arnold rose amidst the sparse jungle of chimneys, parapets and television aerials.

Limping barefoot on the pinching pebbles, Arnold followed to a protuberance of concrete, and a green door to which Sklodovich put his ear before opening it gently.

"Put these on." Sklodovich handed him a pair of sunglasses which, once on, made it doubly difficult to walk down the dimly lighted stairway.

"If anyone asks you, we're on our way to Dr. Keaky for a heat treatment." Sklodovich, too, was wearing dark glasses.

"What if they ask us why we're wet?"

"We just took showers."

"But our robes and pajamas are wet."

"We fell in a pool."

"Is there a pool?"

"I don't know," he said, hurrying down the stairs. "We're supposed to be mentally unstable, remember?"

As they reached another door, Sklodovich raised his dark glasses and paused.

"Remember, we're on our way to see Dr. Keaky for a . . ."

"Heat treatment."

"Right."

Dripping, they stepped into an alcove. Arnold, exhausted,

warm, and perspiring, felt about to collapse.

"Wait here. Dante is on this floor somewhere. I'll check on the room. It'll just take a minute." Too weak to protest, Arnold watched Sklodovich put his huge hands in sopping pockets and step into the hallway, whistling more conspicuously than Arnold thought safe.

The instant Sklodovich turned the corner, an unnoticed door before Arnold opened and a short, dark man stepped into the alcove. One hand calmly rested in the pocket of a black silk robe. The other hand held a pistol pointed at Arnold's stomach.

"You will please step quietly into this room," said the man. "I'm on my way to Dr. Keaky for a heat treatment."

"Nonsense. There is no Dr. Keaky. Please step into this room with no more trouble." Arnold stepped in, leaving moist footprints on the tile floor.

The room, Arnold noticed, was much like his own and the few others he had seen except this one looked more permanent, perhaps because of the simple, unpainted table in the corner, the huge trunk near it, and the reproduction of a Van Gogh sunflower on the wall.

"You will sit on the chair and I will sit on the bed where it will be quite impossible for you to make a move toward me and live. Very good. You did not know that I could open the door, did you? Of course not. You never see the obvious. In many ways you are clever, but in the end your overconfidence betrays you."

"You've got me confused with someone else. Honest to God. I'm a patient just like you. My name's Trewitz. I'm just looking . . ."

"Take off those sunglasses."

The man did not look as dark, but the gun looked much larger.

"We might be able to arrange some kind of deal," the little man whispered.

"Deal?"

"Perhaps. Remember I can always kill you, push you outside and close the door. The others do not know I have this gun or that I can open the door. Do not move."

"I'm not moving."

"First, we will change clothes. You take yours off first."

"My clothes are wet and they won't fit you. Besides, they don't look much different from yours."

"Clever. I give you credit, but in this case you are also right. I advise you not to move."

"I'm not moving. I didn't move."

"Very good. I'd hate to have to shoot you before you served my purpose. You will walk out of this room in front of me as if you were leading me someplace. You understand? My gun will not be visible, but it will be in my pocket trained on your back."

"You're making a mistake. We'll get halfway down the hall and they'll grab both of us. I'm a patient, too. Don't you understand? I'm a patient, too."

"You'd like me to believe that, but I know you have been planted here by Dr. Led. I can always spot you."

"But . . ."

"No more. One more word and I'm afraid I'll have to shoot. Now move to the door."

Before Arnold could decide on the safety of another protest, Sklodovich stepped into the room, cleaning moisture from his face with a dry terrycloth towel.

"Well, what's the scoop?" said Sklodovich.

The little man's eyes darted between his two visitors.

"Do you know this man?"

"It's Arnold. Arnold L. Trewitz."

"What is the 'L' for?" said the man who Arnold now realized must be Dante.

"Lionel," said Arnold.

"Like in trains or Barrymore?"

"What's the difference?"

"World view," said Dante, putting his gun in his pocket and pulling out a brown paper bag which he flipped to Sklodovich who moved quickly to the bed and dumped the contents, dozens of walnuts, on the brown, fuzzy blanket. "Well, my welding friend, what can I do for you and how is the electroslag business?"

"They stole my patent," said Sklodovich, selecting a walnut and crushing it in one hand, "but what the hell." Arnold slumped to the floor feeling that he was about to pass out, but he managed to disguise his collapse as a floor-sitting slide.

"Staff conference will be over shortly," said the little man, looking at his watch. "Suppose we get to business."

Sklodovich looked at Arnold and fished a bit of walnut out of the shell fragments in his hand before responding.

"Escape," he said. Dante grinned.

Eyeing Arnold over his shoulder, Dante stepped to the window and pulled down the shade which he spread out on the bed.

"Your friend is not interested?"

"Arnold."

Arnold rose and staggered to the bed to see an elaborate and confused map of some kind drawn on the back of the shade. Sklodovich assumed an air of rapt attention and continued to crack walnuts and pop them into his grinding mouth.

"Our main problem," said Dante, pointing to something on the map to which Arnold paid no attention since he had quickly ruled the man off as a hopeless lunatic, "is the moat. The drawbridge is down during the day, but well guarded. At night it is up, but the guard is small because they don't fear an attack from the rear, a thrust from within at the bowels of their own vile creation. I know the mechanism of the bridge for I've worked on the greasing detail under heavy guard. That mechanism, gentlemen, is the only way. The moat, as you noticed when they brought you in, is not too deep or too long or wide to swim, but it is filled with deadly little fish that can pick a man clean to the bone before he takes two strokes. Therefore, one man, you, Sklodovich," (Sklodovich nodded) "will overpower the drawbridge guard and you, Lionel, will put on the guard's uniform and answer all calls to the guard station while we then work on the bridge. You speak their language, don't you?"

"Yes," said Arnold, too weary to flee from the madman whose eyes were now gleaming with intrigue.

"Good. Now as long as they don't put the iron mask back on my head this afternoon, and I doubt if they will since it caused a strawberry rash last time and they had to work on me for days to be sure there would be no complaint from the Swiss legation of the Red Cross when they examined me, gentlemen," he added, wrapping his window shade. "Until tonight."

"Dr. Led," said Arnold in an attempt to salvage something from the mad pilgrimage. Sklodovich concentrated on cracking a difficult walnut beneath his huge bicep.

"Nothing to fear from Dr. Nobius-Led," chuckled Dante. "He'd not dare be around at midnight. He knows I've sworn revenge against him."

"That's not what I meant."

"Ah, you're worried about the plan. Believe me, it is the best. There's no chance for a successful tunnel operation.

We'd simply fall into the room below and they'd be even more suspicious."

"Do you know what Dr. Led looks like?"

"Of course. How could I forget my mortal enemy? A tall, gaunt man with fire-red hair flying in all directions and sharply pointed orange mustaches. Glassy-blue eyes trying to escape from their sockets. Not old, but ageless death in doctor's disguise."

"I've never seen anyone here who fits that description," said Arnold.

"Me either," said Sklodovich.

"Nor have I," said Dante. "But I've heard his voice a dozen, dozen times and it told me everything."

"You've never seen him."

"Don't be a fool," Dante said cheerfully. "So I've never seen him. Two words and I know any man. One look at his face and his history is open to me; he stands naked. Dante has learned to observe. Take you for example. Your walk, your voice. As soon as you walked in, I could tell you were a Catholic."

"I'm a Jew."

"Converted?"

"No."

"Well, I could tell you've been married at least five years and have two children."

"I'm not married."

"Liar," hissed the little man and grabbed Arnold by the collar, choking him. Sklodovich's hairy arm appeared before the swimming vision of the teeth-clenched Dante holding Arnold. Dante released him and Arnold reeled back against the wall.

"He was just testing you, weren't you, Arnold?"

"Yes," Arnold gasped, and through clearing eyes saw the

little man's face brighten.

"No patient has ever been allowed to see Dr. Led," said Dante.

"I've got to see him," Arnold said aloud, but to himself. "I've got to see him." Through sobs he told the two walnut-eating madmen what he had heard while crawling up the pipe. After his story, Dante closed his eyes, grinned and spoke.

"Listen, I have a story that will solve your problem. Once the powerful warden of a Peruvian prison called a jailed friend of mine into a large room filled with guards and newspaper reporters. It was late at night and my friend, a revolutionary, had been wakened from a troubled sleep. He rubbed his eyes at the huge crowd and rubbed them again when he saw the rare smile under the warden's black mustache. The warden ordered my friend to a table in the center of the room on which rested a black cloth bag. Conversation in the room stopped and the warden cleared his throat.

" 'In honor of the one hundredth anniversary of liberation, an amnesty has been called for all political prisoners,' said the warden with a sweep of his fat hand. 'However, since this prison contains only the worst and most dangerous elements, our president is reluctant to include this man and his fellows. But our president is a fair man who has instructed me to give this man an even chance to secure his freedom and that of all the others in this prison. In that bag are two small white balls. On one is written FREEDOM; on the other PRISON. By virtue of his rank in the subversive underground revolution, this man has been selected to choose the ball which will determine his fate and that of the others. He will place his hand in the bag and pull out one ball. If it is the one for FREEDOM, he is free. If it is the other, they all remain. You of the press have been invited to prove that our president is a man of his word. Now, take out a ball,' the warden ordered my friend.

"My friend was no fool. He knew that the fat warden with the great mustache hated him and would not let him get away. What, my friend quickly reasoned, would be a better way than to make him the object of hatred among his fellow inmates? Surely, my friend knew, if he selected the ball marked PRISON, the lower elements in the prison would read of it or hear of it and it would fester until one of them could stand it no longer and would kill my friend for his ill luck. My friend pretended to be sleepy as his mind worked rapidly. 'There is no chance of my pulling out the right ball,' he decided, looking at the grinning warden and feeling the breath of the reporters. The truth was obvious. Both balls contained the word PRISON and it made no difference which one he picked. No one would dare challenge the powerful warden, second cousin to the president, by asking to see the remaining ball, least of all my friend who knew that such a move would bring an unpleasant death. My friend made up his mind quickly.

"He strode to the table, plunged his hand into the bag and, without looking, threw the ball into his mouth and swallowed it in one gulp. A gasp rose from the crowd and the warden reached for his pistol.

" 'What are you trying to do?' shouted the purple-faced warden.

" 'Nothing,' said my friend, innocently pretending a combination of stupidity and drowsiness. 'I thought I was supposed to eat it. Anyway, there is no harm done. All you have to do is see which ball remains in the bag and the one I picked is, by elimination, the other one.'

" 'True,' said a sharp-nosed reporter standing near the table. A murmur of approval ran through the reporters who were anxious to discover the fate of the prisoners and were not to be put off by one idiot revolutionary. The warden, teeth clenched, eyes magnificent with hate, dumped the ball on the table. It bounced towards the sharp-nosed reporter, who grabbed it and read it.

" 'FREEDOM,' said the reporter, handing the ball to the warden. 'He ate the PRISON ball.' In an instant the room was clear of reporters rushing to write of my friend's sad selection. Badly shaken, my friend was returned to his cell and several weeks later he was found beaten to death, whether by guards or prisoners no one ever discovered." Dante reached for a walnut to show that his parable had ended.

"Outsmarted himself," said Sklodovich.

"No," said Dante. "Not at all. He had been absolutely right. Both balls had PRISON marked on them. The sharp-nosed reporter had used a perfect opportunity to do a good turn for the powerful warden who rewarded him by attempting to have him imprisoned a few months later on some trumped-up charge. At that time, the reporter told the truth, but it was too late to do my friend any good and, since the warden denied it as the word of a desperate criminal, it did no good for any of the remaining prisoners, either."

"What's this got to do with me?" asked Arnold, shivering with cold from his moist pajamas.

"There's little hope for you, Lionel. Realize this, it makes no difference if you find out who Dr. Led is. If he has made up his mind, you are as surely doomed as my friend and you will have as much choice as he had. Either give in to DRUP or escape. Now gentlemen, if you will forgive me, I've got to get some rest. We have a great deal of work tonight."

The little man guided them to the door, his attack on Arnold obviously forgotten, hands once again in his pockets. Sklodovich scooped up his walnuts, winked at Dante and nodded to Arnold to follow him. Over his shoulder Arnold saw the little man climb into bed behind them and, as Sklodovich closed the door, a loud snore arose from the still, robed figure.

"Is that gun real?" whispered Arnold.

"No mechanism," said Sklodovich, looking down the hall.

"Does he really expect us to come back tonight?"

"Don't know. Doesn't really matter. He wouldn't leave anyway. He can leave whenever he wants to. His door is open. He just won't go out unless a doctor or nurse holds his hand and leads him out. He thinks the floor will give way. Something to do with an accident he had in South America."

The fluorescent corridor was empty and quiet except for a distant muffle of voices. Sklodovich turned toward the door leading to the roof and Arnold felt a sinking, tired feeling in his knees.

"I can't make it," he whispered in panic.

Sklodovich winked and, with a nod, indicated a new direction. Arnold followed him around the corner, down a short corridor and to a door. Walking through the door, Arnold found himself not more than twenty steps from his own room which he had assumed was an odyssey away.

"Why didn't we just come through here in the first place?" he sobbed.

"There are many ways of doing things," said Sklodovich, taking his arm and helping him to the room. "There's always an easy way, but to mean something, sometimes it has to be the hard way. Besides, that wasn't even the hardest way. Hell, I didn't even take you down the wire or make you put on the nurse's disguise. Next time we'll try something different."

Arnold was never sure whether he passed out before or after he reached the door to his room.

THE MAN WHO SHOT LEWIS VANCE

When I opened my eyes, I saw John Wayne pointing a .38 at my chest. It was my .38. I closed my eyes.

The inside of my head seemed to be filled with strawberry cotton candy with little unnamed things crawling through its sickly melting strands. Nausea forced my eyes open again. John Wayne was still there. He was wearing trousers, a white shirt and a lightweight tan windbreaker. He was lean, dark and puzzled.

"Don't close your eyes again, Pilgrim," he said.

I didn't close them. He was standing over me and I slumped in a badly sprung cheap understuffed hotel chair. I tried to sit up and speak but my tongue was an inflated, dry, pebbly football. There was a flat half full glass of brown Pepsi on the stained yellow table in front of me but I didn't reach for it. That glass, and what had been in it, had put me out.

I wasn't sure of the day and the time. When I took that last few gulps of Pepsi, it had been a Sunday night in the winter of 1942. I had been sitting in a cheap Los Angeles hotel room with a guy who had identified himself as Lewis Vance.

Lewis Vance had left a message for me at my office, but I had been out of town filling in for a gate guard at an old people's home in Goleta. It had netted me $20 minus gas. The message on my desk, left in the uncertain hand of Sheldon Minck, the dentist I rent space from, had said I should call

Lewis Vance in Room 303 of the Alhambra Arms over on Broadway. I'd called and Vance had told me to come right over. I didn't even have to drive. My office was on Hoover a few blocks away and I ambled over knowing I needed a shave and worrying about which island the Japanese had taken while I was in Goleta.

My gray seersucker was crumpled but reasonably clean if you ignored the remnants of mustard stain on the sleeve. It was the best suit I had. The sky threatened rain but no one on the street seemed concerned. Soldiers, sailors, overly painted women laughing too loud to make a buck and sour-faced visitors flowed with me. Before the war, the crowds had been thick on Broadway on a Sunday, but tourists didn't make their way to Los Angeles after the first threats of an invasion by the Japanese.

Now Broadway was kids in uniform, waiting women and girls and people who couldn't afford to or were too stubborn to leave. I was one of the latter.

Vance had said he had a job for me. Since I am a private investigator, I assumed it had something to do with my profession. At 46 with a bad back, pushed-in nose, and black graying hair, I was a reasonably formidable sight as a bodyguard. If I were over five foot-nine, I'd probably be busy nine or ten months a year with celebrities who wanted to show they could afford protection they usually didn't need. But there were plenty of muscle builders from the beaches— Santa Monica, Venice—who could be bought cheap and looked bigger and meaner than I did. They weren't meaner, but they were fine for show as almost everything was and is in Los Angeles.

The people who hire me usually get my name from someone who has used me in the past. They really want protection, or a grandmother found, or a stern word or two said to a former friend who owes them a few hundred bucks. Vance hadn't said what he wanted me for.

The lobby of the Alhambra Arms was wilting badly, had been since long before the war. There were four big wooden pots in the lobby which had once held small palm trees. The palms had sagged to the floor years before and now the chipped green pots were used as ash trays and garbage bins. It didn't look too bad because you couldn't see much of anything in the Alhambra lobby. There was a strict policy of not replacing light bulbs as they died. The ceiling was a cemetery of darkened bulbs with a few dusty die-hards still glowing away. Considering the way I looked, I didn't mind the shadows of the Alhambra. I had filled in as hotel detective here twice in the last two years, both times on weekends. There had been no detecting involved, no thefts. The job was to keep the uniformed kids and un-uniformed prostitutes from destroying the place and each other. It had kept me busy. The last time I had held down the duty I had done almost as much damage to the Allies as the Japanese fleet. Two sailors in diapers had taken umbrage at my telling them to refrain from destroying the lobby. Had they been sober I might have had a problem. They walked away from our discussion with a concussion, broken thumb, badly lacerated thigh, and a black eye. The damage was divided rather evenly between them.

The guy behind the desk when I walked into the Alhambra lobby on Sunday was named Theodore Longretti, better known on the streets as Teddy Spaghetti. Teddy was about 50, long, lean and faintly yellow from whatever it is cheap hotel clerks put into themselves to make the world think they are awake and relatively sane. Teddy's once white hair was even turning yellow again, not the yellow it might have been when and if he'd been a kid, but the yellow of white yam dipped in cheap bourbon.

"Teddy," I said, walking across the empty morning lobby and listening to my shoes clap the worn linoleum made to look like Spanish tiles.

"Toby?" he said, squinting through the darkness in my direction.

A desk lamp stood on the counter next to Teddy. Lights bounced off of the center making the welcoming clerk look like the skeleton of Woodrow Wilson.

"You've got a Lewis Vance, 303?" I said, coming near the desk, but not too close. A little of Teddy Spaghetti can go a long way. Besides he thought we were buddies.

"I've got a Lewis Vance," he admitted, looking down at his open book, "and a half dozen Browns, a sprinkling of Andersons, a Kelly or two, but no Smiths. It's a fallacy that people use the name Smith when they go to a hotel. You know what I mean?"

"I know," I said.

"Even people named Smith avoid saying they're Smith. It looks too suspicious," Teddy said seriously, finally looking up from his book. "So what can I do for you?"

"Vance look kosher?"

Teddy shrugged, his yellow face moving into a thoughtful pout. "Never saw him before, but looks like a straight arrow," he said. "But I ask you, if he's so straight, what's he checking in here for?" Teddy looked around, into the dark corners, past the chipped green former palm holders. I had to admit he had a point.

"Thanks," I said and headed for the stairway.

"No trouble, Toby," he stage whispered. "I see you're packing heat. I'm in for two shifts and I don't want to identify the remains of former guests. You know what I mean?"

"I know, Teddy," I whispered back. "The gun's just for

show, to impress the client. You know what I mean?"

I patted the holster under my seersucker jacket and winked at Teddy, though I doubted if he could see me.

"I know what you mean," he said, and I jogged up the stairs.

The holster thumped against my chest as I went up and my back told me not to be so athletic. I slowed down and followed the trail of dimly lit landings to the third floor. Room 303 was next to Room 301 where what sounded like a child soprano was singing "Praise the Lord and Pass the Ammunition" with frequent stops for giggling. I knocked on the door of 303, adjusted my jacket, ran a hand through my hair and tried to look as if I wasn't afraid of anything less than a Panzer attack

The guy who opened the door looked familiar, at least his outline did against the back light. He was tall, good shoulders, a full size nose, and a good head of dark hair.

"Peters?" he said.

"Right," I answered. He opened the door and I walked in.

When I turned to face him, he didn't look quite so much like John Wayne as I had thought, but the resemblance was there.

Vance had a glass of amber liquid in his hand. He was wearing a weary smile and a lightweight brown suit with a white shirt and no tie. It wasn't Beverly Hills but it beat what I was wearing and he was the client.

"How about a drink?" he said, holding up the glass.

"Nothing hard," I said, looking around the small room, seeing nothing but shabby furniture, an open unmade Murphy bed and a dirty window.

"Coke?" he asked.

"Pepsi, if you've got it," I answered, sinking into the worn chair next to the splintery yellow coffee table.

"I've got it," he said, moving to the dresser where a group of bottles huddled together. One, indeed, was a Pepsi. "Even got some ice."

His back was to me as he poured and started to talk. He kept talking as he turned and handed me the glass.

"Job is simple," he said. "I'm John Wayne's stand-in. Maybe you can see the resemblance."

"I can see it," I said.

"I'm doing the Duke a little favor here." He went on swirling his glass and sitting across from me on a wooden chair pulled away from the spindly-legged desk in the corner. "He owes some people and they want to collect. Word's out that the Duke is registered at a downtown hotel as Lewis Vance. Meanwhile, the Duke is out calling in some loans to pay these guys off. My job, our job, is to keep them busy and away from the Duke till he collects and pays them off. Don't worry about your money. We're talking big bills here. He can pay you with pocket money. No offense."

"None taken," I said, picking up the Pepsi. I wasn't offended by the money insult. It was true. It was the story that offended me. It had more holes than the U.S. Navy ships in Pearl Harbor. There were lots of possibilities here, I thought as I took a sip of the Pepsi. First, the story is true and John Wayne is doing one of the most stupid things imaginable. Second, Lewis Vance, who sat across from me watching for a reaction through dancing brown eyes, was a first-class nut who had thought this up for ends I couldn't imagine. Three, I was being set up for something, though I couldn't begin to figure what that something might be. I took a deep drink of the slightly bitter Pepsi and pretended to weigh the offer. What I really wanted to do was get the hell out of this room before I found out what was going on.

I took another sip of the Pepsi, put the glass down and stood up. Vance was bigger than me, younger too, but I was used to getting past people or keeping them from getting past me. He didn't look as if he had too much experience with either. I didn't see anything on him that looked like a gun bulge.

"I think I'll pass on this one, Mr. Vance," I said.

He stood up quickly, not loosening his grip on his glass.

"Wait," he said with real panic. "I can pay whatever your fee is. Duke authorized me to pay. Cash. Just one day's work. He'll really be grateful."

"Sorry," I said. "Truth is, Mr. Vance, you don't smell right to me."

Something went dull inside my head and should have been a warning, but I've taken so many blows over the years that I tend to regard occasional aches, pains, and ringing bells as natural.

"I'll prove it," Vance said, holding out his free hand to get me to wait. "We'll call Duke. He'll tell you."

Maybe John Wayne had gone mush-headed. My head certainly wasn't feeling too good. Maybe the 48 hours straight in Goleta and the drive back was getting to me.

"Make the call," I said. Hell, I needed the money.

"Fine," he said with a smile, his hand still out. "Just sit down again and I'll get him."

I sat down again. Actually, I fell backwards.

"Fine," I repeated.

Vance walked slowly to the phone on the desk, his eyes on me all the time as if to keep me from moving. My upper lip felt numb and my eyes didn't want to stay open, but I forced them to as Vance slowly, very slowly made his call or pretended to. I was rapidly losing my grip on the room and the situation.

"Right," Vance said. He kept looking at me and nodding his head. "Right. Mr. Peters is right here and he wants to talk to you."

Vance was looking at me now with a triumphant and mean little grin. He held out the phone.

"It's the Duke," he said. "He wants to talk to you. All you have to do is walk over here and take the phone."

I tried to get up, but it couldn't be done. It was at that point, long after a lobotomized chimp would have figured it out, that I knew I had been slipped something in my Pepsi. I could but hope that it wasn't lethal as I gave up, sank back and closed my eyes.

It rained while I was asleep. I don't know how I knew it while clowns danced before me, but I knew it and it was confirmed when I woke up with John Wayne, the real John Wayne, holding my gun on me. I looked at the single window and watched the downpour splatter and ask to come in.

"Water," I said.

"That it is, Pilgrim," he agreed, the gun steady and level.

"No, need water," I said, pointing to my tongue.

He nodded, understanding and pointed to the sink in the corner. I made three tries at getting up and succeeded on the fourth. I staggered to the sink, turned on the tap and looked down at the brown stain near the drain. The stain looked a little like the state of Nevada. I put my head under the warm water, cupped my hand and sloshed liquid into my mouth and over my inflated tongue. The tongue deflated slightly and, using the sink for support, I turned around.

Beyond Wayne, who looked at me with his forehead furrowed in curiosity, the Murphy bed stood open and on it lay the former Lewis Vance. He was definitely not asleep, not with that hole through his forehead.

I must have looked sick, surprised, or bewildered.

"You did that?" Wayne said, pointing his gun at the corpse.

"No," I said as emphatically as I could. I even shook my head which was one hell of a mistake. The red cotton candy inside my skull turned to liquid and threatened to come out of every available opening.

Slowly, painfully, I told my tale. The call, the offer from Vance, the drugged Pepsi. Wayne listened, nodding once in a while.

"And," I concluded, "I've got a feeling that hole in Vance's face came from a bullet in my gun, the one in your hand, the one with your fingerprints on it."

Wayne looked at the gun, shrugged and said, "Supposing I believe you. Where do we go now?"

First I asked him why he was in the room, holding my gun.

"Got a call," he said, gun still on me, though he looked over at the corpse from time to time. "Man said I should get over here fast, a friend of mine named Dick Lang had taken an overdose of something. I came fast and walked in to find you out with the gun in your hand and your friend Vance. He's never been my stand-in. I don't owe anyone any money and no one is looking for me. I was planning on going to a party at C.B. DeMille's to celebrate the finish of REAP THE WILD WIND when the call came. I don't think old C.B. is going to be too happy that I didn't come. Won't surprise me if I've worked for him for the last time."

The rain got louder and the day darker.

"Why should I believe you, Peters?"

"When you were a kid you used to go in the driveway of Pevsner's grocery store in Glendale," I said, making my way back to the chair and dropping into it. "About two blocks from your dad's drug store. You used to go to that driveway and throw a ball against the wooden wall. You did that for about two weeks till Pevsner's son came out and hit you in the head."

Wayne's mouth opened slightly and his hand went up to his head, a spot right behind the ear.

"That was you?" he said.

"My brother, Phil," I said. "He's a Los Angeles cop now."

I figured Wayne was about 35 or 36 now, but there was still a little of that kid in him.

"I thought you said your name was Peters," Wayne said suspiciously.

"Professional change," I said. "I thought your name was Marion Morrison."

"You made your point," he agreed. "But knowing your brother beat me up when I was a kid doesn't exactly prove you didn't shoot that fella over there."

I got out of the chair again and started to stagger around the room in the hope of clearing my head and returning my agonized body to its former, familiar level of constant ache.

"Let's go over it," I said, looking at Vance. "Someone wanted me here. Vance or someone else. Let's figure the idea was to set me up for Vance's murder. Vance thought it was for something else. Who knows what? He put me out with the drink and our killer steps in, takes my gun and punctuates Vance."

"And then," Wayne interrupted, "the killer calls me and I come over and step into it. Publicity could ruin the DeMille picture and maybe my career. Could be we're dealing with an old enemy of mine."

"Could be we're dealing with an old enemy of both of us," I said. "The only one I can think of is my brother Phil and I doubt if he'd go this far to get either one of us. Maybe it's a blackmail deal. The phone will ring and we'll get . . . No. It would have happened by now. It's a frame-up, simple and dirty."

"Let's try it another way," Wayne said, furrowing his brow. "Fella over there puts something in your drink. You feel you're going out, get out the gun, put some holes in him and pass out. I come in, find the gun in your hand and . . ."

"Who called you?" I said. My mind was starting to work again, not as well as I would have liked, but that's what I feel even if I haven't had a boiled Pepsi.

"Beats me, Pilgrim." Wayne shrugged.

The knock at the door cut off our further exploration of possibilities. We looked at each other and he delegated me with a wave of the .38 to be the door opener. I opened the door. The woman standing there was more than thirty and less than fifty, but that was about the best I could do with her age. She had a body that could pass for twenty-five. Her hair was red and frilly. So was her tight dress.

She looked at me, at Wayne—who she didn't seem to recognize—and over at Vance on the bed who had his head turned away.

"You didn't say anything about three," she said. "Three is more."

She stepped in, looked at Wayne and added appreciatively, "Maybe not much more." He had pocketed the gun in his windbreaker and was looking at me for an explanation.

"What did I say?" I said. "On the phone."

She put her small red handbag on the yellow table next to my lethal Pepsi, and looked at me as if I had a few beans loose, which I did.

"You said ten at night," she said, looking now at the body of Vance with the first hint of awareness. "It's ten and here I am." Then she turned to Wayne, looked at him enough to get him to look away and added, "You really are Randolph Scott."

"John Wayne," I said.

"Right," she said with a snap of the fingers. "That's what you said, John Wayne." Her eyes stayed on Wayne who gave me a sigh of exasperation and said,

"Thanks for clearing it up for the lady, Peters. I wouldn't want her to forget who she met here."

She took a few steps of curiosity toward the Murphy bed and Vance, and I eased over as fast as my retread legs would let me to cut her off.

"Are you sure it was me on the phone?" I said, putting my face in front of hers.

"You don't know if you called me?" she said, trying to look over my shoulder at Vance. "Voice on a phone is all I know. You trying to back out of this? And what's with the guy on the bed?"

Wayne was leaning against the wall now, his arms folded, watching. He wasn't going to give me any help.

"We're not backing out," I said. "You'll get paid, Miss . . ."

"Olivia Fontaine," she said.

"Classy," I said.

"Thanks," she answered with a smile that faded fast. "That guy on the bed. Is he hurt or something?"

"Or something," I said.

"He's dead, lady," Wayne said, pushing away from the wall. "And we're going to call the police."

"Dead?" she repeated and backed away from me. "I don't want no part of 'dead,' " she said, looking for something, spotted her red bag and clacked her red high heels toward it.

"You're going to have to stay awhile, ma'am," Wayne said, stepping in front of the door. "I don't like this much, but you walk out of here and that's one more complication that has to be unwound."

"You didn't talk like that to Claire Trevor in

STAGECOACH," Olivia Fontaine said with her hands on her hips. "She was a hooker and you was . . . were nice to her, for Chrissake."

"That was a movie, lady," Wayne said.

"Me, other girls I know, love that movie," she said, forgetting for a second the corpse on the bed. "I saw it five times. Hooker goes riding off with you at the end to a new life, ranch or something. Only thing is I thought you were Randolph Scott."

This knock at the door was louder than Olivia's. It was the one-two knock of someone who is used to knocking at hotel room doors. . . .

Olivia, Wayne and I looked at each other. Then Wayne nodded at me.

"Who is it?" I asked.

"Hotel detective," came a familiar voice. "Got a call to come up here."

Wayne shrugged, Olivia looked for someplace to hide, found nothing and sat in the chair I had recently passed out in. I opened the door and he came in. He was Merit Beeson, sixty, a massive white-haired man who had once been shot by a Singapore sailor. The shot had hit him in the neck and when it was clear he would survive, it also became clear that he would never be able to turn his neck again. Hence Merit Beeson became known as Straight-Ahead Beeson. The stiff neck lost him his job as a Los Angeles cop, but it gave him a strange dignity which got him steady, if not high-paying, work in hotels. Straight-Ahead looked like a no-nonsense guy, a stand-up, almost British butler in appearance, with strong ham arms and a craggy face. His suit was always pressed and he always wore a tie. Straight-Ahead avoided a lot of trouble just by looking impressive, but he wasn't going to be able to avoid this one.

He took it all in fast, Olivia, me, Wayne, and the body.

"You know the guy on the bed, Merit?" I said.

He stepped into the room, closed the door behind him, and looked at me carefully.

"Before we talk," he said, without turning his body to John Wayne which would have been the only way to acknowledge the actor, "I want the cowboy to ease the radiator out of his pocket and put it nice and gentle on the dresser. You think we can arrange it?"

Wayne took the gun out and did just what Straight-Ahead wanted.

"Good start," Beeson said, though he hadn't turned to watch. In the thirty years he had looked straight ahead, he had developed great peripheral vision. "I've seen the gent staining the Murphy around the lobby now and then. Gave him a light rousting. Mean customer. Threatened to cut up Merit Beeson. Can you imagine that, Toby?"

"Can't imagine it, Merit," I said, shaking my head for both of us. Something he said hit me gently and whispered back that I should remember it.

"You or the cowboy or the lady shoot him?" Merit said

"None of us," I answered.

"Speak for yourself," Olivia said, jumping up. "I didn't shoot him is all I know."

"Sal," Beeson said, his body moving toward the corpse, "I thought you agreed to stay out of the Alhambra after the unfortunate incident of the trollop and the ensign. You recall that tale?"

"I recall," she said. "I'm not Sal anymore. I'm Olivia, Olivia Fontaine."

Straight-Ahead was leaning forward over the bed in that awkward stiff-back way he had. When Merit moved, people watched.

"And I am now General Douglas MacArthur," he sighed, touching the body carefully. "The former Mr. Vance has been with his maker for maybe five hours. That how you peg it, Toby?"

" 'Bout that, Merit," I agreed.

He stood up, pushing his bulk from the bed with dignity. The springs squealed and the body of Lewis Vance bounced slightly.

"And what do we do now?" he said.

"We call the police," said Wayne.

"That the way you want it?" Beeson said.

"No," Wayne admitted, stepping forward. "It's not the way I want it, but it's the way it has to be, isn't it?" He pointed at the bed and said, "We've got a murdered man here."

"Not the first in the Alhambra," Straight-Ahead said. He now had his hands folded over his belly like a satisfied Sunday School teacher. "You even had one the last time you filled in for me, if my memory serves me, right, Toby?"

"You've got it, Merit," I agreed. "Salesman in 512, but it was suicide, not murder."

"Not that time," he agreed, "not that time." Then to Wayne, "No, you see, Mr. Wayne, hotels usually don't like to promote the number of people who get killed within them. It's not like they keep charts and compete with each other because it will bring in new trade. No, we usually do our best to keep such things from the attention of the populace."

I explained, "It is not unheard of for a corpse to be carted off to some alley by a house dick."

Wayne shook his head and looked at us as if he had been trapped in a room with the incurably insane.

"You mean that you're suggesting that we just take . . ."

"Vance," I supplied, "Lewis Vance."

"Right, Vance," Wayne said. "That we take Vance and

dump him in some alley and walk away?"

"No," I said emphatically.

"Of course not," Straight-Ahead concurred. "Too many people involved now, and you're too big a name. Sal . . ."

"Olivia," she corrected from her chair as she reached for my unfinished Pepsi.

"Olivia," Merit said, "would be happy to walk away and forget it. Toby knows the routine. He'd walk in a twinkling."

I nodded agreement and reached Olivia just as she was bringing the glass to her mouth. I took it from her. She gave me a dirty look, but I weathered it and put the flat, warm drink on the dresser near the gun.

"So," Wayne said. "What now?"

"We get the killer in here and try to work something out," I said.

"That's the way of it," Straight-Ahead agreed.

"But we don't know who killed him," Wayne said, running his hand through his hair.

"Sure we do," said Straight-Ahead, looking straight ahead at Wayne.

"We do now," I agreed. Olivia didn't give a damn.

I moved to the telephone, picked it up and dialed a number.

"The who of it is easy," said Merit, unfolding his hands and scratching his white mane. It didn't do his image much good, but his head clearly itched. "It's the why we have to figure. Then we'll know what to do."

The killer answered the phone on the third ring and I said, "Get up to 303, fast." I hung up.

The rain took this pause in the conversation to get really mad and start rocking the window in its loose fitting. It rocked and rattled and said bad things while we waited.

"Can I go?" Sally-Olivia asked Merit.

"Let's all just stay cozy till we wind it up," Merit said. "That's how you put it in the movies, right?"

"Wrap it up," Wayne volunteered with a sigh. "Call it a wrap."

Straight-Ahead nodded and filed that information for future use.

"You think he might skip?" I asked.

"Human nature is a fickle thing, Toby," Straight-Ahead said, now facing the door, "a fickle thing. He might skip, it's true, but where's he to go? And going will be a confession. No, he'll bluff it out or try. Besides, he doesn't yet know that we know."

"That's the way I see it," I agreed.

Wayne and Olivia looked at each other for an answer, got none and joined Straight-Ahead in looking at the door and listening to the rain and the rattling window. I glanced at Lewis Vance's body, trying not to be angry about what he had done to my head and gotten me into. Then the knock came, almost unheard under the noise of the rain.

"Come right in," Merit shouted.

A key turned in the lock, and the door opened to reveal Theodore Longretti. He stepped in, eyes darting around, and closed the door behind him.

"What is this all about?" he said, his eyes finding John Wayne and fixing on him.

"Murder," I said. "Over on the bed."

Teddy Spaghetti turned his long, yellow face to the bed and registered fake surprise.

"He's dead?" he said.

"You ought to know," I said. "You put the bullet in him with my gun." I nodded toward the dresser, and Teddy's eyes followed me.

"Me?" he said, pointing to his thin chest and looking

around at each of us for a touch of support, a sign of realization that it was too absurd to consider the possibility of his having killed anyone.

"You," I said.

"I'm calling the police," Teddy said, stepping toward the phone. I stepped in front of him.

"Let's just work it through," Straight-Ahead said, turning slowly to look at us. "Then we'll decide what to do about it. Give it to him, Toby."

I stepped away from Teddy knowing I had his attention and that of everybody else in the room. I eased back to the metal railing of the Murphy bed.

"Number one, Vance has been seen hanging around the lobby," I began. "Which means you knew him. But you told me you'd never seen him before."

"I knew him, but . . ." Teddy began looking around the group for support. All he got was distant curiosity.

"I get a call on a Sunday to come to a room in this hotel, your hotel, while you are on the desk. You know me. You know Vance. Nothing tight here yet, but it's adding up. You following me?"

"Toby . . ." Teddy started, but he was stopped by Straight-Ahead who put his finger to his ample lips and said, "Shhhhhh."

"Then Sal . . . Pardon me, Olivia shows up. Someone called her. Someone who knows she is for rent. You know Olivia, don't you, Teddy?"

He looked at her and she looked back at him.

"I've seen her," he said. "I've seen lots of whores."

"Seen is right," she said disdainfully. "Just seen."

"I've done plenty," Teddy said, standing straight and thin.

"We're not questioning your manhood," Merit said.

"We're trying to clean a dirty room. Hush it now."

"Then John Wayne gets a call," I said.

Teddy looked at John Wayne, who nodded.

"And finally, Merit gets a call to come up here," I went on. "Seems to be whoever did the dialing knew a lot about who was coming and going, not just to the Alhambra, but Room 303. You follow my reasoning?"

"No," Teddy said stubbornly.

"We could be wrong," Straight-Ahead said.

"We could be," I agreed.

"But we're not," Straight-Ahead added.

"We're not," I agreed again.

"Hold it just a minute here," John Wayne said, shaking his head. "You mean this fella here set this all up, killed that fella on the bed, fixed it so it would look like you did it, and fixed it so I'd be found here with the corpse, you, and . . . the lady."

"Looks that way to me," I said.

"What in the name of God for?" Wayne asked reasonably.

"You want to answer that one, Teddy?" I asked as if I knew the answer, but was willing to give up the stage to let the supporting cast take over. I had tried to set it up this way with Merit's help and the moment of truth or lies had come. All Teddy had to do was keep his mouth shut and we'd be stuck with having to make a decision. There was about enough evidence to nail him on a murder charge as there was to get Tojo to give up by midnight. A little digging might put him in the bag, but a little digging would mean enough time for the newspapers to make John Wayne and the Alhambra big news. That gave me an idea.

"Publicity," I prompted. "You want to talk about publicity, Teddy?"

Teddy didn't want to talk about anything. He looked as if he were in a voodoo trance, his face almost orange as the thunder cracked outside.

"Teddy," Merit prompted. "I've got work to do and no one is on the desk downstairs."

Teddy shook himself or rather a wave or chill went through him.

"It got all crazy," he said. "I tell you it got all crazy."

Olivia sighed loudly to let us know she had no interest in hearing Teddy tell it, but she had no choice.

"I didn't plan on killing him, you see," Teddy said, playing with his shirt front and looking down. "Idea of it was to get you here, Toby, put you out or something, get Wayne in, and then Sally and have Merit walk in on it. Idea was to give the *Times* a tip about a love nest thing at the Alhambra, have a photographer and reporter maybe right behind. You'd confirm the whole thing and . . ."

"That was one hell of a stupid idea," Olivia said angrily from the chair.

Teddy shrugged. It hadn't worked out the way he'd planned.

"Idea was publicity," he whispered to his shirt.

"That John Wayne was making it with a prostitute in your hotel?"

"You think the Alhambra is such a hot-shot address?" Teddy came back defensively, with a little animation. "Kind of people we got coming it could be a real attraction, you know what I mean? Idea was to set something up like this with a whole bunch of movie people, you know, real he-man types, Wild Bill Elliott, Alan Ladd, you know."

"And then the girls would be kicking back a few bucks to you just to work the rooms," Straight-Ahead said.

"Never thought of that," said Teddy, who had evidently considered just that. "But it was the publicity. Rooms aren't going as good as they should. Management needs it at seventy-eight percent or they'll sell and I'll lose my job."

"Hold it," John Wayne pitched in. He walked over to Teddy, who shrank back, almost flopping like a wet noodle over the coffee table. "This is one hell of a harebrained scheme, Pilgrim, and I've got a mind to snap a few pieces off of you, but I want to know why you shot that man."

Teddy was still backing away from Wayne toward the wall. He almost stumbled over Olivia's stretched-out legs, but she pulled them in just in time.

"An accident," Teddy said. "An accident. Vance called me, said Toby had passed out. I had already made the calls to Sally and Wayne, got his phone number from a friend at Republic. Vance called me up, said he wanted more than the ten bucks I promised him, wanted in on whatever I was doing. I told him I didn't have more than ten bucks to give him, that there might be more money later, but he wouldn't listen. It was not a good situation."

"Not a good situation at all," Straight-Ahead agreed, turning toward him. "So you took Toby's gun and shot Lewis Vance between the eyes."

"He threatened to beat me up, kill me," Teddy whined. "It was self-defense."

"That's the story I'd tell," I agreed.

"It's the truth," Teddy squealed, bumping into the wall with Wayne advancing. I realized what was coming, but I couldn't stop it. It should have been plain to a room in which half the living people were detectives, but it wasn't. Teddy reached up to the dresser at his elbow and came down with my .38 in his right hand. He pointed the gun at John Wayne's stomach, who stopped abruptly and put up his hands.

"You are making me mad, mister," Wayne said through his teeth, but he took a step backward.

"Teddy, Teddy, Teddy," I said, shaking my head. "You

are not going to shoot all four of us. Put the gun down and let's talk."

I could see no good reason why he wouldn't shoot all four of us, but I hoped that the prospect of mowing down citizens would not appeal to the shaking desk clerk whose experience in mayhem, as far as I knew, had been limited to one unfortunate scrape a few hours earlier with an apparently unpleasant third-rate bully. "Think of the publicity."

He thought of the publicity, and his mouth went dry. He reached over and took a sip of the flat Pepsi to moisten it. I didn't stop him. No one moved. We just watched him and hoped he would down the whole thing.

"Five bodies in one room, one a famous actor," Straight-Ahead chimed in. "The Alhambra might have a hell of a time surviving that."

"I can shoot you and get away with it," Teddy reasoned. He took another drink.

"Never get away with it," I said. People always said that in situations like this. My experience was that they very often did get away with it, but you don't tell things like that to killers holding guns. You just hoped they saw the same movies and listened to the same radio shows you did. The room suddenly went quiet. The rain had stopped.

Teddy blinked his eyes, and looked at us. I couldn't tell whether he was considering who to shoot first or was realizing that he couldn't pull the trigger. I never got the chance to ask him.

"I've had just about enough," Wayne said, and took a step, the final step, forward. Teddy, already a little drowsy from the drink, moved his gun-holding hand and fired. It missed Wayne, breezed past me and shattered the window, letting in a rush of rain-smelling air. Wayne's punch slammed Teddy against the wall. The gun fell, hit the floor, bounced a few times, then stopped.

Olivia screamed and Straight-Ahead walked slowly straight ahead toward the slumped figure. Wayne, fists still clenched, stepped back to let the house detective take over. It was a show and a half to see Merit get to his knee, lift the now silent desk clerk up, and deposit him on the chair near the desk.

"Let's go," I said, exchanging a look of understanding with Merit when he turned around.

"Go?" asked Wayne, his dark hair over his forehead. "What are you talking about? This man killed that man and we . . ."

"Can go," I said.

Olivia didn't need persuading. She grabbed her red bag and headed for the door.

"You've never been in this room," Straight-Ahead said to her.

"I've never been in this hotel," she answered. "Nice to meet you, John." And out she went.

"Merit will work a deal with Teddy," I explained to the be-wildered Wayne. "Teddy says he shot Vance in self-defense and no one else was around. Merit backs him up. Story's over. Teddy doesn't want it that way. Merit calls him a liar trying to save his skin, but that won't happen. Teddy will back it up and you're out of it."

"With some embellishments, that's the way it really was," Merit said, looking at Teddy.

"It's . . ." John Wayne began.

"Not like the movies," I finished. "Not this time, anyway. The rain's stopped. You want to stop for a cup of coffee?"

"I guess," said Wayne, shaking his head. "It's too late for DeMille's party." He took a last look at the corpse on the bed and the scrawny killer in the chair. The Ringo Kid wouldn't have handled it like this, but what the hell. He looked at Straight-Ahead, who said, "Go on. It's my job."

Wayne nodded and went into the hall after I said, "I'll be right there."

Teddy was showing no signs of waking up.

"The gun," I said.

"The gun," Merit repeated, giving up on a revival of Teddy Spaghetti in the near future. "We say you left it here for Teddy. Protection. He was threatened by all kinds. That sort of thing. It'll hold up."

"It'll shake a lot," I said, "but it'll hold. Take care."

A breeze from the broken window swirled around the room as Straight-Ahead waved his arm at me and sat slowly in the overstuffed chair to wait for Teddy to wake up. I closed the door quietly, and joined John Wayne in the hall.

"This happen to you a lot?" he said as we got into the elevator.

"When things are going well," I said. "Only when things are going well."

My head began to ache again and I longed for a plate of tacos from Manny's a few blocks away. I wondered if I could talk Wayne into a trip to Manny's.

BUSTED BLOSSOMS

Darkness. I couldn't see, but I could hear someone shouting at me about Adolf Hitler. I opened my eyes. I still couldn't see. Panic set in before memory told me where I was. I pushed away the jacket covering my head. After a good breath of stale air, I realized where I was, who I was, and what I was doing there.

It was 1938, February, a cool Sunday night in Los Angeles, and I was Toby Peters, a private investigator who had been hired to keep an eye on a washed-up movie director who had come in from out of town and picked up a few death threats. I was getting fifteen dollars a day, for which I was expected to stay near the target and put myself in harm's way if trouble came up. I was not being paid to fall asleep.

My mouth tasted like ragweed pollen. I reached over to turn off the radio. When I had put my head back to rest on the bed and pulled my suede zipped jacket over me, Jeanette MacDonald had been singing about Southern moons. I woke up to the news that Reichsführer Hitler had proclaimed himself chief of national defense and had promoted Hermann Wilhelm Göring, minister of aviation, to field marshal. I was just standing when the door opened and D.W. Griffith walked in.

"Mr. Peters," he said, his voice deep, his back straight, and, even across the room, his breath dispensing the Kentucky fumes of bourbon.

"I was on my way down," I said. "I was listening to the news."

Griffith eyed me from over his massive hawk of a nose. He was about five-ten, maybe an inch or so taller than me, though I guessed he weighed about 180, maybe twenty pounds more than I did. We both seemed to be in about the same shape, which says something good for him or bad for me. I was forty-one, and he was over sixty. He was wearing a black suit over a white shirt and thin black tie.

"I have something to tell you," Griffith said.

So, I was canned. It had happened before, and I had a double sawbuck in my wallet.

"I really was coming down," I said, trying to get some feeling in my tongue.

"You were not," Griffith said emphatically. "But that is of little consequence. A man has been murdered."

"Murdered?" I repeated.

I am not the most sophisticated sight even when I'm combed, shaved, and operating on a full stomach. My face is dark and my nose mush, not from business contacts, but from an older brother who every once in a while thought I needed redefinition. I sold that tough look to people who wanted a bodyguard. Most of my work was for second-rate clothing stores that had too much shoplifting, hard-working bookies whose wives had gone for Chiclets and never come back, and old ladies who had lost their cats, who were always named Sheiba. That's what I usually did, but once in a while I spent a night or a few days protecting movie people who got themselves threatened or were afraid of getting crushed in a crowd. D.W. had no such fears. No one was looking for his autograph anymore. No one was hiring him. He seemed to have plenty of money and a lot of hope; that was why he had driven up from Louisville. He hoped someone would pick up the phone and call him to direct a movie, but in the week I had worked for him, no one had called, except the guy who threatened to lynch him with a Ku Klux Klan robe. D.W. had explained that such threats had not been unusual during the past two decades since the release of BIRTH OF A NATION, which had presented the glories of the Ku Klux Klan. D.W. had tried to cover his prejudice with INTOLERANCE and a few more films, but the racism of BIRTH wouldn't wash away.

"Mr. Peters," he tried again, his voice now loud enough to be heard clearly in the back row if we were in a Loews theater. "You must rouse yourself. A man has been murdered downstairs."

"Call the police," I said brilliantly.

"We are, you may recall, quite a distance from town," he reminded me. "A call has been placed, but it will be some time before the constabulary arrives."

Constabulary. I was in a time warp. But that was the way I had felt since meeting Griffith, who now touched his gray sideburns as if he were about to be photographed for *Click* magazine.

"Who's dead?" I asked.

"Almost everyone of consequence since the dawn of time," Griffith said, opening the door. "In this case, the victim is Jason Sikes. He is sitting at the dinner table with a knife in his neck."

"Who did it?" I began.

"That, I fear, is a mystery," Griffith said. "Now let us get back to the scene."

I walked out the door feeling that I was being ushered from act one to act two. I didn't like the casting. Griffith was directing the whole thing, and I had the feeling he wanted to cast me as the detective. I wanted to tell him that I had been hired to protect his back, not find killers. I got double time for finding killers. But one just didn't argue with Dave Griffith. I slouched ahead of him, scratched an itch on my right arm, and slung my suede jacket over my shoulder so I could at least straighten the wrinkled striped tie I was wearing.

What did I know? That I was in a big house just off the California coast about thirty miles north of San Diego. The house belonged to a producer named Korites, who Griffith hoped would give him a directing job. Korites had gathered his two potential stars, a comic character actor, and a potential backer, Sikes, to meet the great director. I had come as Griffith's "associate." D.W. had left his young wife back at the Roosevelt Hotel in Los Angeles, and we had stopped for drinks twice on the way in his chauffeur-driven Mercedes. In the car Griffith had talked about Kentucky, his father, his mother, who had never seen one of his films—"She did not approve of the stage," he explained—and about his comeback. He had gone on about his youthful adventures as an actor, playwright, boxer, reporter, and construction worker. Then, about ten minutes before we arrived, he had clammed up, closed his eyes, and hadn't said another word.

Now we were going silently down the stairs of the house of Marty Korites, stepping into a dining room, and facing five well-dressed diners, one of whom lay with his face in a plate of Waldorf salad with a knife in his back.

The diners looked up when we came in. Korites, a bald, jowly man with Harold Lloyd glasses, was about fifty and looked every bit of it and more. His eyes had been resting angrily on the dead guest, but they shot up to us as we entered the room. On one side of the dead guy was a woman, Denise Giles, skinny as ticker tape, pretty, dark, who knows what age. I couldn't even tell from the freckles on her bare shoulders. On the other side of the dead guy was an actor named James Vann, who looked like the lead in a road-show musical, blond, young, starched, and confused. He needed someone to feed him lines. Griffith was staring at the corpse. The great director looked puzzled. The last guest sat opposite the dead man. I knew him, too, Lew Dollard, a frizzy-haired comedian turned character actor who was Marty Korites' top name, which gives you an idea of how small an operator Marty was and what little hope Griffith had if he had traveled all the way here in the hope of getting a job from him.

"Mr. Griffith says you're a detective, not a film guy," Korites said, his eyes moving from the body to me for an instant and then back to the body. I guessed he didn't want the dead guy to get away when he wasn't looking.

"Yeah, I'm a detective," I said. "But I don't do windows and I don't do corpses."

Dollard, the roly-poly New York street comic in a rumpled suit, looked up at me.

"A comedy writer," he said with a smile, showing big teeth. I had seen one of Dollard's movies. He wasn't funny.

"Someone killed Sikes," Korites said with irritation.

"Before the main course was served, too," I said. "Some people have no sense of timing. Look. Why don't we just sit still, have a drink or two, and wait till the police get here. We can pass the time by your telling me how someone can get killed at the dinner table and all of you not know who did it. That must have been some chicken liver appetizer."

"It was," said Griffith, holding his open palm toward the dead man, "like a moment of filmic chicanery, a magic moment from *Méliès*. I was sipping an aperitif and had turned to Miss Giles to answer a question. And then, a sound, a groan. I turned, and there sat Mr. Sikes."

We all looked at Sikes. His face was still in the salad.

"Who saw what happened?" I asked.

They all looked up from the corpse and at each other.

Then they looked at me. Dollard had a cheek full of something and a silly grin on his face. He shrugged.

"A man gets murdered with the lights on with all of you at the table and no one knows who did it?" I asked. "That's a little hard to believe. Who was standing up?"

"No one," said Vann, looking at me unblinking.

"No one," agreed Griffith.

There was no window behind the body. One door to the room was facing the dead man. The other door was to his right. The knife couldn't have been thrown from either door and landed in his back. The hell with it. I was getting paid to protect Griffith, not find killers. I'd go through the motions till the real cops got there. I had been a cop back in Glendale before I went to work for Warner Brothers as a guard and then went into business on my own. I know the routine.

"Why don't we go into the living room?" Korites said, starting to get up and glancing at the corpse. "I could have Mrs. Windless—"

"Sit down," I said. "Mrs. Windless is . . . ?"

"Housekeeper," Korites said. "Cook."

"Was she in here when Sikes was killed?"

I looked around. All heads shook no.

"Anyone leave the room before or after Sikes was killed?" I went on.

"Just Mr. Griffith," said Vann. The woman still hadn't said anything.

"We stay right here till the police arrive. Anyone needs the toilet, I go with them, even the dragon lady," I said, trying to get a rise out of Denise Giles. I got none.

"What about you?" said Dollard, rolling his eyes and gurgling in a lousy imitation of Bert Lahr.

"I wasn't in the room when Sikes took his dive into the salad," I said. "Look, you want to forget the whole thing and talk about sports? Fine. You hear that Glenn Cunningham won the Wanamaker mile for the fifth time yesterday?"

"With a time of 4:11," said Denise Giles, taking a small sip of wine from a thin little glass.

I looked at her with new respect. Griffith had sat down at the end of the table, the seat he had obviously been in when murder interrupted the game. Something was on his mind.

"Who was Sikes?" I asked, reaching down for a celery stick.

"A man of means," said Griffith, downing a slug of bourbon.

"A backer," said Korites. "He was thinking of bankrolling a movie D.W. would direct and I would produce."

"With Vann here and Miss Giles as stars?" I said.

"Right," said Korites.

"Never," said Griffith emphatically.

"You've got no choice here," Korites shouted back. "You take the project the way we give it to you or we get someone else. Your name's got some curiosity value, right, but it doesn't bring in any golden spikes."

"A man of tender compassion," sighed Griffith, looking at me for understanding. "It was my impression that the late Mr. Sikes had no intention of supplying any capital. On the contrary, I had the distinct impression that he felt he was in less than friendly waters and had only been lured here with the promise of meeting me, the wretched director who had once held the industry in his hand, had once turned pieces of factory-produced celluloid into art. As I recall, Sikes also talked about some financial debt he expected to be paid tonight."

"You recall?" Korites said with sarcasm, shaking his head. "You dreamed it up. You're still back in the damn nineteenth century. Your movies were old-fashioned when you made them. You don't work anymore because you're an anachronism."

"Old-fashioned?" said Griffith with a smile. "Yes, old-fashioned, a romantic, one who respects the past. I would rather die with my Charles Dickens than live with your Hemingway."

Dollard finished whatever he had in his mouth and said, "You think it would be sacrilegious to have the main course? Life goes on."

"Have a celery stick," I suggested.

"I don't want to eat a celery stick," he whined.

"I wasn't suggesting that you put it in your mouth," I said.

This was too much for Dollard. He stood up, pushing the chair back.

"I'm the comic here," he said. "Tell him."

He looked around for someone to tell me. The most sympathetic person was Sikes, and he was dead.

"So that's the way it is," Dollard said, looking around the room. "You want me to play second banana."

"This is a murder scene," shouted Korites, taking his glasses off, "not a night club, Lew. Try to remember that." His jowls rumbled as he spoke. He was the boss, but not mine.

"Someone in this room murdered the guy in the salad," I reminded them.

"My father," said Griffith.

"Your father killed Sikes?" I asked, turning to the great director. Griffith's huge nose was at the rim of his almost empty glass. His dark eyes were looking into the remaining amber liquid for an answer.

"My father," he said without looking up, "would have known how to cope with this puzzle. He was a resourceful man, a gentleman, a soldier."

"Mine was a grocer," I said.

"This is ridiculous," said Denise Giles, throwing down her napkin.

"Not to Sikes," I said. Just then the door behind me swung open. I turned to see a rail of a woman dressed in black.

"Are you ready for the roast?" she asked.

"Yes," said Dollard.

"No," said Korites, "we're not having any more food."

"I have rights here," Dollard insisted.

Now I had it. This was an Alice in Wonderland nightmare and I was Alice at the Mad Hatter's tea party. We'd all change places in a few seconds and the Dormouse, Sikes, would have to be carried.

"What," demanded Mrs. Windless, "am I to do with the roast?"

"You want the punch line or can I have it?" Dollard said to me.

"Sikes already got the punch line," I reminded him.

Mrs. Windless looked over at Sikes for the first time.

"Oh my God," she screamed. "That man is dead."

"Really?" shouted Dollard, leaping up. "Which one?"

"Goddamn it," shouted Korites. "This is serious." His glasses were back on now. He didn't seem to know what to do with them.

Griffith got up and poured himself another drink.

"We know he's dead, Mrs. Windless," Korites said. "The police are on the way. You'll just have to stick all the food in the refrigerator and wait."

"What happened?" Mrs. Windless asked, her voice high, her eyes riveted on Sikes. "Who did this? I don't want anything to do with murder."

"You don't?" said Dollard. "Why didn't you tell us that before we killed him? We did it for you." He crossed his eyes but didn't close them in time to block out the wine thrown in his face by the slinky Denise.

Dollard stood up sputtering and groped for a napkin to wipe his face. Purple tears rolled down his cheeks.

"Damn it," he screamed. "What the hell? What the hell?" His hand found a napkin. He wiped his eyes. The stains were gone, but there was now a piece of apple from the Waldorf salad on his face.

"Mrs. Windless," said D.W., standing and pointing at the door. "You will depart and tell my driver, Mr. Reynolds, that Mr. Peters and I will be delayed. Mr. Dollard. You will sit down and clean your face. Miss Giles, you will refrain from outbursts, and Mr. Vann, you will attempt to show some animation. It is difficult to tell you from Mr. Sikes. Mr. Peters will continue the inquiry."

Vann stood up now, kicking back his chair. Griffith rose to meet him. They were standing face to face, toe to toe. Vann was about thirty years younger, but Griffith didn't back away.

"You can't tell us what to do. You can't tell anyone what to do. You're washed up," Vann hissed.

"As Bluebeard is rumored to have said," whispered Griffith, "I am merely between engagements."

"See, see," grouched Dollard, pointing with his fork at the two antagonists. "Everyone's a comic. I ask you."

I sighed and stood up again.

"Sit down," I shouted at Vann and Griffith. The room went silent. The mood was ruined by my stomach growling. But they sat and Mrs. Windless left the room. "Who called the police?"

"I did," said Korites.

"I thought no one left the room but Griffith?" I said.

"Phone is just outside the door, everyone could see me

call. I left the door open," Korites said. He pushed his dirty plate away from him and then pulled it back. "What's the difference?"

"Why didn't you all start yelling, panic, accuse each other?" I asked.

"We thought it was one of Jason's practical jokes," said Denise Giles. "He was fond of practical jokes."

"Rubber teeth, joy buzzers, ink in the soup," sighed Dollard. "A real amateur, a putz. Once pretended he was poisoned at lunch in . . ."

"Lew," shouted Korites. "Just shut up."

"All right, you people," I said. "None of you liked Sikes, is that right?"

"Right," Korites said, "but that's a far cry from one of us . . ."

"How about hate?" I tried. "Would hate be a good word to apply to your feelings about the late dinner guest?"

"Maybe," said Korites, "there was no secret about that among our friends. I doubt if anyone who knew Jason did anything less than hate him. But none of us murdered him. We couldn't have."

"And yet," Griffith said, "one of you had to have done the deed. In THE BIRTH OF A NATION—"

"This is death, not birth," hissed Vann. "This isn't a damn movie."

Griffith drew his head back and examined Vann over his beak of a nose.

"Better," said Griffith. "Given time I could possibly motivate you into a passable performance. Even Richard Barthelmess had something to learn from my humble direction."

There was a radio in the corner. Dollard had stood up and turned it on. I didn't stop him. We listened to the radio and

watched Sikes and each other while I tried to think. Griffith was drawing something on the white tablecloth with his fork.

Dollard found the news, and we learned that Hirohito had a cold but was getting better, King Farouk of Egypt had just gotten married, Leopold Stokowski was on his way to Italy under an assumed name, probably to visit Greta Garbo, and a guy named Albert Burroughs had been found semiconscious in a hotel room in Bloomington, Illinois. The room was littered with open cans of peas. Burroughs managed to whisper to the ambulance driver that he had lived on peas for nine days even though he had $77,000 in cash in the room.

I got up and turned off the radio.

"You tell a story like that in a movie," said Korites, "and they say it isn't real."

"If you tell it well, they will believe anything," said Griffith, again doodling on the cloth.

The dinner mess, not to mention Sikes' corpse, was beginning to ruin the party.

"Things are different," Griffith said, looking down at what he had drawn. He lifted a long-fingered hand to wipe out the indentations in the tablecloth.

"Things?" I asked, wondering if he was going to tell us tales about his career, his father, or the state of the universe.

"I am an artist of images," he explained, looking up, his eyes moving from me to each of the people around the table. "I kept the entire script of my films, sometimes 1,500 shots, all within my head." He pointed to his head in case we had forgotten where it was located.

"This scene," he went on, "has changed. When I left this room to find Mr. Peters, Mr. Sikes had a knife in his neck, not his back, and it was a somewhat different knife."

"You've had three too many, D.W.," Dollard said with a smile.

I got up and examined Sikes. There was no hole in his neck or anywhere else on his body that I could find.

"No cuts, bruises, marks . . ." I began, and then it hit me. My eyes met Griffith's. I think it hit him at the same moment.

"We'll just wait for the police," Korites said, removing his glasses again.

"Go on, Mr. G.," I said. "Let's hear your script."

Griffith stood again, put down his glass, and smiled. He was doing either Abe Lincoln or Sherlock Holmes.

"This scene was played for me," he said. "I was not the director. I was the audience. My ego is not fragile, at least not too fragile to realize that I have witnessed an act. I can see each of you playing your roles, even the late Mr. Sikes. Each of you in an iris, laughing, slightly enigmatic, attentive. And then the moment arrives. The audience is distracted by a pretty face in close-up. Then a cut to body, or supposed body for Sikes was not dead when I left this room to find Mr. Peters."

"Come on . . ." laughed Dollard.

"Of all . . ." sighed Denise Giles.

"You're mad . . ." counterpointed Vann.

But Korites sat silent.

"He wasn't dead," I said again, picking up for Griffith, who seemed to have ended his monologue. All he needed was applause. He looked good, but he had carried the scene as far as he could. It was mine now.

"Let's try this scenario," I said. "Sikes was a practical joker, right?"

"Right," Dollard agreed, "but—"

"What if you all agreed to play a little joke on D.W.? Sikes pretends to be dead with a knife in his neck when Denise distracts Griffith. Sikes can't stick the fake knife in his back. He can't reach his own back. He attaches it to his neck. Then you all discover the body, Griffith comes for me, Sikes laughs. You all laugh, then one of you, probably Korites, moved behind him and uses a real knife to turn the joke into fact. You're all covered. Someone did it. The police would have a hell of a time figuring out which one, and meanwhile, it would make a hell of a news story. Griffith a witness. All of you suspects. Probably wind up with a backer who'd cash in on your morbid celebrity."

"Ridiculous," laughed Korites.

"I was the audience," Griffith repeated with a rueful laugh.

"Even if this were true," said Denise Giles, "you could never prove it."

"Props," I said. "You didn't have time to get rid of that fake knife, at least not to get it hidden too well. D.W. was with me for only a minute or two, and you didn't want to get too far from this room in case we came running back here. No, if we're right, that prop knife is nearby, where it can be found, somewhere in this room or not far from it."

"This is ridiculous," said Vann, standing up. "I'm not staying here for any more of this charade." He took a step toward the door behind Griffith, giving me a good idea of where to start looking for the prop knife, but the director was out of his chair and barring his way.

"Move," shouted Vann.

"Never," cried Griffith.

Vann threw a punch, but Griffith caught it with his left and came back with a right. Vann went down. Korites started to rise, looked at my face, and sat down again.

"We can work something out here," he said, his face going white.

A siren blasted somewhere outside.

"Hell of a practical joke," Dollard said, dropping the radish in his fingers.

No one moved while we waited for the police. We just sat there, Vann on the floor, Griffith standing. I imagined a round iris closing in on the scene, and then a slow fade to black.

IT COMES WITH
THE BADGE

Statement: Taken by Officer R. F. Rnzini
November 3, 1941, Los Angeles, California
From Witness Richard A. Mann, 1488 Sagamore, Cleveland

"My name is Richard A. Mann. I live at 1488 Sagamore in Cleveland, Ohio. I'm a salesman. I usually stay at the cheapest clean hotel I can find. You know, profit margin, but I've been a little down on sales. I'm not the only one. No one's sure this Depression is really on the way out no matter what Roosevelt says. They don't want to buy. Tell the truth, if I knew just how bad this place really was, I wouldn't have stayed.

"It was about one in the morning, maybe an hour ago. Couldn't sleep. Read the news and Li'l Abner. Got up, lathered my face for a shave. Threw a towel around my neck. This place is made out of balsa wood. The guy above me had been pacing back and forth for hours. I had half a mind to go up and tell him to sit down, but I've had nights like that on the road, you know. So, I figured, let the guy alone. Maybe he's got enough troubles. Live and let live.

"I was in the room by the bed, shaving cream on my face, you know. Not much room to wander with one small room and that little bathroom. I could tell exactly where the guy upstairs was and I'm sure the guy below me knows where I was. Well I was standing next to the bed deciding whether to watch the wallpaper peel for a few hours or listen to the radio after I shaved when I heard the shots. Loud, really loud. And I knew right away where they came from. A blast and an echo. For a second I thought the building's boiler blew. Probably happen some day. Radiators rattling all night. Probably hasn't been checked in years. Well, there I was ready to shave just standing there for a second. I put everything down and went out into the hall. My face still covered with cream, towel over my shoulder, you know.

"The Belvidere doesn't have a lot of curious tenants. In a place like this people have their own problems and aren't about to get into anyone else's trouble. But there were a few people in the hall. One old guy with white whiskers looked like a scared bird. He had on an undershirt with a big hole in it. His mouth was open like he was going to say something, but nothing came out.

" 'Shots, upstairs,' I said, and went for the stairs. Maybe I should have minded my business, but I didn't think. The pacing guy might have killed himself or someone else. Those shots were too damn close.

"The stairs sagged as I went up. You can see I'm not a little guy, but hotel stairs should be made to hold a lot more than me. This whole damn place is coming apart. When I got up to the next floor there were maybe three, four people in the hall. One woman looked like . . . well, officer, you know this place better than I do. Most of the doors were closed and quiet like they hadn't heard what they must have heard.

" 'In there,' I told them, and I pointed at the door of the room above mine. I must have looked like a foaming screwball. They backed away and I knocked on the door. No answer. The door was locked. I told everyone in the hall to get back and I went with my shoulder against the door. It snapped away banging open. I think my ten-year-old daughter could have gone through it. Then I saw him. Lying on the bed covered with blood, a red lump shaped like a human. He was holding the gun in his hand just the way he is now. I'll never forget it. I went back into the hall before any of the others could see it. I was sorry I had seen it. I told the nearest guy, a thin guy in his 60s, I think, to call a cop. Then I went back into the room to see if he might still be alive. Believe me, I didn't want to check and I didn't think he could be, but you know, there might have been a chance. He was dead. I yelled at the people in the hall not to come in, not to touch anything, and I just waited till you got here. Now if there's nothing else, officer, I'm feeling kind of shaky and I'd like to get back to my room and clean up. If you need me, I'll be in the room right below."

Lieutenant Philip Pevsner was worried when he entered the Hotel Belvidere less than an hour after Officer Rnzini had taken the statement from Mr. Mann and the few others who would acknowledge that they had heard anything. Lieutenant Pevsner was in a bad mood. Lieutenant Pevsner was always in a bad mood. It wasn't his mortgage, his three kids with the flu, his wife with anemia, his sagging gut that he couldn't control, his 51 years which he couldn't ignore, or the likelihood that he would never be promoted. It was none of these things. Surliness was a way of life for Phil Pevsner. He was a cop at war and the world was full of enemies. Crime was a personal thing with him. Each murder was an added burden to his life, another problem to add to the others. And they never stopped. There was no conclusion to being a cop. You cleaned up some garbage and there was a bigger pile the next day. The killers existed to make his life miserable. He hated them and all criminals. Each pain they caused in his head and stomach diminished his health. Little by little the criminals were killing him.

Which was why Lieutenant Pevsner was not a Captain. He did not treat suspects with respect. He did not treat colleagues with respect. He viewed everyone on every case including the duty cops and medical examiner with suspicion. He was never taken in by a pretty or ugly face, a good story or a tear. He never smiled. It made him a pain to work with.

When he hit the hotel lobby, the desk clerk came around the counter and moved toward him, his mouth open to speak. Pevsner held up his hand to stop him from saying anything and over his shoulder to his partner, Sergeant Steve Seidman, a pale cadaverous man, he said, "Talk to him."

Officer Rnzini was waiting at the elevator, sweat at his collar, his LAPD star tarnished, his face pale.

"Elevator's out, Lieutenant," Rnzini said. "It's on the fourth floor."

"I think I can walk it without a heart attack," Pevsner shot back.

"I didn't mean . . ." Rnzini began, but Pevsner was already taking the stairs two at a time, trying not to pant, not to smell the building's rancidness of decay.

"It's crazy," Rnzini whispered confidentially behind him, keeping pace. "The guy looks like he was shotgunned, but he was alone in a locked room, window locked tight, looks like it hasn't been open in years. Doesn't make any sense."

Pevsner stopped suddenly on the stairs and Rnzini had to throw himself against a wall to keep from bumping into the lieutenant, who looked like an angry refrigerator. Pevsner had stopped to catch his breath, but he masked the stop by turning on the cop behind him.

"Maybe you did it," he said. "Just to confuse the police department. Maybe because you're bored. Maybe because seeing crime has warped your brain."

Rnzini started to smile and stopped. Pevsner wasn't smiling.

"Lieutenant, I'm a Catholic," he said.

"Of course," Pevsner answered and went back up the stairs. Rnzini stayed a bit farther behind him.

There was a small crowd on the fourth floor and a uniformed cop of about 60 was standing guard outside a room with a broken door.

"You talk to all of them?" Pevsner called over his shoulder.

"All the ones who admit hearing anything," Rnzini said, catching up.

Pevsner elbowed his way past two young Mexican kids. One of them turned an angry face toward the burly cop and Pevsner looked back at him.

"Something on your mind, Chico?" he said.

The two kids backed away.

Inside the small room, Pevsner looked at the body and then around the room.

"Your notebook," he spat at Rnzini and pulled it from the sweating cop before he could hand it over. Pevsner went into the small washroom and read through it slowly. Rnzini stood trying not to breathe or think. In ten minutes or so the gaunt Sergeant Seidman came into the room and looked around. Then he walked into the washroom. Pevsner rubbed his eyes and opened his already open tie even further. He handed the notebook to Seidman who began to read it as the lieutenant walked back into the room with Rnzini.

"Rnzini," he sighed, his hands balled into fists. "You know who that is on the bed?"

"No . . ."

"His name is Greenberg, also known as Greenie, a mob muscle man. You heard the name before?"

"I think maybe I did, but . . ." Rnzini started.

"He was thinking of testifying against Bugsy Siegel on a murder rap. You heard of Bugsy Siegel?" Pevsner asked with more venom than sarcasm.

"Sure," said Rnzini.

"He's heard of Bugsy Siegel," Pevsner shouted over his shoulder toward the washroom. Rnzini could see the thin figure of Sergeant Seidman nod his head in acknowledgment without lifting his head from the notebook.

Pevsner sat on the bed next to the dead man and looked at Rnzini. Looked into him and through him.

"He had that gun in his hand and the door locked because he was afraid that someone might be looking for him who wished him no good. Make sense to you, Rnzini?"

"Sure."

"You know who killed him, Rnzini?" asked Pevsner.

"No," Rnzini answered. He felt like giggling and confessing himself, but he knew he hadn't done it.

"You should," sighed Pevsner. "By God, you should."

"He's right," said Seidman, coming back into the room and handing the notebook back to Rnzini. "It's right in your book."

Rnzini stared at the black book wondering if someone had written something in it he hadn't seen.

Without looking at the body, Pevsner said in a rumble of anger, "Look at our friend Greenie here. Pellet holes in him from a shotgun with a narrow pattern, powerful. Pellet holes in his feet, from the bottom up. Strike you as strange, Rnzini?"

"He was shot while he was lying in the bed," the cop tried.

"No pellet holes in the bed by his feet. Lots of blood, but no holes. Blood on the floor," said Seidman, looking around the room and at the floor.

"Someone moved him, Rnzini," said Pevsner, looking at the wall. "Any idea of who?"

"It wasn't me," Rnzini said defensively.

"Well, that eases my mind and narrows the list of possibles," the lieutenant said. "Any ideas beyond that?"

"You've got a guy alone in a room," Seidman went on. "He's got a gun and he's afraid someone is after him. Supposing you were after him and found him here, what would you do?"

Rnzini tried to think, but nothing came, nothing except the thought that being a cop might not be such a good profession after all. After all, he had only invested a year in it. He could always go into the cleaning business with his old man and brother in Fresno, and . . .

"Rnzini," Pevsner interrupted.

"I don't know, Lieutenant."

"Well, in a tin-can hotel like this," Pevsner said, looking at the imitation circular oriental rug on the floor that had long since lost its pattern, "you might get a room next door or below the guy you were after. You might get a shotgun with a hell of a kick, listen to our old friend Greenie pace the floor for a few hours, figure out where he was standing and send a blast through the wall or floor or ceiling. You see any holes in the wall or ceiling, Rnzini?"

Rnzini looked. There was nothing, but there was nothing in the floor either.

"Five will get you ten if you move that rug," said Pevsner, "you'll find a hole in it."

"Mr. Mann from downstairs?" said Rnzini.

Pevsner winked sourly and Rnzini got on his knees and moved the rug. The pattern was nearly symmetrical. The room below through the holes was dark.

"Mr. Mann," Sergeant Seidman began, "put shaving

cream on his face, threw a towel over his shoulder, sat down and blasted old Greenie here."

"Put down the shotgun," Pevsner continued, "ran out in the hall and started to yell about the gunshot upstairs before anyone had a chance to say or think that the shot might have come from his room. He went up the stairs and got to the door of Greenie's room, broke it down and told everyone to get away, call the cops. He made sure Greenie was dead. Then he put the body on the bed, moved the rug over to cover the holes and waited for a cop to show up. Then he told you his story."

"But," said Rnzini, "why the shaving cream?"

"Hide his face," said Seidman. "Desk clerk wouldn't remember what he looked like when he checked in. And when he finds out we want Mr. Mann, the desk clerk will forget what little he knows. A cop might remember."

"The towel," Pevsner said softly, turning to give Greenie another look.

"Probably used the towel to move the body," said Seidman, "keep from getting blood on him."

"But he had the towel when I got here," Rnzini said.

"Oh, Christ," shouted Pevsner. "He just walked into the washroom over there and took another one. Bloody one's probably under the body or the bed. Then he gave you his story, walked down to his room, packed up and went out the door."

One of the two forty-watt bulbs in the ceiling fixture sputtered and died. Pevsner pointed downward.

"We can go downstairs now and find an empty room with no fingerprints," he said. "Then we can start doing the leg-work."

"His statement was a lie?" Rnzini said, looking from one of the detectives to another.

"Outside of his name and profession and home town, everything he told you was probably true," said Seidman. "It's not what he told you. It's what he left out."

"I didn't . . ." Rnzini started.

"You didn't ask enough questions," Pevsner said. "You weren't suspicious enough. You didn't make everyone sit down someplace where you could keep an eye on them. You get a crime and a witness you sit them down until someone who knows what he's doing shows up. I don't care if it's your own mother or your priest."

Rnzini had nothing to say. He thought about his sweat-stained uniform. He wondered who he hated more, the murderer who called himself Richard A. Mann, or the two detectives who were turning him into a pants-wetting kid.

"He had a scar," Rnzini whispered.

Pevsner looked up suddenly. The shadows from the single light above turned him into a hulking monster.

"A scar?"

"Left cheek," said Rnzini. "His face was covered with shaving cream, but there was a ridge on his cheek and you could see that it was darker under it. My Uncle Carlo's got a scar on his chin and when he shaves . . ."

Pevsner and Seidman exchanged looks which could have meant anything.

"Could be," said Seidman softly.

"Sounds like him," said Pevsner. "Rnzini, could you give a positive identification on this guy from a photograph?"

"Yes," said Rnzini.

"Shaving cream and all?" added Seidman.

"Yes," said Rnzini firmly.

Something like a smile touched Seidman's lips.

"Come with us," growled Pevsner, bulling his way to the door without looking at the young policeman.

"What's with him?" Rnzini whispered to Seidman who looked more corpse-like with the single-bulb light.

"He's a cop," said Seidman, walking to the door. "If you stick around a couple of dozen years, you've got a chance at being as good a cop and as miserable a man as he is. Comes with the badge."

BLOWOUT
IN LITTLE MAN FLATS

"The last murder in Little Man Flats was back in, let me see, 1963, before Kennedy was shot by who knows how or why," Sheriff George Fingerhurt told his prime suspect. "Want some tea? Do you good in this heat."

"No . . . thanks."

"Suit yourself."

Fingerhurt sat back drinking his herbal peppermint tea from the Rhett Butler cup his daughter had brought him from Atlanta. George Fingerhurt liked Rhett Butler and herbal tea. Rhett was cool, never mind the temperature—like today, pushing a hundred in the shade.

"Got a theory about tea, got it from my grandfather Ocean Fingerhurt who was half Apache. Grandpa Ocean said hot tea cooled you off. Since Grandpa Ocean had got lost and wound up in Little Man Flats, New Mexico, back in 1930, when he thought he was in southern California, he was hardly a man to trust, at least not about directions. He was better about tea. Sure you don't want to change your mind?"

"Okay," said the suspect. "I'll have some tea."

"Gets dry out here," said the sheriff, pouring a cup of dark-green tea into a Scarlett O'Hara cup and handing it to the truckdriver, whose name, as he had told the sheriff, was Tector (Teck) Gorch. "Careful—hot."

"Obliged," said Teck.

They drank for about a minute, and Teck looked out the window.

"Quite a crowd," the sheriff said.

"Umm," Teck grunted.

There were eight people outside the one-story adobe town hall and sheriff's office. One of them was Ollie Twilly, from the feed store, wide-brimmed Stetson shading his eyes as he leaned back against the front fender of his '88 Ford pickup. Ollie had reason to be there. His brother Stan was one of the three people who had been killed, probably by the trucker sitting across from George drinking herbal tea.

The trucker was, George figured, maybe thirty-five, forty. One of those solid mailbox types. Curly hair cut a little long, could use a shave, but considering what had happened, made sense he hadn't considered the social graces. Teck the trucker was wearing slightly washed-out blood-specked jeans and a bloody T-shirt with the words I'M HAVING A BAD DAY written across the front in black. Amen to that sentiment, George thought.

"Last murder, back when I was a boy," George explained after a careful sip. "Indian named Double Eagle out of Gallup on a motorcycle went ravin' down 66 and plowed into Andrew Carpenter. Jury figured it was on purpose. Not much point to it. Andrew was near ninety. Am I getting too folksy for you? I haven't had much practice with murder cases. Haven't had any, really."

Teck shrugged and tried to think. The tea was making him feel a little cooler, but the sheriff was making him nervous. Fingerhurt was wearing matching khaki trousers and short-sleeved shirt. His black hair was freshly cut, combed straight back, and he looked a hell of a lot like the crying Indian in the TV commercials about polluting the rivers.

A sweat-stained khaki cowboy hat sat on the empty desk.

"Hey," said Fingerhurt, pointing out the window. "Crowd's growing. Those two are Mr. and Mrs. Barcheck, what passes for society in Little Man Flats. Own a lot of the town, including the Navajo Fill-up."

Teck looked out the window for the first time.

"Nice-lookin' woman," the sheriff said. "Not enough meat for me, but we're not in Santa Fe, so one's voyeuristic choices are limited. You wanna just tell your story? State police'll be here in a half hour, maybe less, to pick you up. Won't have a good report on what it looks like up there till Red comes in." Teck held his cup in two hands, feeling warm moisture seep into his palms.

"Red's my deputy, one you saw out at the Fill-up."

"His hair isn't red," said Teck.

"Never was. His father had red hair, was called Red. Deputy was Little Red. When his daddy died, deputy was just plain Red."

"Interesting," said Teck.

It was the sheriff's turn to shrug.

"Say, listen, information like that counts for lore in Little Man Flats."

He looked out the window and observed, "Crowd's getting bigger. I'd say twenty out there, coming to take a look at you. Four, five more people, and practically the whole town'll have turned out. State troopers are gonna be here soon, asking if I found anything. You want to tell your story? I'll take notes."

"I'm arrested? I need a lawyer?"

"You're here for questioning in the murder of Miss Rose Bryant Fernandez, Mr. Stanley Twilly, and a man who had a wallet in his back pocket strongly suggesting he was Lincoln Smart. You know the man?"

"Trucker, like me," said Teck. "Knew him to say hello. Where's my rig?"

"Safe, gathering dust out at the Fill-up, where you parked it. Wanna tell me what happened out there?"

"Someone cut your population almost in half," said Teck without a smile.

Sheriff Fingerhurt shook his head. He put down his Rhett Butler cup and folded his hands, looking unblinking at the trucker.

"Educated?"

"A little too much," said Teck. "Almost finished college. Almost a lot of things."

"Feeling a little sorry for yourself?"

"Considering, I think I've got a right."

"Maybe so. Story?"

Teck sat back, looked out the window at the gathered crowd, focused on a little boy about nine, who was looking directly back at him and covering his eyes to shade out the sun.

"Came thundering in a little before four in the morning," Teck began, nodding his agreement to the sheriff, who had pulled a tape recorder out of a desk drawer. Fingerhurt pushed the button and sat back.

"Came thundering in before four in the morning," Teck repeated. "Wanted to make Gallup, usually do. Never stopped at the Navajo Fill-up overnight before. One bad tire out of sixteen didn't stop me. I'd have even tried outlasting the knock in the diesel, even with nothing but desert for fifty more miles. Rain and backache did me in. Learned enough in eleven years in the high cab to know that when the back says stop, you stop, or you will have one hell of a tomorrow."

Sheriff Fingerhurt nodded and shook his head.

"Grit and sand on my neck, air conditioner gone lazy, shirt sticking to my chest, back, and deep down into my behind," Teck continued. "I was a sorry mess by one in the A.M. I never stopped in your town before last night except for diesel. I don't know the two locals who got killed, and I barely knew Linc."

"Lincoln Smart, the other driver?" asked the sheriff.

"There was only one rig in the opening beyond the pumps. Linc's big silver-and-blue, bigger than mine. I own my truck out there, and I've got a load of furniture from a factory just outside of Baines, Arkansas. Taking it to a pair of stores in Bakersfield."

"Where you from, Teck?"

"Tupelo. Tupelo, Mississippi."

"Elvis's town?"

"Yeah."

"You ever see the King himself?"

"He was long gone when I was growing up."

Sheriff Fingerhurt sat back, shaking his head.

"Well," Teck went on, "I—"

"Married?" asked the sheriff.

"Divorced. One kid. A boy, about seven or eight."

"You don't know?"

"Seven. His birthday's February 11. I just forget the year. Haven't seen him for three years. My ex-wife won't let me."

"Sorry," said Fingerhurt.

"I got bigger things to worry about today," Teck said, putting down his now empty cup.

"Yeah," said the sheriff.

"Got out of my rig, with my rain poncho over my head, duffel in my hand, locked up, and went inside the café. Woman behind the counter was reading a paperback."

"Remember what it was?"

"Make a difference?"

"Who knows?" said Fingerhurt.

"Woman behind the counter looked up at me like I was a

204

surprise she could have done without," Teck went on. "People tend not to be overjoyed when I walk in, but this woman—"

"Rosie Fernandez," Fingerhurt supplied.

"I guess," Teck said with a shrug, looking out the window.

The small crowd had grown. There were more men now, and they were talking, arguing.

"You ever have a lynching in this town?" Teck said, his eyes meeting those of Ollie Twilly, whose Stetson was now tilted back on his head. Ollie either had a very high forehead or he was bald. Bald or balding, he was clearly in one hell of a bad mood.

"Not a white man," said the sheriff. "Last Indian was shot in 1928 by a mob for drunk talk to a white woman."

"Your grandfather picked one hell of a town to settle in," Teck said.

"He was lost."

"We keep this up, I won't get my story told before the troopers get here," Teck said.

"Go on. Rose Fernandez was behind the counter, reading a paperback."

"Dean Koontz. It was Dean Koontz."

"Read one by him," said Fingerhurt. "People turned into machines in a small town. Scared shit out of me."

"I asked her for a room and something to eat," Teck went on. "I wasn't particular as long as it wasn't trout. I'm allergic."

"We don't have much call for trout in New Mexico," the sheriff said.

Outside the window, the crowd was getting louder, and there was, the sheriff noted, a very bad sign even a white man could read. The children were being sent off, as if there might be something the adults didn't want them to see.

"I think they're working themselves up to come here and lynch me," said Teck, following the sheriff's line of vision.

"Closest yucca that'll hold your weight is two miles out of town," said the sheriff, reaching for his hat. "Shoot you is what I'm thinking."

"Like the Indian in 1928?"

"Something like that," George Fingerhurt agreed. "But we'll stop 'em."

"We?"

"Me and Red. He's pulling up."

About twenty-five yards beyond the window where the crowd had gathered, a dust-covered pickup pulled in and a man in jeans, a khaki shirt, and a hat climbed out.

People flocked around him as he strode forward, shaking his head.

"He found something," the sheriff said.

"How can you tell? Your Indian blood?"

"Got the look. Known Red for almost forty years. You know things like that about people you know."

The door behind Teck flew open, and voices from outside came in, full of fear and anger. Red closed the door and stepped in. He was thinner and, considering the mood of the mob, less formidable than Teck would have liked. Red looked at the sheriff and then at Teck.

"Wanna talk in the other room, George?"

"What'd you find?" asked the sheriff.

"You sure you—"

"You found what, Red?"

"Troopers came with a truck. All over the place. Told me I could go. They'd be here quick. Said we shoulda held Gorch at the murder site. Found this under Rosie's body. Said you should have a look at it."

Red stepped to the sheriff's desk, avoiding Teck's eyes,

pulled a crumpled paper bag out of his jeans pocket, and handed it to George Fingerhurt. The sheriff held the bag open behind the desk, looked into it and then out the window and then at Red.

"Damn," said Fingerhurt.

"Damn right, damn," said Red.

"Sheriff. . . ." Teck tried, but the door behind him opened with a jolt. He turned and found himself facing Ollie Twilly, both Barchecks, and a variety of others, mostly with the look and matching intellect of bewildered cattle. Twilly was carrying a shotgun.

"We want him," said Ollie, pointing his shotgun barrel at Teck, who jumped up and stood with his back to the wall behind the still seated sheriff.

"You all want him? You too, Mrs. Barcheck?" Fingerhurt asked.

"Yes," she said.

She was, indeed, a fine-looking woman, freckled brown with yellow hair tied back, could have been any age from thirty to fifty, Teck thought, and wondered how he could do such thinking with a shotgun cocked and aimed in the general area of his gut.

"And what'll you do with him?" asked the sheriff.

"Take him out. Shoot him," said Twilly. "Shoot him through the brains like the dog he is."

The shotgun came up toward Teck Gorch's face, and Ollie Twilly continued with:

"You shot my brother like a dog, and I'm—"

"How'd you know Stan was shot, Mr. Twilly?" the sheriff asked, as two of the more oxlike men stepped toward Teck.

"Red told us," said Andrew Barcheck, who was decidedly a slouching Saint Bernard to his wife's well-groomed poodle.

The sheriff closed his eyes and shook his head before he

looked up at Red, whose left cheek twitched.

"George, you and Red go out for a shake at Veronica's," said Ollie Twilly. "When you come back—"

"No, Mr. Twilly," said the sheriff.

"We'll have your goddamn job, George," Twilly said through gritted teeth.

"You couldn't live on my salary, Mr. Twilly. You take him. You shoot him. Red and I arrest you for murder," said the sheriff. "Is it worth going to jail for, Mr. Twilly?"

"Yes."

The two bovine men were now about three feet in front of Teck, who had sucked in his stomach, feeling more than a little sick.

"Rest of you feel the same way?" the sheriff asked. "You got murder looking at you, conspiracy, impeding a lawman in the dispatching of his duty. Hell, folks, you're looking at a lot of bleak years in the state house."

"No jury will convict us. Not after what he did."

"Act your age, Ollie," Mrs. Barcheck said. "There isn't a jury that wouldn't convict us."

"Then by shit and a wild pig," shouted Twilly, "I don't give a crap. I'll shoot him right here."

The two bulls in front of Teck jumped out of the line of fire.

"Man was telling his side when you came in," said the sheriff. "Think you can hold off till he finishes? Give him that?"

"Let him speak, Ollie," Mr. Barcheck said.

Someone behind the front line let out a groan and an "Oh, shit."

"Miguel, that you?" the sheriff called.

A heavy, hard-breathing dark man with bad skin worked his way forward through the crowd.

"Let him say," Miguel said.

"No," said Twilly, the gun now firmly against the chest of Miguel.

"My sister got killed last night too," Miguel Fernandez said. "We can listen. Who knows what Leon Harvey Oswald would have said if the Jew guy hadn't shot him?"

"Lee. Oswald's name was Lee," Mrs. Barcheck corrected.

"And the man who shot him was Jack Ruby."

"This isn't goddamn Trivial Pursuit," screamed Twilly. "Can't you see Fingerhurt's stalling till the state police get here?"

"I'll look out the window," said Miguel. "We see them coming, and you can shoot."

Defeated for the moment, Ollie Twilly let the shotgun point toward the floor.

"Finish your story, Tector," the sheriff said.

Teck, back to the wall, looked at the faces of anger, hate, and confusion around the room.

"I don't think I. . . ." Teck began, and then said, "I walked in, soaking wet, told the woman I needed a room for the night and a mechanic in the morning. She said . . ."

Teck's eyes met Miguel's and then went to the sheriff.

"I don't . . ."

"Tector," said the sheriff, "I don't see a hell of a lot of choice here, do you?"

"She said all she had was eggs any way I wanted 'em, and if I wanted company in bed for a couple of hours, she could handle that too, for a reasonable fee."

Teck's eyes were watching Miguel Fernandez. Fernandez betrayed nothing but heavy breathing.

"I said I'd think on it," Teck went on.

"A fine-looking woman, Rosie," said the sheriff. "Some meat on her bones. Nothing to hold back here, Teck. Rosie was the town—begging your pardon, Mrs. Barcheck—lady of the afternoon and evening."

"She was a whore, yes," said Miguel, "but she was a good person. Anybody in this room say anything else?"

No one in the room had anything else to say relating to Rosie Fernandez's behavior, so the sheriff nodded at Teck, who went on.

"She said she'd make me two over-easy sandwiches with mayo and onions and figured from the onion order that I wasn't interested in company. I said I wanted to change into something dry, and she told me to go up the stairs off in the corner and go into room three, where I could shower and get decent and dry."

"What else?" the sheriff said.

"Jukebox in the corner near the window was playing Patsy Cline," Teck said hopefully.

"She was reading Dean Koontz and listening to Patsy Cline," the sheriff said.

"Stairs were dark. I started up. This guy passed me coming down."

"Guy?" asked Fingerhurt. "What'd he look like?"

"Don't know. Wasn't really looking. About my height, weight. Maybe."

"Met himself coming and going," said Twilly. "We heard enough here yet?"

"Wait," Teck said. "He had a big silver belt buckle."

"Every man in this room and a few of the women are wearing big silver belt buckles," the sheriff said. "Even me and Red."

"I'm telling you what I remember," Teck pleaded. "I'm telling the truth."

"Okay. Sha-hair-a-zadie," said Ollie Twilly. "Keep going."

"Not much more to tell. I went to room three, got my clean jeans, socks, and the shirt I'm wearing out of my bag, took a quick shower, got dressed, and headed back down. Patsy Cline was still singing, eggs were burning bad, and Miss Fernandez was laying there in the middle of the room, dead and bloody. I tried to help her, but she was—"

"And you were covered in her blood," the sheriff said.

"Yes."

"And then?"

"I called for help. No one answered. The rain was harder. It was pushing dawn. I ran back up the stairs and knocked at doors and yelled. No answer. One of the doors was open. Linc Smart was naked, bloody, and dead. I kept opening doors. One was an office. Bald man was laying across the desk, dead."

"That was my brother. That was Stan," cried Ollie. "You lying son of a bitch and a half."

"No," said Teck, holding up his hands to ward off the anticipated shotgun blast. "No lie. I found the phone, called the operator, told her that someone had murdered who knows how many people at the Navajo Fill-up. And that was it."

The sheriff's eyes met Teck's and then moved for an instant to the running tape recorder before returning to Teck's face.

"Question, Mr. Gorch," the sheriff said. "You didn't hear gunshots when you drove up to the Fill-up and walked in?"

"No. It was raining hard. Whoever it was must have shot Linc and the other guy before I got to the door."

"How many times were they shot, Red?" the sheriff asked.

"The trucker three times, Mr. Stanley Twilly twice. Then Miss Rosie twice."

"Why," the sheriff asked, "did Miss Rosie sit there reading a Dean Koontz and offer you eggs and companion-

ship if she just heard five shots?"

"Yes," said Miguel, turning angrily toward Teck.

"I don't know," said Teck.

"And why didn't you hear Rosie getting shot?" the sheriff went on.

"I was in the shower. It was raining hard. I don't know."

"This is the stupidest damn story," Ollie said. "Everybody step back. Fairy tale's over."

The shotgun came up toward Teck again.

"Why would I kill those people?" Teck said.

"You thought Rose was alone," said Ollie. "You went for her behind the counter. She fought you, threatened to call the sheriff. You shot her. Then you panicked and went to look for any witnesses who might have seen you. You shot that truckdriver and my brother."

"And then I called the police?" Teck cried.

"Maybe you were trying to be tricky," Miguel Fernandez said. "Maybe you just got damned confused, decided you couldn't get away, tire tracks, whatever. So you made up your story."

"No," cried Teck. "Sheriff."

"What'd he do with the gun?" Sheriff Fingerhurt asked.

"Threw it away, maybe buried it couple hundred yards off in the desert," said Barcheck. "What's the difference?"

"Troopers are coming down the street," said Miguel softly, turning his eyes to Teck's frightened face.

"That does it," said Ollie. "Everybody stand back. We in this together?"

The two bulls who had approached Teck grunted something. The rest of the crowd was shuffling, silent now that the troopers were a minute or two away.

"I've got one thing I can't figure," said the sheriff. "If his story is true, why didn't Rose call me and Red, or go upstairs to see what was happening? Why did she sit there reading a book?"

"He made up a dumb story," said Miguel.

"Miguel," said the sheriff, "how long I know you?"

"Your whole life."

"What if Rose did hear the shots? What if Rose knew Stan and the trucker were dead when Gorch came in looking for a warm room and meal? What if he surprised her, she picked up a book, looked as if she didn't want company, and then, to keep him from getting suspicious, offered to bed down with him for the night, not forgetting to say it wasn't free. Gorch goes upstairs. Killer comes down. Rose tells him about Gorch. Killer gets the idea of blaming everything on the dumb trucker. Sorry, Tector."

"No offense," said Teck.

"Why would anyone want to kill my brother?" Ollie said.

"Property, money's my guess," said Sheriff Fingerhurt. "Killer probably considered burying Stan and the dead trucker and having Rose say Stan just got fed up, grabbed some cash, and took off for northern California."

The troopers' car door opened and then slammed shut a beat later. All eyes turned to the window. Two troopers were walking toward the Little Man Flats municipal building, where most of the adult population was gathered in the sheriff's office.

"That's crazy," shouted Ollie.

The sheriff lifted his right hand and displayed a crinkled brown paper bag.

"Red found this on the floor under Rose's body," he said, pulling a bright silver buckle out of the bag and holding it up for the congregation to see. The silver was hammered into the shape of a buffalo, with huge horns in relief.

"So," said Miguel, "everybody around here has a belt

buckle like that, something like that. It could be this guy's, this truckdriver's."

"Right," said the sheriff, "but he's got a buckle on his belt, and he had time to look for it if Rose pulled it off in a struggle with him. But the killer, the killer heard the shower go off, made a decision not to kill the trucker, and ran without finding the buckle. Hell, maybe he didn't even notice till he got home or too far to turn back."

The door behind the crowd opened, and a deep voice said: "What the hell is going on in here?"

"I'm not interested in who has a buffalo-head silver buckle," said Fingerhurt, ignoring the troopers who were muscling their way forward through the gathering. "I'm interested in who *doesn't* have one anymore. With the cooperation of the troopers who have just arrived, I'm going to ask a few of you who I know have buffalo buckles to go back to their houses with me and show me the buckle. Miguel, Dan Sullivan, Mr. Barcheck, and you, Ollie."

The troopers were in front now, near twins, well built, unwrinkled uniforms, hats flat on their heads and brims perfectly parallel to the ground.

"What's going on, George?" the older of the two said.

The sheriff held up a finger to show that he needed only a minute more.

"All right with me," said Barcheck.

"Me too," said Miguel.

"I'm wearing mine," said Danny Sullivan, stepping forward to show the buckle in question.

"Mr. Twilly?" Sheriff Fingerhurt asked.

"Lost," he said defiantly. "I looked for it a few days ago. Someone stole it."

"You wore it yesterday, Oliver," Mrs. Barcheck said.

"Hey, that's right," said Danny Sullivan. "You sat next to

me at Veronica's for lunch. You were wearing the buckle. You had the meat loaf with chilies, and I had . . . who the hell cares what I had?"

"Is there a punch line here, George?" the older trooper said, doing a magnificent job of hiding his complete confusion.

"I think Mr. Twilly here has some questions to answer," the sheriff said.

The shotgun was coming up again, but before Twilly could level it at anyone, Teck Gorch pushed himself from the wall with a rebel yell and threw himself at the armed man. The shotgun barrel was still coming up toward Teck's face when Miguel Fernandez punched Twilly in the gut. Twilly went down with Teck on top of him, and the shotgun spun around in the air like the bone at the beginning of *2001*.

Three people made it out the door. Some went for the floor. Barcheck pushed his wife against the wall. The troopers and Red dived behind the desk, where Sheriff George Fingerhurt sat shaking his head.

The gun hit the ceiling, dropped quickly to the floor with a clatter-clack, and didn't discharge.

It took Red about twenty seconds to clear everyone but the troopers, the sheriff, Teck, and Ollie out of the room.

It took Ollie Twilly two minutes and some resuscitation from the younger trooper to revive enough to deny everything, from his affair with Rose to the murder of his brother. He even managed to deny a variety of crimes, including felonies of which no one had yet accused him.

Within four minutes, the troopers were being led by Red, with Ollie in tow, for a tour of Ollie's home and office.

"Can I go now?" Teck asked when he was alone with the sheriff again.

"Nope," said Fingerhurt. "You're our key witness."

"But . . ."

"Up to the troopers now," the sheriff said. "They can let you go when they take you off my hands, but who knows. Maybe they'll get a statement and let you deliver your furniture to Bakersfield."

"Okay if I go back to my rig and pick up some clean clothes?"

"Sure," said the sheriff. "I'll give you a lift."

George Fingerhurt backed his wheelchair from behind the desk and carefully maneuvered it through the space between it and the window. From that point, it was out the door, down the ramp, and another day starting.

THE VOICE OF A CHILD

The chubby, yellow-haired boy, his thick glasses perched on the end of his nose, sat quietly in the corner with his legs dangling several inches from the floor. His head tilted forward toward the open book on his lap and he seemed to pay no attention to the two men sputtering on the other side of the room about murder and suicide and the like.

The boy's only observable reaction to the adults was an occasional grimace against Doctor Fairbanks's billowing cigar smoke that threatened to engulf the chief of police's office in a gray cloud.

"It can't be, Doc," said Chief Witt with a sigh as he spotted the boy's crinkled nose and rose to open a window. "It just can not be, I tell you."

In the full-length mirror on the door beyond the desk, Witt saw himself as the doctor must have seen him, a neat, good looking uniformed man in his early forties with graying hair and a perplexed look on his face as he scratched his head.

"How," Witt said glumly, "can a dead man commit murder by stabbing another man? It just can't be, Doc."

He threw open the window and a haze of smoke drifted out. The white-haired, white-mustached little man seated on the other side of the desk expelled a huge gray puff as if to help fill the vacancy left by the retreating smoke.

"You wanted a medical opinion, Leonard," the man said,

brushing gray ash from his sleeve. "When you ask my opinion, you will get it. It is also my opinion, contrary to prevailing belief in this community, that use of television and radio does not contaminate the air, one need not lie on his right side when sleeping to keep from interfering with the heart, there is no medicine that can be taken by mouth to dissolve gallstones, a cold cannot be broken up, daily bowel movements are not necessary for health . . ."

"Doc," said Witt, sinking back into his swivel chair.

"Well, my opinion on such matters is good enough for you while you question my judgment on the subject about which I know most, death and its causes. As chief pathologist for Delft-Highwood County, I resent your insinuation. I especially resent it in view of the fact that the job is without salary and I have held it for twenty-five of the most frustrating years of my prolonged existence." The old man smoothed his mustache and chuckled.

"I'm not amused," said Witt, restraining his hand, which sought to scratch his nervously itching scalp again.

"Go ahead and scratch," said the doctor, pointing to Chief Witt's head with the glowing cigar. "It might do you some good—get the blood flowing, induce internal secretions to the brain and give you some answers."

Len Witt lifted a stapled and typed report. "Doc, I've got a witness, two witnesses. It's nice and simple, or it was until you complicated it. Are you sure?"

"Len, do you know that tomato juice causes heart disease?"

"Doc, I—"

"Well, it doesn't. And ice water won't cause heart trouble either, watermelons won't cause polio, cooked cereals do not heat the blood, grape juice and dried poke berries are useless for treating arthritis, and parsnips do not cleanse the kidneys."

"All right, Doc. You're sure, but—"

"My grandfather says alfalfa tea cures rheumatism," said the little boy in the corner without looking up from his book.

"See?" said Doc Fairbanks, twisting in his chair to look at the boy. "Everybody in Delftwood thinks he's a doctor and your sergeant is the worst offender. If Breedlove continues to practice medicine without a license, I will personally retaliate by making citizens arrests on all the clods in this town who spit on the sidewalk."

"I'll talk to him, Doc. But please," Witt pleaded, "I've got two reporters out at the front desk waiting for a statement. Now let's get this straight. The boy was right there all the time. He was sitting in Professor Dockstader's living room with the professor's niece last night when it happened. Foreman came in, went to the professor's room right off the hall, stepped in, stabbed him, and then went out in his car and shot himself. Foreman couldn't have killed himself before he killed the professor."

The old doctor snapped his head around to the chief who, startled by the sudden movement, dropped the report on the desk.

"Thanks to the presence of mind of that young man and the speed with which he got to a telephone, both you and I were at Dockstader's home within fifteen minutes. I examined both bodies then, and I have just spent the night working on both of them. I tell you, in lay terms, that Dockstader died within seconds after being stabbed directly in the heart. The blade pierced the aorta.

"Allowing for fibrillation and the fact that his heart was weak in any case, I tell you he died after Foreman. Crudely stated, Foreman died of a bullet in the brain. Suffice it to say that judging from body temperature, in spite of the unseasonably cold weather, plus pupil contraction and a number of other factors, I can affirm that Foreman was dead at least ten minutes before the professor."

"But how—do you have a few minutes, Doc?"

"No, but I'll take them."

Witt picked up the phone on his desk, pressed a button and said, "Come in here, please, with your notes."

Almost instantly Sergeant Breedlove, a huge, overweight yet powerful looking man in a rumpled police uniform, lumbered in. His freckled, bald head was tanned as was his face over a crumpled, open tie. He looked a decade younger than his sixty years.

"Breedlove," rasped Doc Fairbanks, "you've been filling that boy's head with some more foolishness."

"Please," said Witt, standing with hands apart and palms out as if to restrain the tiny doctor from attacking the gigantic sergeant.

The doctor made a sour face and Breedlove, paying no attention, patted his grandson on the head and eased his bulk into an oversize chair in the corner.

"Sergeant," Witt said, pouring a glass of water into a paper cup from a dusty pitcher on the desk, "will you tell us what you found?"

Doc Fairbanks shot a cloud of smoke toward the sergeant and held his cigar as if it were a dart.

"Well," said Breedlove, flipping through a battered notebook, "it seems Professor Dockstader and Harv Foreman have been at each other for years, or so says the professor's niece, Lucy. Foreman wanted to marry Lucy a few years back, but Dockstader cut it all off, said he didn't want a sick, ignorant, money-grabbing janitor in the family."

"We all know that," grumbled the tiny doctor. "Town's been kicking that around for years. Dockstader was no prize of a man, but you know and so does everyone else around here that Foreman was after the girl's money. Just look at her."

"What's wrong with Lucy?" came the voice of the boy in the corner.

"Nothing," Doc Fairbanks sighed. "She's a fine woman, fine woman. I hope he left her a pile of money after all those years of looking after that old grouch. But it was a waste of effort if Foreman did it. Dockstader couldn't have lasted much longer."

"Professor Dockstader was sick?" asked Witt.

"Cancer. Now that he's dead I don't see any reason for secrecy. Doctor Griggs has operated on him several times in the last few years. Well, go on, Sergeant, I've got to get some sleep before office hours," Fairbanks grumbled.

"Anyway," Breedlove continued, "murder threats have been going both ways for months, especially since Foreman has been trying to see Lucy and Lucy has started to think about accepting Foreman in spite of the professor. Then yesterday the professor tells Lucy that Foreman is coming over to settle things and that she is to just sit quietly in the living room till it's all worked out. Well Pete, my grandson—"

"We know he's your grandson," mumbled the doctor.

"Pete gets along fine with Lucy and he was over at the professor's in the living room with her having cake when, sure enough, at about nine Foreman comes through the front door, and steps right into the professor's room before Pete or Lucy can even stand up. Right away the professor lets out a scream."

"He yelled, 'put that knife down!' " said Pete Breedlove from the corner.

"So Pete and Lucy got up, but before they could even move Foreman is in the hall, locking the professor's door and running out the front door. Pete and Lucy tried to open the professor's door but it was locked, so they ran outside to get in through the window, but it was locked from the inside and the curtains were drawn.

"They broke the window, climbed in and found the professor dead with the knife in his stomach. We live just a few doors down, so Pete came and got me and called into headquarters while I ran over."

"Boy has more sense than a lot of adults," said the doctor, examining his cigar.

"The professor was dead all right and we found Foreman in his car around the corner right away as soon as we looked. His car was locked from the inside and we had to break a window to get in. The gun was in his hand and he was dead. Then Lucy fainted and by the time I got her back in the house you two were there."

"There," exclaimed Chief Witt slapping down on his desk. "You see, Doc? How could Foreman be dead first when you tell me both of them died almost instantly and I have witnesses who saw Foreman commit the murder?"

"One of your witnesses is in no condition to give sensible testimony," said the doctor standing, "and the other is a boy. Did you know that punctures from rusty nails are no more dangerous than those from clean, shiny nails?"

"No, I didn't, Doc," said Breedlove in obvious awe.

"Well, it's true. You accept it when I tell the both of you but when it comes to pathology, you suddenly know more medicine than I do."

"Now look here, Doc," said Witt, standing and leaning toward the little man, who glared at him defiantly. "Somebody's wrong."

"Bollo," the boy whispered.

"Not now, Pete," the bulky sergeant said.

"But I've got to get back to school and I've been sitting here almost an hour."

"Let the boy go," said Doc Fairbanks.

"But Chief," the boy said, "if you will just let me ask a few questions, I think I know what happened."

"Why not?" said Witt, crunching his empty water cup and throwing it into his waste basket as he sat in his swivel chair and folded his arms. A few minutes of childish babble might calm some jumpy nerves.

"Okay," the boy said, examining some notes he had been taking in a black spelling book. "First, were there any fingerprints on the knife?"

"No," replied Breedlove. "We figured Foreman wore gloves."

"Was Foreman wearing gloves when you found him, Bollo?" continued the boy, chewing on a yellow pencil.

"No, but there was a pair in the car. We figure he took them off to hold the gun."

"What are you getting at, Pete?" said Witt, suddenly attentive.

"Let the boy go on," Doc Fairbanks said through teeth clenched tightly on the dwindling cigar. "He seems to be the only one around here besides me doing any thinking."

"Some things seem mighty funny to me," said Pete. "Like why did Mr. Foreman stab the professor? Why didn't he just shoot him? He had a gun."

"Too much noise," Witt said.

"But Lucy and I were there. We saw him go in and out. Noise wouldn't have made any difference."

"He was crazy," Witt said "He didn't think. Maybe he didn't mean to stab the professor. Then when he did it he went out in the car and shot himself."

"No such thing!" the doctor bellowed. "Foreman died first."

"Why last night?" said the boy.

"What do you mean?" asked Witt.

"I've been thinking," Pete continued. "There was something funny about last night. First off—"

"Don't say 'first off', Pete. Just say 'first'," Sergeant Breedlove corrected.

Doc Fairbanks glared at the sergeant and Len Witt slumped back with his hand to his forehead.

"First, last night was the first cold spell we've had this year—which might not mean anything, but it might," said Pete, ticking off a note in his book with the pencil. "Second, last night was the first time Professor Dockstader didn't complain about me being around. He didn't like kids. Usually Lucy comes over to our house to visit. Right, Bollo?"

"That's true," Breedlove agreed.

"He was afraid of Foreman and wanted someone else around for protection," Witt ventured.

"I'm just a kid. If he wanted protection, he would have asked Bollo to come. He wanted Lucy and me sitting in the living room, where we could see the door but not do anything."

"What's your point, Pete?" asked Witt.

"Don't you see?" wailed Doc Fairbanks, squinting at the boy with admiration. "He may be wrong, but he's got imagination."

"See what?" Wilt and Breedlove said in unison.

"Professor Dockstader killed Mr. Foreman and then committed suicide, not the other way around," the boy said.

"Certainly would account for the fact that Foreman died first," said the doctor.

"Can't be," Breedlove said, tapping his black notebook. "You and Lucy saw Foreman come in, heard the professor scream, saw Foreman leave. The professor's room was locked from outside by Foreman and we found the key in his pocket.

The windows in the professor's room were latched from the inside. Besides, we found Foreman dead in his locked car."

"A hodge-podge of data," said the old doctor throwing the remains of his cigar in a waste basket and reaching for another one, "but valid points to contend with. Can you contend, boy?"

Pete's lips formed a pout. "I think so. If the professor did it, he picked last night for a reason and that reason was that it was cold. Lucy said she saw Foreman come in and I don't see so good—"

"So well," Breedlove corrected.

"Sergeant, if you interrupt that boy once more—" Doc Fairbanks threatened.

"I don't see so well, but all I could tell was that a man in an overcoat and hat came in fast and was in the professor's room almost before I could look up. He was partly turned away, too. The professor had told Lucy that Foreman was coming at nine. So, when someone came in at the right time, wearing a coat and hat just like Foreman's, Lucy thought it was Foreman. She couldn't see his face clearly with the hat down and the collar up."

"If it wasn't Foreman, who was it?" asked Witt.

"Professor Dockstader, of course," Doc Fairbanks snorted. "They were about the same height and weight, but a coat and slouch would make up the difference."

"Right," Pete said. "He waited for the first cold night so he could wear a coat and hat just like Foreman's. He came in, stepped into his own room, yelled so Lucy and I could hear him and think he had been stabbed. Then he comes out with his back to us, locks the door, and is out of the house before Lucy and I can get across the room. It all happened fast and that's what he wanted. The thing that got me thinking was why, if Foreman did it, did he lock the professor's room?"

"I don't know," said the perplexed Witt, reaching in his desk for a bottle of aspirin.

"Because the room was empty," the doctor said triumphantly. "Dockstader didn't want Lucy and the boy to get over there, open the door and find no body."

"Right," said the serious Pete Breedlove. "The professor had left the window open. He ran around the house quick, climbed through the window, locked it and stabbed himself before Lucy and I could get in. So, the suicide looked like murder."

"But why?" sputtered Witt.

"Simple," said the gleeful Fairbanks, stroking his mustache. "I told you Dockstader was sick. He didn't have long to go, so he decided to get rid of Foreman, knowing that after he was gone Foreman would be sure to marry Lucy and get his money. I don't know if he was more bothered by the prospect of Foreman getting his money or marrying Lucy, but he found a way to get rid of Foreman and go out as a poor, sympathetic murder victim."

"The way I figure it," said the boy, pushing his slipping glasses back on his nose, "Professor Dockstader called Foreman and told him to park around the corner at about a quarter to nine, where they could talk things over without Lucy knowing. The professor climbed out his window, met Foreman in the car and when he saw he was wearing the right coat and hat, he climbed into the car, shot him, left the gun, locked the car after dropping a duplicate key to his room in Foreman's pocket.

"Then, wearing a coat and hat he had bought just like Foreman's, he went back through the front door, where Lucy and I thought he was Foreman."

"Fantastic," Witt's hoarse voice cracked. "Wait a minute. Wait a minute. What about the locked automobile?"

"I can answer that one, Chief," said Breedlove glancing proudly at his grandson. "Foreman's car is a Ford. You can lock it from the outside with no trouble and no key."

"Then there should be a duplicate key to the professor's room," said Witt. "You say there was such a key in Foreman's car. Well, Professor Dockstader didn't have time to drop the key in the car after his little show. If this story is true, there is a key somewhere around that house, and what about the hat and coat?"

"That's just it," said Pete Breedlove, moving toward the door. "That's what proves I'm right. Professor Dockstader hid the hat and coat right where nobody would look for it, especially if we thought he was murdered. He put it in the only place he had time to put it, in the closet in his room. He just hung the coat in his closet and put the hat on the shelf. I've got to go now, Chief. I've got a math test this afternoon. Can I go, Bollo?"

"Sure, Pete," said the proud, confused sergeant.

"Breedlove, go over and check that closet," said Witt. "I don't think you'll find anything, but—"

"He'll find it all right," said the boy, with his hand on the doorknob. "I stopped by at the Dockstader house this morning to see Lucy, and I checked the closet. A coat and hat just like the ones on Foreman are in there and there's a key in the coat pocket. I could feel it from the outside."

Doc Fairbanks, laughing and choking, stood up and walked over to the boy. "Peter, my boy, it would be an honor if you would permit me to drive you to school, during which trip I can try to guide you toward a career in medicine. This town is sorely in need of another intelligent voice."

The old man and the eleven-year-old boy left the office and the two policemen stared at each other in silence for half a minute. With a grunt Breedlove lifted his massive weight from the chair and moved toward the door.

"Send those reporters in," Witt called to the closing door.

He scratched his head, fanned away a final cloud of cigar smoke and wondered what reaction he would get from the city council if he hired a part-time preteenage detective.

Or—he shuddered—if he told them the real story of what had happened this day.

LISTEN, MY CHILDREN

A man can't commit a murder if he is miles away from his victim and directly under the eyes of the police.

Sergeant Bollo Breedlove of the Delftwood police savored this thought as he sat comfortably in his police car munching a Mars bar and occasionally shifting his bulk to get a better view of the small gray house across the street. The weary one-story wooden home sat alone in the snow with the nearest neighbor on each side a safe forty yards away, as if to avoid contamination from the peeling paint.

The police car with its bright blue star on the side was clearly visible from the lone house, but it made no difference to Breedlove. He blew his nose on a wrinkled blue handkerchief and flipped on his car radio.

"Anything doing, Art?"

"Nothing, Bollo," replied the bored voice of Art Bluet, who was parked in the alley behind the little house. "But I might need a tow out of this snow if we ever leave here."

"You see him?" asked Breedlove, searching through his unkempt glove compartment for another candy bar.

"Moved through the kitchen about a minute ago," said Bluet.

"Right, Art. Just sit tight."

Breedlove flipped off the radio, scratched his bald head without removing his worn police cap, and removed a gnarled pencil from behind his ear. He made a note on a yellow pad on the seat just as a car turned the corner and skidded to a stop in the snow before the gray house.

Breedlove watched as the well-bundled driver hurried out, carrying a brief case which seemed to weigh him down, and dashed up the snow-covered walk and through the door without knocking.

The dashboard radio sputtered and spat before Breedlove could turn it on to relay his news about the visitor.

"Breedlove. Breedlove. Bollo, where are you? This is Chief Witt. What the devil happened there? Answer."

"Nothing happened, Len, except someone just came and ran into the house," the sergeant answered in semi-confusion.

"I don't care about that. How did Dexter get out of the house?" The radio had a few faulty tubes that distorted the sound, but Breedlove could hear the voice about to crack.

"He never left the house, Len. Art and I can see every wall, every window. There's not a footprint in the snow, not a. . . . He hasn't left here since you talked to him this morning. I swear it."

"Then how do you account for the fact that ten minutes ago he made good on his threat and shot his partner—shot Ramsden? Shot him right in front of a witness, who gave a positive identification."

"He couldn't have, Len."

"Ramsden's secretary saw the whole thing. She's known Dexter for fifteen years. Now stop telling me he didn't do it. See if you can get in there and look for a bundle of money, cash. The secretary says he took everything in the safe, between seven and ten thousand dollars."

"But, Len—" The radio went dead and Breedlove sighed, buttoned his coat without noticing that one of the buttons was about to come off, checked his gun and flipped on the radio.

"Art?"

"I heard, Bollo," said Bluet. "Damn it, Dexter hasn't left the house."

"Let's just get in there like the chief said."

Breedlove eased his way out of the car, his stomach pressing tight against the steering wheel. His feet crunched noisily in the snow as he lumbered across the street.

Looking like an overstuffed dragon, he clutched his yellow pad in one hand and raised a gloved paw to knock at the door. Bluet, a thin, worried-looking man, wore only his light jacket.

He seemed unaffected by the cold as he joined Breedlove before the door.

Behind the door he knew Dexter stood waiting to greet him with a smile or a look of surprise. Early that morning Breedlove and Witt had hurried to this little house making the first tire tracks in the fresh snow.

Earl Ramsden, senior partner in Ramsden and Dexter, Delftwood's oldest and only moving company, had called the chief at home and said that his partner had just threatened to kill him before the end of the day.

Dexter, who reminded Breedlove of a wilted piece of celery, had met them at the door wearing a satisfied smile and a shabby flannel robe. The prematurely gray-haired man, looking much older and more mature than his thirty-five or so years, had invited them in and calmly explained that Ramsden had been cheating him into poverty for years, although he couldn't prove it. Ramsden was too adept at juggling the books. Since nothing could be proved, Dexter planned that afternoon to go to the office, shoot his partner and take whatever money was in the safe.

"But why tell us?" Witt had asked. "We can lock you up

right now for threatening his life."

"What good would that do?" Dexter had replied, passing around coffee which both policemen had accepted. "How long can you keep me in jail? No, I have a much better plan. I'll give you a sporting chance. If you keep me from killing Ramsden today without locking me up, I'll abandon the idea."

"You're nuts," Breedlove had cried, almost dropping the coffee.

"By the time you get someone to agree to that assertion and have me detained for observation, the day will be over," Dexter had answered calmly, handing him a dry chocolate chip cookie. "Besides, I would consider that a violation of our agreement."

"Look here, Dexter," had been Chief Witt's reply as he ran his hands nervously through his well-groomed, gently graying hair. "I'm going to have your house watched all day, front and back, and if you make one move to leave, I'll haul you in for questioning."

"That's fair enough," Dexter had replied. "Now if you will excuse me, I have a great deal to do."

"I haven't made any deal," Witt said, taking a step forward. Both the well-built, tall police chief and his massive sergeant towered over the little man, but he had made no move to back away and had given no sign of fear.

The man had given Breedlove a creepy feeling and he stood now, hesitating to knock. He couldn't have gotten out. Witt had remained in the house while Breedlove called Bluet. For the past six hours the two officers had sat there watching the house, waiting for the figure of Dexter to make a spindly-legged dash past them. But nothing had happened.

No one had entered or left the house. According to a call several hours earlier from Chief Witt, there wasn't even an outside chance that he had dug a tunnel. A check with the Delftwood planning board revealed that Dexter had requested an inspection on the claim that he wanted a zoning grant to expand his small basement. The inspector was sure there was no tunnel.

Breedlove knocked. The whole thing was screwy and beyond him.

"Ah, sergeant," said Dexter. "What a surprise."

"This is Officer Bluet. Can we come in?"

"Of course." Dexter, still wearing his flannel robe, stepped back with a smile.

"You don't have to answer any questions," Breedlove recited, automatically removing his gloves and ear muffs. "Anything you say can be taken down and used in evidence against you. And if you want a lawyer—"

"It's not necessary, Sergeant. Please step into the living room and meet my brother."

Breedlove followed him with the growing hope that the man who had dashed into the house a few minutes before would be an exact twin, a reasonable facsimile, a ready-made murderer. But he wasn't. The brother, introduced as Sidney Dexter, was a foot shorter than the man who had threatened murder. Not only was he shorter, but they looked nothing alike. This brother, although thin, had a reddish face, small nose and dark hair. They looked nothing alike and Breedlove's hope sank.

"Mr. Dexter, would you mind if we had a look around your house?"

"Not at all," replied Dexter with a sweep of his hand.

Breedlove nodded to Bluet, who went to work.

"Now," said Breedlove, examining the notes on his pad as if they might give him some clue as to what he should say next.

"You want to know how I killed Ramsden," said the taller Dexter, sitting next to his placid brother.

"How did you know he was dead?" said Breedlove.

"That metallic object behind you is a radio," Dexter said indicating the direction with a flick of the wrist. "It was announced just a second before you walked through the door."

Breedlove turned and placed his bare palm on the radio.

"If you were just listening to it, why is it cold?"

"Sergeant, I didn't say I was just listening to it," Dexter said, obviously enjoying himself. "I said I had a radio and that the announcement was made on the radio. Actually Sidney heard it on his car radio. He was just around the corner so he drove over immediately to tell me."

"That's right," said Sidney Dexter in a deep voice which startled the rotund sergeant. He had expected a high, nervous voice from the man who sat there with his hands on his lap.

The yellow pad gave him no ideas and Bluet had disappeared into another room. He had the feeling that both Dexters were laughing at him, challenging him, but he had no idea of how to meet the challenge.

A car pulled up outside and Breedlove, stalling, strode to the window to see the welcome sight of Chief Witt's unmarked Fairlane. The chief jumped out quickly, followed by a well-wrapped, short-legged little creature that waddled after him in oversize boots.

"Visitors?" said Dexter, rising. "I'll let them in, Sergeant. Just entertain yourself."

In a few seconds, Chief Witt was ushered in by Dexter and both were followed by a small boy, almost invisible under his winter clothing and behind his scarf.

"Pete," said the sergeant, looking from the chief to the boy.

"Chief Witt picked me up in front of the house, Bollo," said the boy.

"I want him here," said Witt removing his coat to reveal a perfectly-tailored gray suit, "unless Mr. Dexter has some objection."

"None," said Dexter with an amused and slightly puzzled twist of his lips.

Breedlove helped his grandson out of his jacket and boots. For some reason, all four of the men in the room watched silently as if the shedding coat and scarf would give them a few seconds of calm.

The pudgy, bespectacled boy moved to a chair in a corner, wiped his nose with his sleeve, and looked at Sidney Dexter, who avoided his glance. Although the boy was eleven, he looked younger and seldom bothered to correct adults who treated him as a toddler.

"Now Dexter, Alvin R. Dexter, I want to warn you that—" Witt began.

"I've already done that, Len," Breedlove broke in lightly, glad to be free of the responsibility of carrying the burden of investigation.

"All right," said Witt. "Who is that?"

"I'm Sidney, Alvin's brother. I was driving past when I heard on the radio about Ramsden's death. Naturally, I stopped by to tell my brother."

"That sounds well rehearsed," said Witt. "Where's Bluet?"

"Searching the place, Chief."

"He won't find anything," said Witt. "If Dexter let you look, you won't find anything. Look here, Dexter, I don't feel like playing games with you. You killed Ramsden."

"But Mr. Witt—" said Alvin Dexter with little emotion.

"You killed him," continued Witt, "and you used us as an alibi. I've got a positive identification on you and I'm going to find out how you did it."

"I hate to bring this up," said Dexter, pouring himself a cup of coffee from a pot on the table before him, "but I have two excellent witnesses, both police officers, who will have to swear that I have been in this house all day. Isn't that right, Sergeant?"

"Well," grunted Breedlove, pointing to his yellow pad with a thick finger, "he didn't leave this house. That's a fact."

"Would you mind telling that boy not to stare at me?" Sidney Dexter's voice broke in. His hands were still clasped in his lap and his tone was deep and matter-of-fact, but Witt thought that his face was just half a shade more red.

"If the boy makes you feel guilty about something—" Witt began but was cut off by the other brother.

"My brother can tolerate the boy's lack of manners for a few minutes, but I would appreciate it if you would ask your questions and go, or, if you insist on looking foolish, you may arrest me. But please do one or the other or I'm afraid I shall call a lawyer."

"What have you got on the time sheet, Bollo?" Witt said, running a hand through his hair and wondering what kind of explanation he would have for the mayor, the building commissioner and the rest of the party leaders if this fell through. For Witt police work was a constant set of traps. If he got past each case cleanly and without getting caught, he would have a promising political future.

If one of the bigger cases resulted in bad publicity, his chances were set back as much as a year or more. With the help of the not overly-bright sergeant with the memory of an elephant and his grandson, he had managed to get past several big ones. It was just a matter of making it cleanly to the next primary. Only the smirking Alvin Dexter stood in his way.

"Not much on my sheet, Captain," said Breedlove, "and nothing on Art's."

"You call me?" shouted Bluet from the next room.

"No," shouted Witt. "Did you find anything?"

"No, Len," replied Bluet. "But this place is as messy as Bollo's glove compartment."

"I've got two notations on my sheet," said Breedlove. "At eleven the mailman walked up to the door, put the mail in the box and left. Dexter stuck his head out, looked over at me, and brought his mail in."

"And the other entry?" said Witt, glancing at the boy, who continued to stare at the seated Dexter brother.

"Three minutes past two a laundry truck pulled up. A uniformed laundry man with a big bundle on his shoulder came in here and came right back out again with a bundle of dirty laundry. Oh, and this fella Sidney Dexter, he drove up and came in just before you called me."

"That laundry bag," said Witt, turning his eyes to the amused Dexter, "how much was in it?"

"No, chief," sighed Breedlove, "it was heavy, but not as heavy as Dexter and not big enough either. Besides, how did he get back in even if he got out?"

Dexter chuckled and rested his hand on the shoulder of his seated brother. "Gentlemen," he said, "do you have any questions?"

Witt and Breedlove looked at each other in the hope that a question would come to mind, but none came. Witt looked at the boy, who beckoned with a finger. Witt walked over to him and leaned over to accept a whisper. The sounds of the boy's whispers came across the small room, but the Dexters and Breedlove couldn't make out the words.

After about thirty seconds, Witt rose and turned, looking as dignified as he could but realizing that dignity had to suffer when you accepted consultation from a small boy in front of a suspect.

"Bollo, when the laundry man came through the door, did you see Dexter? Did he open the door?"

"Well," the sergeant said, closing his eyes, "the laundry man just walked up and the door swung open. I didn't actually see Dexter, but I figure he saw the laundry man come up the walk and opened the door for him."

"Fine," said Witt, looking over at the boy, who nodded as he pushed his slipping glasses back on his nose. "And how long would you say the laundry man was in here? Did he come all the way in or just drop the bundle at the door?"

"He came all the way in," said Breedlove, "but he wasn't in here more than a few seconds."

"Did you see his face when he came out?"

"Well, no, he had the bundle over his shoulder and—"

"Well, I'll be," said Witt with a slight smile.

"I can make a few guesses about what you will be, Mr. Witt," Dexter said. "But I don't think you would find it very constructive. You seem to think you have some explanation of how I could have gotten out of here to commit this murder. But how did I get back in here—and where is the money I am supposed to have taken?"

Breedlove looked in bewilderment at Witt and his grandson.

"Art," Witt shouted, "did you find anything?"

"No luck," replied Bluet's voice.

"Did you find a bundle of laundry?"

"Yeah, right on the bed," came the puzzled reply.

"What company?" shouted Witt keeping his eyes on the less composed Dexters.

"Let me see," shouted Bluet. "Royal Laundry."

"Shall we just call that laundry and find out if they made a delivery here this afternoon?" said Witt.

"Please do," said Dexter. "Be my guest."

"Chief," said the boy, climbing down from the seat.

Witt looked dazed and confused. Dexter's answer wasn't right.

"Chief," said the boy again, "can I ask a few questions?"

"Uh, yes."

"Mr. Dexter," said the boy squinting at the seated brother, "where do you work?"

"I don't think that's any of your business," said Alvin, tightening his grip on his brother's shoulder to keep him quiet.

"It won't be hard for us to find out," said Witt, stepping forward.

"I work for a firm in town," said Sidney Dexter.

"The Royal Laundry?" asked Pete Breedlove.

"As a matter of fact yes, but—"

"And did you make a delivery here this afternoon?"

"Yes, this is one of my regular stops. Why shouldn't my brother be one of my customers? I object to being questioned like this. Alvin is the suspect, not me." Sidney Dexter started to rise but his brother pushed him down.

"After you left here, where did you go?"

"Look here, I didn't feel well. I called in and told the dispatcher that I was sick. I have a bad stomach and—"

"You recovered quickly," said Witt.

"I was on my way to the drug store when I heard the news broadcast and hurried over. I'm not feeling particularly well now, so if—"

"I don't get it," said Breedlove scratching his freckled head.

"It's simple, Bollo," said the boy, reaching for a cookie which was pulled out of his reach by Alvin Dexter. "Alvin was standing inside the door when his brother came with the laundry. They had it all worked out, knowing you'd be watching. Alvin was wearing one of his brother's uniforms.

"When Sidney stepped in with the clean laundry, Alvin stepped out with the dirty laundry over his shoulder to keep his face covered. Alvin then went over to kill Ramsden while his brother was in here calling the laundry and saying he was sick. He moved around in here so you'd see someone and not know it wasn't Alvin."

"But—" Breedlove began.

"And," Pete continued, eyeing the cookies, "dressed in his brother's clothes, he drove back here and came in. He gave his brother the coat and put on the robe just before you came in."

"But the money," said Breedlove.

"It's probably right out in the car," said the boy.

"You mind if we search that car, Mr. Dexter?" asked Chief Witt.

"You don't touch that car without a warrant," shouted Sidney Dexter, pushing his brother's hand aside and rising.

"Well," smiled Witt, "we can get that without too much trouble. We might even find a gun in there."

Sidney Dexter sank back in the chair and looked at his brother, whose face turned white. He was lifting the heavy cookie tray above his head with a look of hatred directed at the boy, who was turning around.

Breedlove leaped forward and landed on the murderer with a house-shaking thud that sent a snowfall of cookies into the air and a metal cookie tray clattering against the wall.

"What's going on?" said Bluet, rushing back into the room, pistol in hand.

"We caught a murderer," said Witt, grinning at the little boy, who picked up a chocolate chip which had fallen on the nearby sofa. "Have a cookie."

IT'S A WISE CHILD
WHO KNOWS

Chief Witt pulled his cap forward and slouched slightly, hoping that he would not be recognized by a passing pedestrian. Delftwood's chief-of-police did not want even a hint of suspicion to leak out that he was about to consult a twelve-year-old boy about a murder case. Political careers had been ruined by far less.

He shifted his weight and smoothed out a crease in his neatly pressed uniform as he glanced at the hulking, unkempt man at his side who drove quickly and expertly through the dark afternoon rain. "Bollo" Breedlove's ever-present smile broadened as he took his eyes off the road for an instant to look at Witt.

"Sergeant Breedlove, will you please keep your eyes on the street?" Witt pleaded.

"Yes, sir. I'm sure it's important, Chief, or Pete wouldn't have asked you to come to the house. If his leg wasn't broken, he'd come down to headquarters, like he did last year with the Decker case."

"All right, Breedlove. I'm not saying the boy didn't give us a lot of help on that case, but that was different. We've got no problem here. Everyone knows Mike Quell killed the old woman and that's that. Plenty of evidence, motive, everything we need. Will you keep your eyes on the road?"

"Right, Chief," whispered the huge driver, removing one

hand from the wheel to reach under his worn police cap and scratch a balding, freckled head.

"And besides," Witt continued, "he's been in bed with a broken leg since she was murdered. How can he have any information that we don't? Who does he think did it if it wasn't Quell?"

"Don't know," Bollo Breedlove chuckled, turning the car into a narrow driveway. "Let's see what he has to say."

"I should have my head examined," Witt muttered, getting out of the parked car and waiting while Breedlove lumbered out to join him. "What could your grandson know about this that we don't?" Breedlove smiled and shrugged. The two men made their way to the front porch of the well-maintained, but aged little frame house.

"I'm home," Breedlove said, stepping into the warm living room. Witt walked in behind him, removing his cap and brushing back his neatly combed gray hair.

Witt had been in the house a few times in the five years he had been Delftwood's chief of police and the atmosphere always made him sleepy. Breedlove, his daughter-in-law and his grandson lived quietly and comfortably, seldom mentioning Walt Junior, who had died in Korea.

"Chief Witt, it's nice to see you again," said Kate Breedlove, coming into the room with her hand outstretched. "How is your wife and the children?"

"Fine," Witt replied, noticing the tiny blonde's flour-marked hands and apron. "Don't let us keep you. We just stopped by to see Pete."

"Well, he's still in his bed so you won't have any trouble finding him." She sighed. "I think I'll throw a block party when he gets on his feet and back to school. Did you ever try to keep a bed-bound twelve-year-old boy from getting bored? Don't bother to answer. Would you like a drink, Chief? Walt?"

The two men refused and Kate returned to the kitchen. Breedlove grinned and led the way down a short hall and into the small bedroom. A chubby, blond boy in blue flannel pajamas with white circles paused in his attempt to scratch an itch under the plaster cast and looked up at the two men.

"Hi, Bollo. Hi, Chief. This thing really itches like crazy."

Breedlove cleared a pile of books from the bed and sat down next to the boy, whose hair he ruffled playfully. Witt sat in a straw chair next to the bed and cleared his throat.

"About the murder, Pete," said Witt.

"You mean Miss Quell, or the one I figured out last year?" replied the boy, trying again to scratch his covered leg.

"I thought we decided that we worked together last year," said Witt.

"Yeah, I guess we did. Well, with Miss Quell, I know who killed her."

"We all know," added Witt quickly. "It was Mike, her nephew."

"I read that in the Delftwood *News-Director*, but that's wrong. Bollo told me about the case, and I—"

"Wait," said Witt. "The facts are simple. Miss Beatrice Quell—"

"Quashy Quell, we called her," mumbled the boy. "Fattest woman in Delftwood."

"Pete, you don't talk that way about the dead," said Breedlove.

"Sorry, Bollo."

"May I continue?" Witt whispered. "Thank you. At exactly nine o'clock Monday night, just as the church tower bell rang, Miss Quell called headquarters and Officer Lydecker answered the phone. She said, and he recognized her voice, 'This is Beatrice Quell and—' Before she could say more, and while the tower bell was still ringing, Lydecker heard a shot over the phone and that was it.

"Lydecker sent a car over and called me. I immediately had her three nephews picked up. Had them within ten minutes. Meanwhile I got to Miss Quell's house about the same time as the patrol car. Both doors were locked. All windows were locked from the inside. We broke down the back door, went in and found Miss Quell, all two hundred forty pounds of her, on the living room floor with the phone in her hand and a bullet in her heart. All clear so far?"

"Sure," said the boy who had stopped scratching and was now chewing on his pajamas.

"Fine. We check and find from one of the nephews, Al Quell over at Quell's Drug Store, that the locks at Miss Quell's had been changed that morning and only the three nephews and the old woman had keys. We found hers in her purse.

"We checked with the locksmith and he says no other keys were made and only those keys could open the doors. The nephews all had their keys on them when we picked them up. No one knows whose idea it was to change the locks, but the old woman was a bit of a nut anyway.

"So, with all the doors locked, the logical conclusion is that someone with a key, one of the three nephews, killed the old lady, locked the door and ran. They all stand to make a lot of money. She was loaded. So we began to check alibis, and—"

"Chief," said the boy, "did you check the locksmith's alibi?"

The chief grinned for the first time.

"Yes, we checked him for nine o clock. He was at an Elks meeting; plenty of witnesses. We also checked the possibility of a duplicate key being made. It's a tricky lock and it would have taken a few days to get the right matrix from Chicago. So, excluding the possibility that one of the nephews had an accomplice, we started to check their alibis for nine o' clock."

"I know why it couldn't be an accomplice," the boy said brightly. "Because if the nephews had the keys on them just a little after the murder, someone would have had to give it to them if that someone were the murderer, and except for Mike, the others were too far away from the house a few minutes later, and no accomplice would have had time to meet them."

"Very clever," said Witt.

"Sure is," agreed Breedlove.

"To continue," Witt went on, "at nine o' clock Al Quell was locking his drug store a mile away. Plenty of people around. Steven Quell—"

"Skinny Minnie Quell," mumbled the boy.

"Steven Quell," Witt went on, "was walking down Center Street and saw his brother locking his store. He remembers seeing who was with him. Half a block further down Center Street he saw the Collins twins in front of the Fox Theater. Both twins remember that it was exactly nine, because the—"

"Church bell was ringing," said Pete Breedlove.

"Right," continued Witt with a frown, "and they were just in time for the feature, which started at a minute after nine. Not only that, but Steve Quell saw Officer Jack Meany giving a ticket to a short, fat man, and Meany's report for the night shows that at exactly nine o' clock he stopped under a street light at First and Center to give a ticket to a Mr. Katz, a short, fat man who had smashed his car into a light pole. I think that is sufficient alibi for Steve Quell."

"He used to be a bird watcher," Pete replied, reaching over the side of his bed and pulling up an old notebook.

"Yes, but it has nothing to do with the case." Witt shifted slightly. "Well, to continue. Mike Quell, a surly ba—son of a gun, has less than an alibi. Claims someone called him and told him to get down to the old boat house in Cove Woods, behind Miss Quell's house. This so-called caller said they or he'd found something valuable belonging to Mike.

"So, according to a half-sober Mike Quell, at exactly nine he was alone, about one hundred yards from the scene of the murder. Item two, Mike Quell admits owning a thirty-eight automatic, which is now missing. Miss Quell was killed with a thirty-eight. Item three, all the nephews knew they would share the old woman's estate when she went, but Mike is the one who seems most anxious to get his hands on it.

"Add to this the public knowledge that Miss Quell had been threatening to cut him out of her will unless he stopped drinking, and you've got a pretty good motive."

"Mike Quell is the best shortstop Delftwood High ever had," said Pete, looking absently through the notebook.

"That doesn't make him innocent," Witt added quickly.

"He didn't do it," said the boy. "Did he, Bollo?"

The fat man scratched his head and shrugged.

"If I show someone else could have done it, will you get me a new baseball glove?" said the boy slyly.

Kate Breedlove walked into the room with coffee for the men and a glass of chocolate milk for Pete, who downed it in two long gulps before Kate had stepped out of the room.

"If you show that someone else did it, or could have done it, I'll give you a new baseball glove," said Witt, sipping at the welcomed coffee which might help to hold off the migraine he feared was on the way.

"That's a deal, Chief. You heard it, Bollo."

"Yup, but wipe the milk off your mouth."

"Well," the boy beamed, looking down at his notebook, "there are a couple of things to get straight first. Miss Quell's house is way up on Cove Hill over Delftwood. The living room where she was found faces out into the woods away from town."

"This is not new information," said Witt, spying with some distaste a still existent chocolate mustache on the boy's upper lip.

"I know, but listen. Nobody heard the shot, Bollo says, because it's a pretty thick old house and there aren't any neighbors nearby."

"Wait," Witt said. "Officer Lydecker heard the shot over the phone."

"Sure, but—" Pete's excited arms were in the air. "Just listen. When Bollo told me about the murder, some things hit me as pretty funny. Like the murder taking place at exactly nine and the murderer letting her use the phone, and the locks being changed that morning and the murderer locking the door behind him."

"Coincidence," Witt sighed, finishing his coffee. "Locking the door was Mike Quell's mistake. If he had left it open, we'd never have been able to narrow it down to the nephews. It happens all the time. Mike had a fight with the old lady. She got mad when he pulled out a gun and started a fuss. She called the police. He shot her, panicked, locked the door, ran into the woods and threw the gun away. He couldn't even come up with a decent story."

"But," said the boy, reading from his notes, "if Mike is telling the truth, then someone has done a good job of making it look like he's the murderer. Now who would do that but one of the other nephews? With Mike gone they would split the old lady's money only two ways."

"Is that what kids do now?" Witt addressed Breedlove. "Sit around thinking about murder?"

"Chief," the boy said. "So maybe one of the others wanted it to look like Mike did it. Maybe the one who did it wanted everyone to know she was killed at exactly nine, when Mike was in the woods at the boat house. If that's true, then the killer must have set up an alibi for nine to cover himself."

"I'd say both of the others have perfect alibis," Witt said, placing his empty cup on the floor.

"That's it, that's it!" shouted Pete Breedlove. "They both don't have perfect alibis. At nine Al Quell was closing his drug store. A customer saw him and Skinny Minnie, I mean Steve Quell, saw him too. But who saw Steve Quell?"

Witt tried to hide the look of disgust as he vowed to tell Bollo Breedlove to stop discussing cases with the boy.

"Look," Witt said, lifting his right hand and counting off the fingers, "Steve was on Center Street, a mile from the murder. He saw his brother close his store at exactly nine. He saw the Collins twins in front of the Fox Theater at exactly nine. He saw Officer Meany giving this guy Katz a ticket at exactly nine."

"That's what I mean," said the boy, laying his notes aside and gritting his teeth for another assault on his itching leg. "He saw them all at exactly nine. The Fox Theater is a block away from the Drug Store. Meany, according to Bollo, was another block down. At exactly nine, Steve Quell saw three things taking place about two and a half blocks from each other."

"Wait a minute!" Witt grinned and put up a hand. "Al Quell might have closed a minute or two early. Meany might have been a minute or two off. The twins were sure of the time, but—"

"But nobody saw Steve Quell," Pete insisted. "To see all that he would probably have to hurry down the street, but no one saw him, and how come he didn't say anything about seeing that guy Katz's car against the pole? Bollo says it was where he would have to pass at about nine."

"He forgot," said Witt.

"Maybe," said the boy. "But Bollo checked and Steve says he might have seen the wreck, but didn't pay any attention. That seems pretty funny unless he didn't see the wreck at all. So I had an idea. Bollo went up to Miss Quell's last night to see if there's a room in back of the house where you can see Center Street."

"Breedlove," Witt whispered grimly, feeling the headache coming. "Did you go up there without telling me?"

"Well, Chief, you see—"

"We'll talk about it later."

"So," said the boy, "Bollo did find one room. With a pair of binoculars, he could see some good lighted—"

"Well lighted," Breedlove interrupted.

"Yeah, well lighted places on the right side of Center Street like the drug store, the front of the Fox and under the light where Meany gave the ticket. But he couldn't see the left side, where the wreck would have been."

"Hold on!" Witt shouted and stood up. "Where was this room?"

"Top floor," said Breedlove. "In back."

"Right," said Witt with a smile. "How could he be on the fourth floor in the back establishing an alibi at exactly nine, while he was murdering his aunt in the living room? And don't tell me he killed her up there and dragged her down to the living room. She weighed a good two-hundred-forty, compared to his soaking wet one-hundred-thirty or one-hundred-forty.

"By the time he got the body down, we would have been there. Besides, there wasn't a mark on her to show she had been bumped or dragged. Even if he could have lifted her, it would have taken him five or six minutes to get her to the living room."

"It would have taken at least ten minutes to get her down," Breedlove whispered. "Pete had me take a keg of nails down from there."

"Yes," said Pete, "and Bollo's strong and the nails only weighed one-hundred-fifty pounds."

"Well, I'm not all that strong," said Breedlove, blushing.

"Save the family compliments for some other time," Witt shouted, placing a hand on his forehead. "You admit he couldn't have got her down."

"Oh, yes sir," said the boy. "But there is a telephone in that room."

"So?"

Pete Breedlove leaned forward and spoke softly.

"Suppose he shot her in the living room before nine, and then went up to the back room on the fourth floor. Then suppose he had a tape recorder with a tape of her voice saying 'This is Beatrice Quell.' That wouldn't be hard for him to get. So he stood at the window with his binoculars, dialed police headquarters, and when he heard Lydecker, turned on her voice and the pre-recorded shot that he could have got any time.

"While Lydecker was listening, Steve Quell was looking down at Center Street. Then he hung up the phone, ran down the stairs, took the living room phone off the hook, locked the door and left."

"No, wait a minute," cried Witt. "This is—where would he get binoculars and a tape recorder? Why?"

"He's a bird watcher," said Pete Breedlove. "He watches birds, records them in Cove Woods."

Witt's eyes wandered around the room as his headache swelled. A University of Illinois pennant danced over the quilted bed. Autographed photos of ball players surrounded him.

"But," Witt gasped, "the gun. We picked him up just a few minutes after nine. Officers Meany and Carl picked him up and he had no gun."

"Threw it in Cove Woods. Probably stole it from Mike."

"The binoculars and tape recorder," Witt muttered, sitting down again. "He couldn't throw them away. We might find them, trace them to him."

"Easy," said the boy. "He could erase the tape on his way downtown. He wanted to get to Center Street fast. Was he carrying anything when Meany and Carl found him?"

"Yes," said Bollo proudly. "I told you yesterday, Pete."

"But," said Witt, "he didn't have binoculars or a tape recorder in his briefcase."

"Are you sure?" asked Pete. "Or did you just ask them to search him for a gun?"

Witt pulled himself together and stood again. "We can settle it easily enough. I'll just call Meany." He went to the phone next to the boy's bed and dialed a number.

"This is Chief Witt. Is your father there? Hello, Meany. Listen. You and Carl searched Steve Quell the night of the murder. I know he had no gun, but did he have a small tape recorder and a pair of binoculars in his briefcase? I see. No. I'll see you in the morning." He hung up and turned to the two Breedloves, who looked up at him with wide eyes.

"Tape recorder, yes. Binoculars, no," mumbled Witt.

"No binoculars?" the boy sighed.

"No," said Witt, fumbling in his pocket for a migraine pill. "But he did happen to have a collapsible telescope."

"Should I pick up Steve Quell, Chief?" Breedlove said with a wide smile and proud glance at his scratching grandson.

"Yes," said Witt. "We'll question him in my office. And Breedlove, let's just keep quiet for the time being about Pete's part in this."

"Right, Chief." Breedlove rose and shook his grandson's pudgy hand.

"Okay with you, Pete?" said the fat man.

"Sure. I think I'd like a Maury Wills model."

"What?" said the chief.

"Maury Wills model baseball glove," explained Bollo Breedlove on his way out.

"Of course," Witt sighed and stood up to follow the sergeant.

As he turned to the door a chubby, blond twelve-year-old boy reached under his pillow for a stack of baseball cards. The top card was a full-color reproduction of Maury Wills.

HERE COMES THE INTERESTING PART

CHARACTERS

MORT, a young man, about 30 years old

EDDIE, a slightly younger Negro man

WALTER, a derelict

WOMAN

FARBER, Mort and Eddie's boss

MAMA, Mort's mother

BARTENDER, a friend

OLD MAN, a realist

NOTE: *the same actor should play FARBER, MAMA, BARTENDER, and the OLD MAN.*

SCENE: *An alley. Three doors, rear exits of small stores, are visible. There is a light above the center door. A fire escape climbs to a window above the door on the right. Trash barrels are stacked under the fire escape and there is a barrel in front of each door. Above the door on the left is a small platform which remains in total darkness except during flashbacks. It is about 2 A.M. on a March morning.* MORT *and* EDDIE *enter from left.* MORT *is short, stocky, and about 30 years old. He is wearing a turtleneck sweater and carrying a heavy, battered gym bag.* EDDIE *is a tall, thin Negro a few years younger than* MORT. *In one hand,* EDDIE *carries a trumpet case. In the other, he carries a dolly (a flat, thick*

*slab of wood about two feet square with small wheels mounted in
each of four corners.*) EDDIE *is wearing a leather jacket. They put
their bundles on the ground and look at the doors.*

MORT: There it is.

EDDIE: Which one? They all look alike.

MORT: They all look alike to you. Behind that door is a
small, fat safe filled to the hinges with one, two, five, ten, and
twenty dollar bills.

EDDIE: Well, which one? How do you know which door it
is?

MORT: How does a salmon know it should swim up-
stream? How does a duck know it should fly south? How does
a lemming know it's suicide time? Trust me, Eddie. I know
what I'm doing. Maybe for the first time in my life, I know
what's to be done.

EDDIE: Then let's do it, Mort. Let's do it and get the car
back to my brother.

MORT: Did you leave the motor running?

EDDIE: It's running. Honest to God. It's running. Now
let's go, huh?

MORT: Hurry, hurry, hurry, hurry, hurry. How many
years are we going to hurry around in little circles? Do you
know what I've got in my head?

EDDIE: A cold.

MORT: No, Eddie, ideas. I've got ideas for a great novel in
my head and I'm going to stop hurrying and write it. And that
takes time and you've got to buy time. And that costs money.
You understand now?

EDDIE: Hell no, Mort. Let's get going. My brother finds
out I took the car he'll tear my arm off.

MORT: I'll explain.

EDDIE: You've explained, a thousand times. If you've
got to do it again, wait till we get out of here. I'm getting

cold and someone might come.

MORT: What have you got in your head, Eddie?

EDDIE: Please, Mort.

MORT: What have you got in your head? I'm trying to make a point. Stop worrying about that car. Stop worrying about warm beds, thick steaks, happy relatives, smiling bosses, ugly cops, the finance company. Worry about where you're going. Eddie, you've got music in your head. That music should come out. It shouldn't be bottled up with income tax and grocery bills. What do you think about all day while you put handles on long lines of plastic suitcases?

EDDIE: Women, music, beer, baseball.

MORT: You are a goddam artist. You think about playing your trumpet. I watch your fingers moving, your mouth humming, your thoughts flying.

EDDIE: Music. When I work a wedding, I play the "Anniversary Waltz, Hail, Hail, the Gang's All Here" at every union meeting, and every bar mitzvah I play happy bar mitzvah boy to the tune of "My Wild Irish Rose." A goddam artist. Now let's get that door open and get out of here.

MORT: I tell you there is beautiful music in your head. It floats around your brain and into your chest. I've heard you play like you were going to break into flowers. Am I right?

EDDIE: I guess.

MORT: You know what that money can do? It can buy you a lifetime of beautiful music and it can get me away from all the hands that have been holding my pants legs for thirty years.

EDDIE: Man, it can buy me a car, a warm bed and all that goes with it. Beautiful music is all right, but when you're cold, you're cold and I'm cold even in the long, hot summer.

MORT: You've got no imagination, but you've got a soul. I forgive you because you've got a soul.

EDDIE: And my brother's got a car standing over there eating gas. He may be a heavy sleeper, but if he happens to hear one of the kids crying and gets up, and sees the car is gone . . . Mort, I can't play my trumpet in jail and you won't get much writing done there either.

MORT: I could write in jail. Look at Malory, Cervantes, Boethius, Sir Walter Raleigh.

EDDIE: I don't know them, but if they were as cold as I am, they'd get the hell out of here. My brother's car. . . .

MORT: Cars and brothers, [*As he speaks, he takes a crow bar from the black satchel he was carrying, advances to one of the doors, and begins to work on it.*] worries and bills, bombs and babies, disease and religion.

[*Stage lights dim and platform above the door on the left is illuminated revealing* MR. FARBER, *a cigar-chomping, sleeves-rolled-up, loose-tied, sixty-five-year-old self-made boss. There is a large barrel in front of him with the word "Glue" clearly stenciled.*]

FARBER: You call this glue? This matzo meal could not hold together two very thin sheets of toilet paper. You want glue, not kiddie paste. [*He stirs the glue with a broom handle.*] Morton, your mother told you I used to sew together potato sacks when I first came to this country? I used to. Now look. I got a factory, thirty-four workers, a partner with an ulcer, union troubles, a bad back, a daughter with a dumb, bum husband, a grandson who burps in my face. I'm what you call a success. You want to know how I got this way? I worked day and night, thirty-seven hours a day, every day including Sundays. [*over his shoulder*] Right, Meyer? What do you know. How is that left gasket holding up, Morton? Good. Your mother wants I should tell you something. How old are you, may I ask? Your mother tells me you sit in your room writing stories, you drink beer, you don't get married. You're a large boy. You are a good worker. Right, Meyer? Ah, what does

Meyer know, I say you're a good worker. Listen, while I think of it, don't put the handles so close together when they come off the line. It blocks the paint. You look at me like you're looking through me. You think maybe I don't know what's in your head? I know that belt in front of you. There's a white scratch on it. Every six and three-quarter minutes that scratch comes back around the belt. How many times do you see that scratch each day, each week, each month, each year? I know. I know. There's a fact in that glue barrel, my boy. If you don't want to count scratches on a belt all your life, you mix good glue now instead of thinking about how you'd like to be in some fancy New York apartment with hundreds of girls running around in clean underwear. Even Farber never had such things. Right, Meyer. Confidentially, if Meyer were not my son, I would fire him as quickly as I could spit. Providing of course he wasn't a union member, God forbid. Now this is glue. And Morton, here comes the interesting part, that's all there is to life . . . mixing good glue, reading a good book, having a few bucks, not hurting anybody. You understand what I mean? So go back to the machine, turn out lots of handles and be careful you don't get your finger caught in the gears like Julius a few years ago. [*over his shoulder*] No, Meyer, you can't go home. Because it's ten in the morning, that's why. Morton, try to keep the glue like this. A twenty-cent an hour raise next month would not be an impossibility. [*Fades out. Stage lights rise revealing* MORT *working on the door.*]

MORT: We won't ever have to go back to that factory again, Eddie.

EDDIE: Except to pick up our pay checks for last week. Say, Mort, how much do you figure is in the safe?

MORT: More than $20,000.

EDDIE: Are you sure?

MORT: For weeks I've been watching him. I've been going in that store for weeks buying root beers and looking at the old man from behind dark glasses. He piles every penny in that safe. He never goes to the bank. He never leaves the store. My mother can hardly remember when he moved in. He must have been here for forty years. Forty years putting dollar bills in that safe. Forty years giving out sticky jaw breakers and bottles of coke. And why? That old jerk has been going around in circles his whole life and some morning he'll wake up dead and some cop will get that money or some relative who hasn't sent him a birthday card since 1936.

EDDIE: Stealing money from an old man though.

MORT: What about us? We can't help it if everyone wants to sit around waiting to die so someone can sell their bones to a costume jewelry factory. You understand me?

EDDIE: You feel lousy about it, don't you, Mort.

MORT: All right, all right. So I feel lousy, but have you got a better idea? Should we forget about it and go back to the factory? I tell you if there was a devil to sell my soul to I'd do it, but I've tried calling him and no one comes. We've got to do it ourselves or it won't get done.

EDDIE: The factory isn't so bad.

MORT: Factory, filling station, candy store. I tell you it's death. Thirty or forty years from now I'll drop dead on my way home with half a sandwich from lunch under my arm. Some guy'll run up to me and with my last breath I'll say, "Be sure to have Eddie dye that last batch of handles before they go on the line." What kind of last words are those for someone who has a head full of thoughts and a body full of feelings?

EDDIE: Okay, okay. Then let's get it over before someone comes.

MORT: Nobody is going to come at this time of the

morning in this rotten weather.

EDDIE: What about a cop?

MORT: We tell him we're electricians just like we planned.

EDDIE: We don't look like electricians.

MORT: How do electricians look? If you tickle them, do they not laugh? If you torture them, do they not cry?

EDDIE: Who the hell is talking about tickling and torturing electricians? I just said we don't look like electricians. We don't know anything about electricity.

MORT: Alternating current is a current the direction of which reverses at regular, recurring intervals. Unless distinctly otherwise specified, the term alternating current refers to a periodically varying current with successive half waves of the same shape and area.

EDDIE: Where did you get that?

MORT: A library book.

EDDIE: It's real pretty, but what does it mean?

MORT: I don't know. It's magic or maybe it's Russian. I don't know everything. My head is filled with ideas not facts. If you get too many facts in your head, they make you a scientist and you invent color television, stamp plans, and hydrogen bombs.

EDDIE: How are you going to get a cop to listen to you talk about alternating current?

MORT: I'll get it in somehow and when I get it in he'll feel ashamed and shrink back from the magic incantation of science.

EDDIE: Let's give it up, Mort. Let's go to Charlie's, have a beer and go home.

MORT: Go home. You know how much of my novel I've written in the past five years? Eleven pages. Eleven stinking pages. If I walk away from here now, I'll never finish it. Never. There's too much in the way. The factory is in the way. [*He takes a hammer and chisel to the door and speaks as he starts working again*] Rent is in the way. Laziness is in the way. Fear is in the way. My mother is in the way. Hunger is in the way. . . . [*Stage lights dim and the platform where* FARBER *stood is illuminated again. On the platform a woman,* MORT'*s mother, sits in front of a television set with its back to the audience.*]

MOM: Mort? Is that you? Don't forget to take your shoes off and step on the newspaper. Your dinner is on the table. Eat your barley and cabbage soup first. So you don't like it. It's good for you. A lot of things I don't like, but I do them. Just because you make the money is no reason you should be fresh to your mother. Eat your soup. Thank you, but I don't want any soup. I don't like soup. So it's the same color you used on the suitcase handles today. Listen, Morton, I've got bad news. Aunt Estelle's sister died. Of course it's too bad. Is that all you've got to say? An aunt's sister dies and you got nothing to say. Sure you know Aunt Estelle. Your father's cousin. The one who lives in New York. Such a young woman, her sister. Only sixty-eight. I never actually met her. Once on the phone I talked to her. All the New York relatives got on the phone and one of them was Aunt Estelle's sister. At least that's what your father said. I'm sick from the news. You want some butterscotch pudding? Of course it's instant pudding. You think I would stand swizzling pudding for an hour? Look. All those decays. Such young children and all those decays. Her sister got all the good toothpaste and that poor little girl will have to carry around a mouth full of gold. Now look. Such a headache that poor man has. Of course he'll take one of those little tablets and be all right, but look at him suffer. So he's an actor. I shouldn't feel sorry for him because he's an actor? I knew several actors in the Yiddish theater who were not such bad people. Your father knew an actor. His name, the actor not your father, was Tishman. So let me finish. See. He took the pill and he's smiling and playing golf. So Tishman fooled with the girls. But that's another story which I will tell you when you get married. You just came in and already you're going out. You got a girl? What's the matter, Eddie can't come over here? I tell him the truth, don't I? A boy like that should be a freedom rider. He should be organizing sit-ins. But he sits like a lump. Both of you sit like lumps. Your father, God rest his soul, was trying to organize sit-ins twenty years ago. He got the union into Farber's factory, didn't he? So you don't like union dues. That's the interesting part. You don't like union dues. You don't like television. You don't like relatives. You don't like nice girls. So where you running? You didn't finish your butterscotch pudding. [*She shrugs, turns to the television set. The platform darkens and* MORT's *voice is heard as the alley again becomes visible.*]

MORT: And I'm in the way. Four walls and a roof are in my way and you want to know what can get rid of them?

EDDIE: An operation?

MORT: Money. And it's on the other side of that wall. [*He swings hammer against chisel.*] Your brother must be a lousy mechanic. This damn chisel is blunt. The drill is dull. How can he fix cars with them when I can't use them to tear down a door?

EDDIE: What's one thing got to do with the other?

MORT: I don't know. I don't know. What do you think I am, a genius or something? I can't keep the details of a thousand trades in my head. It's a waste of time. You get some professor who spends ninety-nine years filling his head with knowledge and what happens?

EDDIE: How should I know? You're the one who's not a genius, not me.

MORT: I'll tell you what happens. Bango. He's dead. His

head swells with facts. His mind bulges with fears. That is the plain unscientific truth. He doesn't die immediately. He leaves his facts in brown and green pebble-covered books that get moldy in dark sub-cellars of college libraries. [*He makes another attempt to open the door and stops.*] I'm in rotten shape. You work on it for a while.

EDDIE: You know what your trouble is, Mort. [*He takes some tools and works on the door.*] You're an anti-intellectual.

MORT: Now where did you get that nutty idea?

EDDIE: You told me yesterday. You said, "Eddie, I'm a damn anti-intellectual, and that's a fact."

MORT: I'm anti a lot of things.

EDDIE: I was thinking I'd better turn the motor off. My brother finds out I used all that gas. . . .

MORT: Small. Thinking small. It gets us all. Day after day after year and then it's too late and we're dead. About a year ago after playing basketball at the Y.M.C.A. I was taking a shower in the locker room and singing Greensleeves when all of a sudden I felt that I was going to slip on the floor and crack my head. I could picture rivulets of blood and people jumping over my body. I reached for the wall and inched my way past a fat man with a mustache. I got back to my locker, dressed and stopped playing basketball. The hell with your brother. The hell with everything. [*He goes to the door again.*] Let's get this door down.

EDDIE: Okay, but let's hurry up.

MORT: It will be opened when it's opened. Now relax.

EDDIE: I'm trying.

MORT: [*He throws himself against the door and the door flies open.*] We did it. [*He steps in.*]

EDDIE: Did you find the safe? Do you want the dolly? Mort? Mort. Are you in there? Mort, answer me or I'm going to get the hell out of here.

MORT: [*comes out slowly.*] Eddie.

EDDIE: It's the wrong door, isn't it?

MORT: We should have known. We should have expected it. If you expect it, it's not so hard.

EDDIE: Let's go, Mort. We can still get the car back before my brother finds out has car is missing.

MORT: Eddie. Look around you. What do you see?

EDDIE: Let's just get out of here.

MORT: What do you see?

EDDIE: An alley.

MORT: That's right. But outside this alley there's another alley and another one and another one, but it's painted different colors so you don't know it's an alley. You never look around at the garbage cans. Everybody walks around with one eye on the ground looking for pennies and one eye in the sky looking for pie or missiles. So they're always bumping into people and things they should have seen half a block away.

EDDIE: This is an alley, isn't it?

MORT: On the other side of one of those doors is a safe. Inside that safe is money. With the money in that safe you can get away from this alley to some nice little place on a hill overlooking a nice little lake.

EDDIE: I don't like water, I'm scared of drowning. I don't like high places. I don't want to be on any hill. I see an alley and you better start seeing alley.

MORT: Things aren't going your way so you have to get nasty again.

EDDIE: How come every time I tell you what's really going on, you tell me I'm getting nasty?

WALTER: [*popping up from behind a garbage can*] Because he is human; crude, imperfect, but human, nonetheless.

MORT: All right, mister. You're going to have to clear out

of here. We've got some dangerous wiring to take care of here. We're electricians and. . . .

WALTER: [*climbing out from between the garbage cans*] Static electricians. I forgive your masquerade, however, and bless your enterprise. I merely would like to take a small share in your profits. Let it be clear that I am begging, not borrowing.

MORT: I tell you we're electricians and we've got no time to waste. The wiring has to be done by morning.

WALTER: You have the nerve born of desperation. I've seen it before and sympathize with you.

MORT: Is that right? Well, do you know that alternating current is the current the direction of which reverses at irregular recurring intervals. Unless distinctly otherwise specified, the term alternating current refers to a periodically varying current with successive half waves of the same shape and area.

WALTER: Is that your general incantation for making evil spirits return to the netherworld? If so I should point out that the direction reverses at regular, not irregular intervals. Now you young men can save a lot of time by just continuing with your work while I pretend to be asleep and unconcerned.

EDDIE: Let's give him a few bucks, Mort, or let's get out of here.

MORT: You think all he wants is a few bucks? He wants a share and I don't intend to go into socialized burglary.

WALTER: I can't decide if you are an abnormally young man for your age or you are a fool. Inside that door you will need four or five years to discover what I know. To discover there is nothing to discover. If you're not lucky, you'll never find out. I am a bum, a seeker of the usable refuse of others. The more usable the refuse, the happier I am. Therefore, I will be quite satisfied with one-third of whatever you get in there. Of course it is understood that I am just a poor bum, perhaps a drunken one, who knows nothing about your project.

EDDIE: I'll tell you what, mister. You can have the whole thing. I'll give you a hammer and we'll get out of here. Mort, let's get out of here.

MORT: [*to* WALTER] You're in, but for a fourth, not a third.

WALTER: I'll not quip and quibble about percentages. I seek not personal gain, but personal comfort. In fact I will settle for two hundred dollars cash right now. Enough to buy some new clothes, a shave, many meals and relaxation, but not enough to tempt me into Indian wrestling at the super-market.

EDDIE: He's drunk or nuts. Let's get out of here.

WALTER: Young man, I wish you would stop saying, "Let's get out of here." It's very annoying.

MORT: We're staying. I saw him in a dream last night and he's not going to stop us.

WALTER: Divine portents. What was your dream? I am no oracle, but I have read the pocketbook of dreams.

EDDIE: I can really wait till later to hear about it.

MORT: I dreamed I was reaching out for a pile of cash when you jumped in front of me and said, "I am a messenger of God. Touch that and man will vanish from the earth for your sin."

WALTER: What did you do?

MORT: I kneed you in the groin, took the money and ran.

WALTER: In my case . . . it is much easier to give me the few dollars I beg. Besides I am an expert in Karate [*he makes a few passes with his hands*] or I may be. In life, unlike dreams, it is easier and more profitable to compromise for a few dollars with a faded gentleman in an alley than it is to slay an angel in a dream. That is a new American proverb which I just created.

Stuart Kaminsky

MORT: Let's get the door open. [*He returns to door.*]
[*Lights dim to end scene.*]

SCENE TWO

(*Stage is dark, but a smooth jazz record can be heard, probably Duke Ellington's "Mood Indigo." Platform lights up, but with a colored light, probably blue, to reveal the* BARTENDER. *The* BARTENDER *is the same actor who plays* FARBER *and* MOTHER.)

BARTENDER: So how is it outside tonight, Mort? In here, day and night, it looks like a steam bath. See those kids playing shuffleboard? Would you think they're twenty-one years old? I must be getting old. I feel like a criminal serving them, but what can I do? Why don't you go over there and beat their pants off in a shuffleboard game or two till Eddie comes? You look terrible. I mean even in here you look white. Is there something wrong? Did I tell you, Rita is coming in tonight? All right, you don't care. I wish I could have a beer. It's miserable to sit here all day giving it out and watching them forget their lives while they watch the ball game on color television. It's my ulcer. You think only Edsel Ford can have an ulcer? Sure, I'm a philosopher. All bartenders are philosophers. It's too dark in a bar to read and you got nothing to do all day but think. But you. I don't like to lose business, but you're here just about every night, you and Eddie. A smart kid like you should be out hustling girls, making a buck or writing that book you're always talking about. Okay, okay, don't get sore. I don't care when you write your book. You pay cash and you treat Rita nice and you never cause trouble so why the hell should I care? Did I tell you my wife has a gall bladder problem? [*The music changes and a rock and roll song comes on.*] Those kids. I forgot I even had that thing on there.

Maybe they'll run out of nickels, get a little drunk and join the Peace Corps. [*Music gets louder.*] Here, you kids, don't turn that juke box up. It's loud enough. All right, you're not kids, you're men. So men turn the music back down. Thank you. And leave it that way. I must be getting old. Did I tell you about my wife's gall. . . . [*Lights fade and he disappears in darkness as stage lights rise to reveal* MORT, EDDIE, *and* WALTER.]

WALTER: How are you gentlemen doing?

MORT: We're doing all right. Nothing's going to stop us, nothing. [*He hammers at door.*]

WALTER: You are a poor fool convinced that fate will stop at nothing to make you suffer unless you meet her with a hammer in your hand. So sure that chance will punish you for living. Jobian self-interest like yours deserves the pain it inflicts upon itself.

EDDIE: Talking, talking. You two keep talking and not saying anything. Let's do something. My brother is mean and big and if I don't get that car back before he misses it, he's going to bounce me down the stairs and no words or pile of dollars will ease the landing.

WALTER: The voice of reality. I admire it. I was once a realist. I was so afraid my head would get wet when it rained that I never ventured outside. I stayed home, repaired bicycles in my shop, read books, agreed with my wife's insistence that we needed more money, smiled at my children who had the bad fortune to look like me, and watched the daily papers to see if my obituary had yet appeared.

EDDIE: You're nuts. I tell you, Mort, he's nuts.

WALTER: That's what I thought too, at first. I looked around and could see nobody else looking for his obituary in the paper and I saw many people walking the streets without worrying about the rain. So I put down my bicycle pump, threw a rain coat over my head and rushed to the drug store

hoping and praying the pharmacist could cure me with a tran-
quilizer. The pharmacist smiled, said it might not rain, sold
me some ice cream and postage stamps and asked how much
I would charge to fix his son's new Schwinn. I decided I
should remain insane and stop worrying. So I left the drug
store with a pint of fudge ripple and have wandered ever
since, waiting. [MORT *thrusts his shoulder against the door and
bursts through.*]

EDDIE: [*looking into the doorway*] I'll back the car up and
get some rope. Do you need the flashlight? Mort, for
Chrissake answer me. [MORT *comes out slowly, teeth clenched
in anger.*]

WALTER: There is one great consolation. We know for a
fact that the next door is the right one.

EDDIE: Mort, I don't want to be a pest, but I've had it. I'm
taking the car and getting out of here.

MORT: One more door. You'll never forgive yourself if you
go now. You'll dream about that door and that money. One
more door.

WALTER: There is always one more door. That's the
secret. You get through the last one and find it's not the last
one. There's one right behind it and you keep going through
them until you die or you give up and decide to live on this
side of the door, which you find intolerable.

MORT: You shut up with your paperback philosophy. I'm
telling you, Eddie, if you go away you'll never stop thinking
about the food, women, cars, clothes.

WALTER: While in my garbage can I do recall an echo
speaking of art in the alley.

MORT: Eddie, please. For me.

EDDIE: All right, but let's get that door open quick. [*A
woman enters from the left. She is about forty, wearing a robe, in
curlers.*]

WOMAN: What is going on here? What is all this noise and who are all of you?

WALTER: Madame, are you taking a formal survey or just displaying normal curiosity?

WOMAN: I am a mother and as a mother I have a right to know. I have a duty, both as a mother and as a citizen, to be sure that nothing immoral or indecent is going on in this alley. My husband, a hard-working man, spends many hours each day in the rubber cement factory. Right now he is trying to sleep. He has to get up in a few hours. He was up late watching "Drifters on the Range" with Ken Maynard and his horse Tarzan. In a few hours, I have to make him breakfast. I also have to make breakfast for my son, Lucius Eban Allen, who is not doing well in school, but he, as they have assured me, is a slow learner, not unlike his sainted grandfather, God rest his soul, after whom he is named. I hope you understand me. Now who are you and what are you doing in this alley?

WALTER: In reply to your very moving family history, I can only say that I am a bum. I cannot, however, speak for these gentlemen.

MORT: We're electricians, lady. Do you know that alternating current is current the direction of which reverses at regular occurring intervals? Unless distinctly otherwise specified, the term alternating current refers to a periodically varying current with successive half waves of the same shape and area. [*He looks at* WALTER *who nods in agreement.*]

WOMAN: Young man, you are no more an electrician than I am president of the Great Atlantic & Pacific Tea Company. Why don't you go home, shave, go to bed and see a baseball game tomorrow. If you can't get there in person, watch it on television. It is good, clean sport and never interrupted by news bulletins. My son, Lucius Eban Allen, will grow up to be second baseman for the Houston Colts and possibly speaker of the house.

EDDIE: We were just leaving, lady. We're all through, aren't we, Mort?

WOMAN: You are a credit to your race.

MORT: [*throwing down the chisel*] We are not through.

WALTER: [*stepping between* MORT *and the* WOMAN] Allow me to explain, Madame. My name is Hiram Tinklepaugh and these are my sons, Shem and Ham. We are account executives with a Peruvian advertising agency. As a publicity stunt we are walking from Lima to Fairbanks, Alaska, and leaving gift certificates along the way to certain lucky people. [*He pulls out a sheet of crumpled paper and hands it to her.*] You, Madame, are one of these lucky people. This certificate will entitle you, if redeemed within thirty days of today, to a full year's supply of Pinkwitz Peruvian Beer, the beer that makes your tummy tingle, your glands palpitate and your husband shout "Carrumba." I am sure you read about us and our product in last Sunday's newspaper, a lage ad facing the comic section.

WOMAN: You are an idiot. If the three of you are not out of here in two minutes, I will call a policeman. Nora, my neighbor, has a brother, Max, who plays handball with a policeman.

EDDIE: We're already gone. [*He starts gathering tools.*] *You* heard the lady, Mort. Let's go.

MORT: Lady, on the other side of that door is a safe. In that safe is a pile of money, unmarked. In about four minutes we will have that door open and the money out. Now if you will just stand back a few feet and pretend that you are a hostage, you will walk away from here with a pile of cash and no one will know about it. If you give us trouble, we leave and no one gets a penny. Do you understand?

WOMAN: I have seldom been so insulted in my life. Do you realize that I am a respected member of this community, a loyal churchgoer? Do you think I can be bought for a few dollars?

WALTER: No one wants to buy you. He is merely trying to bribe you.

MORT: A thousand dollars.

WOMAN: A thousand dollars?

MORT: Fifteen hundred. What do you say?

WOMAN: You will please remember that I am a hostage and do your best to hurry. I am quite cold.

MORT: [*returning to door*] We'll hurry.

WOMAN [*to* EDDIE] I don't normally do such things, but I could use the money in my club's campaign against obscene literature. You know we do a very good job. With money we can send out pamphlets, support rallies. Ends do not generally justify means; unless, of course, as in this case, the means is the lesser of two evils.

WALTER: You are absolutely correct. Incoherent, but correct.

WOMAN: [*to* EDDIE] You understand what I mean? You see that I am doing the right and necessary thing?

EDDIE: I don't know, lady.

MORT: Right is what you think is right. Now please be quiet so I can get this door open.

WOMAN: You realize, of course, that I do not approve of what you are doing, but I strongly feel that pornography which spins around on little wire racks in drug stores should not be put into the hands of innocent boys like Lucius Eban Allen. Drug stores are for ice cream and newspapers, not dirty books. Those books should be . . .

WALTER: Confiscated?

WOMAN: Appropriated?

271

WALTER: Appropriation without representation.

WOMAN: Yes. It is certainly less evil to appropriate some money, which I am sure is insured, than to allow the moral fiber of our American youth to be weakened and twisted by vile volumes of filth.

WALTER: You have expressed my own sentiment clearly, concisely, and with great eloquence. With proper attention my own son, who is now a missionary in the jungles of Guam, would have been saved at an early age and would not have felt obligated, driven and tormented into devoting his brief candletime on Earth to the cleansing of heathen souls. Madame, we are in accord. Do not rest until the blight is removed from the path of our youth.

WOMAN: My feet are beginning to get cold. [MORT *breaks through the door.*]

MORT: This is it. Eddie, this is it. [*He goes through the door.* EDDIE *picks up the dolly and follows him.* WALTER *and the* WOMAN *peer in after them. From inside the* door MORT *says:*] Well, lift it up, lift it up, lift it up so I can get this thing under it.

EDDIE: I'm trying. I can't.

WOMAN: Damn it. Try harder.

EDDIE: Okay. I got it. [EDDIE *and* MORT *come out pushing and pulling the safe on the dolly.*]

MORT: Get the car back here, Eddie. Hurry. [*Eddie runs offstage.*] We'll hook the chain to this door and the money will flow out. I'll buy a little place somewhere where there's air and time and I'll write that novel.

WOMAN: And I'll continue my campaign.

WALTER: Perhaps.

EDDIE: [*panting*] It's gone.

MORT: What's gone?

EDDIE: The car. It's gone.

MORT: It's not gone. It's not gone. It's right by the street where you left it.

WOMAN: If you're talking about a short, black car with slightly rusty chrome, I saw two boys about my son's age drive away in it when I walked in here.

MORT: Then we'll push it home and open it there. We'll cover it with something and push it home. When we get it open, we'll buy your brother a new car.

EDDIE: Oh, Christ. Mort, I'm going to call the cops and tell them the car's been stolen.

MORT: I tell you, Eddie, we'll buy your brother a new one.

EDDIE: We can't push that safe down the street.

WALTER: I'll have to agree with the young man and withdraw my blessing from this enterprise.

WOMAN: You mean we're not going to get the money?

MORT: I tell you we're going to get into this safe. [A *light goes on above the door and an* OLD MAN *sticks his head out. He is wearing an undershirt.*]

OLD MAN: And what may I ask is going on here, the witches sabbath?

MORT: We're electricians. The power line broke and electricity is escaping all over the neighborhood. [*He stands in front of the safe, with* EDDIE *to hide it from the* OLD MAN*'s view*] You'd better close the window and get back in bed before you get some electric fallout.

OLD MAN: I don't smell no electricity.

WALTER: Pay no attention to my son. The world situation being what it is and the touch of arthritis which he inherits from his sainted grandfather, a famous Indian fighter in Mexico, have made him feverish.

OLD MAN: Ah, arthritis, I know, but what, may I ask, are you all doing in the alley?

WALTER: Sir, we are a group of traveling troubadours trying, in our small way, to revive the spirit of America's past and revitalize the pride in Americana, to bring back the heritage of the past, George Washington, Edgar Allan Poe, Lucius Eban Allen, Westbrook Pegler, Dominic Dimagio. We are, in short, traveling minstrels, playing for pennies, collecting ballads. This, sir, is my wife Corrine, a voice like a lark. My son Clive, who suffers from arthritis and fear, you have met. Clive recites from the great new novel he is writing about our great land. That gentleman is our faithful retainer, Dawson, who has been with us for generations. He plays beautiful music of the people on his dulcet horn.

OLD MAN: What?

WALTER: He plays trumpet.

OLD MAN: Gypsies. Please depart from my alley, please. I got to open in a few hours.

WALTER: You doubt us. Clive, recite your opening lines to that vast and mysterious work which you are writing about our wonderful land.

MORT: [*Gropes in his pocket and pulls out a scrap of paper. He reads:*] In this and any other age of demons when the sagging jowls of cities salivate on innocent and vile alike, one maddens, turns to Gods unknown or stands to face the snap of teeth, uncertain, angry, afraid, but determined to act his own image of Man. So saying, I suck in my dancing nerves, fold back my nightly dreams of nothingness and take a step. But is it a step forward?

OLD MAN: You are a sad boy. You think too much. It's better you should go on a nice vacation to Florida or find a nice girl. But take from me a suggestion. Stop writing that kind of stuff. Nobody wants to hear it. You gotta write, write funny stories. Make people laugh. Heh. I got news for you. Most people don't like you should tell them what they're already thinking if they don't like what they're thinking.

WALTER: Now, sir. You must hear my dear wife sing a plaintive folk song which was taught us by the town jailer in a little place called Pebble Rock, Arkansas, famous for its corn syrup factory. Sing for the gentleman, my dear.

WOMAN: [*Steps forward a bit frightened, pauses and begins to sing in a wooden voice. As she sings, she begins to enjoy the attention*] Won't you come home, Bill Bailey, won't you come home. You've danced the whole night long. I'll do the cooking honey, I'll pay the rent. I knew I done you wrong. Remember that foggy evening I threw you out with nothing but a fine tooth comb. I know I'm to blame, but ain't it a shame, Bill Bailey, won't you please come home.

OLD MAN: A Dinah Shore you are not.

WALTER: Ah, but you have yet to hear from Dawson; originally of Argentine blood, his family has passed on its musical lore for posterity. Display your heart and soul. Play, Dawson, play with the weight of a hundred years of oppression on the Pampas wrung into the beauty and pain of music.

EDDIE: Play here? What about the car?

MORT: Play. [EDDIE *takes out his trumpet, looks around, sighs, and begins to play "My Wild Irish Rose" as softly as he can.*]

OLD MAN: That's a folk song of your people? My advice to you is get a good job someplace and try to sleep nights. Now why don't all of you go home, be nice people and stop sneaking around alleys trying to steal safes from old men. [*closes the window and then reopens it*] By the way, I called the police a few minutes ago. My nephew Harold, that's my sister's middle boy, he wanted to be a physical therapist but he couldn't pass the test. Now he's a policeman. Maybe it's not the same as being president of IBM, but a bad job it's not. Harold will be here with some friends in a few minutes. [*to*

MORT] And you, young man. Thank you for buying all those root beers and if you're in the neighborhood some time stop in again. Now go home and try not to hurt anybody. There ain't much else worth doing, believe me. [*closes window*]

WOMAN: I believe I'd better be going. I have several all-night drug stores to visit later where particularly vile books have been reported. [*She exits quickly and nervously.*]

WALTER: Gentlemen, I have enjoyed our brief acquaintance. If you would like to adjourn to the nearest tavern for a nice quiet talk . . . I can see you would not. Well, I think I will seek a small, inexpensive hostel for the night if one of you can come to my aid with a few dollars. I'm not borrowing it, remember. I'm begging.

EDDIE: [*pulls out some bills and change.*] Take it.

WALTER: Thank you. And cheer up. Tomorrow is coming. [*He exits.*]

EDDIE: Mort, Mort, I think I hear the police car. Let's get out of here. Let's go report my brother's car stolen. Maybe they'll get it back. So my brother'll crack my skull. It won't be the first or last time.

MORT: [*leaning on the safe*] That old man doesn't know what the hell he's talking about. I'm to be a great writer and you're going to be a great trumpet player. All we need is some money. That's all. And next time. Next time we get it. [EDDIE *gathers all their bags together and starts offstage.*]

EDDIE: Right, Mort. Next time.

MORT: I've already got a plan. You know those ice cream trucks you see driving around. We can buy one and work ourselves into a whole chain in one summer. We can be rich.

EDDIE: Okay. But let's talk about it tomorrow. [*He goes offstage.*]

MORT: [A *siren is heard.*] Stop worrying about the car,

Eddie. We're going to have enough money to buy a string of cars. Stick with me and we'll go places. [*He follows* EDDIE *off-stage. The lights on stage indicate that daylight is coming. The curtain falls.*]